I0639029

Ghostly Echoes

Sarah sees and hears ghosts. For her it is a normal and mostly ignored part of her daily life. Only a few close friends know. Sarah hates publicity ...but the police know and so do the spirits who seek her help (and some ghosts, especially children, are very hard to ignore). All Sarah wants to do is to live quietly, however, a quiet life is difficult to achieve when the recently dead keep intruding. Worse, her daughter might also be psychic and, without realising it, is walking into danger ...so a missing woman and child may soon be the least of all their worries!

~~Deadly Shades of Grey~~

Originally published as Deadly Shades of Grey, the first of the ORIGINAL Shades of Grey series – long before any of a number of other Shades of Grey were published by other people, this book is a Ghost Story – with little or no sadomasochism in its content! Well, to be precise, it hasn't any! We, the publishers and the Author, give up. Our books came first – our titles were out first – our books are beautifully written and crafted – and we are fed-up with the assumption that this series is in some way a spinoff from any other when, in fact – we repeat – it was written and published FIRST!

In whatever order you read her books, Mai Griffin's series of supernatural thrillers ~~Shades of Grey~~ Ghostly Echoes will grip you (once you get over the title and the total lack of spurious sex).

First published in Great Britain in 2007 by
U P Publications St George's House, George Street, Huntingdon, Cambridgeshire, UK PE29 3GH

Cover design copyright © G. M. G. Peers 2007, 2010, 2014, 2020

Extracts are taken from "Anon - A Book of Unknown Quotes" a private publication copyright © G. M. G. Peers 2007

A CIP Catalogue record of this book is available from the British Library

Originally released as Deadly Shades of Grey under

ISBN 978-0-9557447-0-9
and Second Edition ISBN 978-0-9557447-7-8

This is the Third Edition (the First as Ghostly Echoes)

ISBN 978-1-908135-51-3

9 3 7 8 5 6

Published by U P Publications

www.uppublications.ltd.uk
www.maiwriting.com

Ghostly Echoes

~~Deadly Shades of Grey~~

Mai Griffin

U P Publications
2007, 2010, 2014

With grateful thanks to Janice Brown and Gisela Mountford for their help and encouragement at the beginning...

Although the characters are fictitious, the creation of Sarah and Stephen Grey was inspired by my late parents to whom the Original Shades of Grey series (now known as Ghostly Echoes) is dedicated.

In Life and Death there is no Black and White,

No core construct that always must be right,

No path or light that clearly shows the way

But filters through a Deadly Shade of Grey.

When some can hear and others single sight

How can they find a soul to lead them to the light?

Ghostly Echoes make confusion and tend to disarray,

So pander to the madness of what the seers say

Anon

Prologue

Bewildered and filled with dread, the boy opened his eyes and slowly sat up. He put a hand to his brow – the agony had been fleeting but surely, it must be bruised or cut. He pressed gently over his eyes and across the smooth unbroken skin of his forehead. How could that be...? Incredulity changed to relief until his hand moved higher ...and his fingers sank into a deep cavity, matted with blood and hair.

Sickened with revulsion, he collapsed again, stunned into insensibility.

In fleeting flashes of awareness, realising he was not in pain, he felt calmer. The grass was cool beneath him and he could see treetops laced against blue sky above, so surely things couldn't be as bad as he'd thought! Cautiously, he risked feeling his head again, but it felt so shockingly unfamiliar that his stomach lurched and he lapsed into a troubled dream, having no conception of time as his mind drifted. Sometimes he shouted for help but no one came.

Gradually gaining a small measure of coherent thought, he tried to deal with the weird jigsaw of emotions – anxiety, fear and fury – which consumed him. Although his head didn't ache, he could not bring himself to examine it again and was reluctant to move from where he lay, supine on the soft ground. The physical pain had been mercifully brief but an indefinable anguish tormented him, as if he had done something bad.

He felt guilty ...but of what?

As the shadows deepened, he gradually became aware of sounds nearby: the lazy trickle of water: the faint hiss of wind through dry leaves. A memory surfaced; vibration …a throbbing engine? No, it was gone! He hovered unhappily between a shifting chimera and devastatingly dark oblivion that, on the brink of recollection, repeatedly frustrated his fleeting fronds of memory before they could solidify.

A sudden stab of certainty startled him out of his inertia. He had been in the cabin of a boat. It was night. Stealthy footsteps betrayed someone moving on the deck above. Moonlight penetrated the shadows, revealing a halo of fair curls framing the delicate face of a child, pathetically small – and transparently white in death. The shocking impact of the vision broke his fragile hold on reality. Yielding again to the pull of the sable black void, he heard his own impotent howls of anguish mingling with the frightened cries of a child.

1 – Friday July 20th ...

Ethel Mead wiped her arm wearily across her brow. She now regretted having started baking. It was far too warm to be in the kitchen with the oven going full blast – especially as the back door and windows were shut because of a wasp nest hanging in a nearby tree. Little Katy had to play out of sight in the front garden because the pernicious pests crawled drunkenly through the sparse grass, in and out of the fallen apples, unable to fly far but not too sleepy to sting if stepped on, or when poked by an inquisitive finger.

Before rolling out the pastry, Ethel covered it with a cloth and went, yet again, to the living room window, to check on her daughter. All was well. A cool breeze wafted the curtains and she stood quietly, enjoying the change of air, watching the three-year old playing 'hospitals' with Rosebud, her doll. Ethel's thin, plain face was transformed, momentarily, by a wide smile.

She recalled how, a few weeks ago, a carelessly waved paintbrush had splashed a red gash on Rosebud's arm. Tommy, Kate's big brother, declared that it was "no big deal" but she was inconsolable until he demonstrated how to bandage it with a handkerchief – promising that it would be better the next morning. Tommy had 'cured' the painted streak by surreptitious washing, so 'Nursing' had become Kate's favourite game.

Her baby face wore a concerned frown and her golden curls bobbed as she rocked the toy cradle where poor wounded Rosebud lay, hardly visible under a voluminous head dressing. Satisfied that all was well, Ethel returned to her baking.

The early evening paper clattered through the letterbox a few minutes later and, as the last batch of jam tarts had just gone into the oven, she decided to put the kettle on. She would read it and enjoy a cup of tea in the fresh air with Katy. The paperboy, Ozzy, often baby-sat for the children, much to the disgust of ten-year-old Tommy who considered himself quite capable of doing the job himself, especially if they paid him!

Kate adored Ozzy and greeted him eagerly.

Surprised to see her at the front of the house he asked, "What are you doing out here young lady?"

"I have waps in my garden," Kate explained. "Waps hurt people! Pease don't go," she called after him accusingly as, without pausing, he hurried away down the path. Kate pursed her lips in consternation. "Naughty Rothebud fell off daddy'th ladder. Her head ith hurted," she lisped, wanting to show him.

Ozzy had taken the delivery job to keep fit and had no intention of being trapped, so hastily pulling the gate behind him he continued jogging along the lane, ignoring the dull thump as the heavy gate swung open again. Eagerly scrambling to her feet, Kate grabbed her doll and ran after him.

It took only a few minutes to wash up and add Kate's orange juice to the tray, so while the kettle boiled Ethel collected the paper. Sunlight streaming through the tinted glass door panel in the front door reminded her to pull the curtains over the side windows – the hall carpet was fading badly and they couldn't afford a new one yet. As she did so, her glance strayed beyond the frilled edge. The gate gaped wide – the faulty latch had stuck again! Where was Kate? ...Kate had gone!

Throwing open the door Ethel rushed out and down the path, panic-stricken, praying that her baby hadn't wandered into the road. Then, looking sideways over the low hedge, she saw Ozzy returning, holding Kate's hand – bringing her back. Ethel sighed with relief and stopped to catch her breath as a car, scarcely noticed, flashed past the gateway ahead of her.

There was no way she could have known how desperate she would soon be, to recall anything and everything about that fleeting moment!

2 – Saturday August 4th…

Clarrie Hunter was upset. She regretted the impulse that had made her pull off the main road, although actually heading for Henley. Within thirty yards, the stony track narrowed and ended abruptly, with no space to turn the car, and the undergrowth ahead looked impenetrable. How could she have been so stupid – she should have left the car near the road and explored on foot, but being certain the river was near, she switched off the engine. With the air-conditioning off and the windows down, the running water sounded very close; she wouldn't drive down this far again but it was certainly worth investigating now.

Picking her way through a patch of shrubs, glad to be wearing jeans, she soon reached a roughly grassed clearing at the edge of the water. The view across the river and to her left was stunning. No buildings, pylons or billboards spoiled the expansive sweep of the fields and a line of overhanging trees on the nearer bank provided interesting detail in the foreground.

Clarrie had been dubious about agreeing to paint "a quiet stretch of the Thames in full sunshine". Harsh contrasts of light and shade weren't always easy to handle but, seeing how the weeping fringe of willows softened the dark water's edge, she was suddenly enthusiastic about the commission. It had seemed a perfect place to site her easel. For three hours, as the day brightened, while working on the general layout of the picture, she had gradually become aware that instead of growing warmer the air was intensely cold. For weeks, the hot weather had been causing some people to grumble incessantly, but Clarrie enjoyed it and was comfortable in lightweight shirts or smocks.

When the nape of her slender neck began to ache as though exposed to an icy draught she was puzzled but expected that the sun's rays would soon penetrate the trees. Unclipping her long hair, allowing it to flow freely over her shoulders, gave only temporary comfort – her hands soon became almost too numb to continue holding the palette and brush. It was ridiculous. This was supposed to be the hottest summer since 1911... Penguins at Bristol zoo were receiving daily cold showers of water to prevent them from dehydrating!

Eventually, in an effort to restore some body warmth, Clarrie walked up and down the limited area, stamping her feet to bring back circulation. A sharp contrast, between cold and warm air, occurred abruptly at the edge of the copse and the incongruity made her apprehensive. Feeling strangely threatened she stared about her, reluctant to remain in isolation. Surely, she was alone. Among the thinly clumped bushes on the opposite bank of the small inlet, concealment was virtually impossible – she would have seen anyone loitering. Yet she did dimly recall voices, an hour ago perhaps, and a shout, obviously too distant to cause alarm.

She might have dismissed a fancied threat but could not endure physical discomfort so had to give up. It was a nuisance having to move her equipment; starting to paint again from a different viewpoint would render the morning's work wasted unless she found a similar clearing nearby – one more sheltered from the cold perhaps, if it didn't envelope the whole bend of the river.

The distant roar of traffic, made her feel less alone so, having packed her gear away, Clarrie paused to assess the terrain. Away from the river, the ground rose sharply and the heavily treed area adjoining the road should have afforded protection but perhaps even a light breeze might be deflected by the steep bank, creating a chilling swirl of air where water undermined the low bank before surging round the bend.

It was too cold to stand and wonder for long and a relief to settle back in the warmth of the car. Normality soon returned to her extremities and she eventually lowered the windows again to reverse to the main thoroughfare.

Clarrie was more than upset. She was thoroughly annoyed that she hadn't stuck to her original plan, to paint in Henley. If only …but regrets were futile. She drove slowly away, ignoring the impatient drivers who collected behind her on the narrow road – reluctant to abandon the area – determined to explore even a footpath, if it went in the right direction. Her natural optimism was rewarded when, within a few hundred yards she was able to pull into a lay-by, where the river could actually be glimpsed beyond a small copse.

A footpath led down to the water and although the bank was narrow it was wide enough for her to work. Cigarette ends and scuffed grass showed that others had used the secluded inlet – probably anglers. Clarrie decided to stake her claim immediately as the view was almost identical to the other. The location was actually better as it was not hidden from passing traffic. Her mother would certainly approve. Sarah always worried about her working alone; such monstrous things happened nowadays.

With little loss of time Clarrie began work again, satisfied that the painting already started needed few alterations. Occasionally, in spite of her concentration, her gaze was drawn to the place, less than a hundred yards distant, where she had first stopped. Could she have heard a voice? No, it must have been the wind moaning lightly. But if someone had been lurking in the shadows beneath the trees, could they be watching her still? No! How ridiculous she was being.

Gradually her insecurity faded as she became engrossed in her painting. By four-thirty, the sun was losing its brilliance, so she stopped work to photograph the view. She preferred working on location but photographs were a worthwhile insurance in case the weather changed. The wide-angle lens revealed the bank she had had to abandon and when it came into focus she could scarcely believe her eyes. In a small inlet just beyond it, surely visible from there, a small cabin cruiser swayed at anchor – but she had neither seen nor heard it arrive!

It must have approached down-river, from Henley, during

her move. Anyway, it accounted for the voice and a nearby presence. The boat provided an attractive splash of colour so she clicked the shutter; she might include it in her final painting. In spite of the false start, it had been a good day. Even as she returned her paraphernalia to the car the sun still shone warmly. It was surprising that such a short distance away it probably still felt like winter.

Clarrie tended to lose track of time with a brush in her hand, but today she would arrive home early; Sarah would be surprised and pleased. Even though both were widows and shared a home, they spent little time together. Her mother did almost all the cooking and they shared evening meals, after which Sarah usually went to her own room to read or watch television, leaving Clarrie free to relax in any way she chose. Sarah, not wishing to encroach on her daughter's freedom any more than could be helped, had insisted on this arrangement before moving in.

As the car crunched over the gravel drive Clarrie saw her mother's slight figure at the front door with Maud, one of her closest friends.

"Oh, Clarinda, what a lovely surprise, I'm so glad you're home before dark," Sarah called out happily. "I can't help fretting when you're late."

Maud wrinkled her nose scornfully. "Why you worry I shall never know. Being psychic you would be sure to know if something terrible happened!"

With an amused smile, Sarah agreed she might, but not in time to stop it. God expected one to help one's self and in her opinion that meant not taking unnecessary risks.

Maud, not for the first time, thought how lucky Sarah Grey was to have Clarinda. They behaved more like sisters together than she and Norma, who actually were! It had been pleasant to get away for a few hours – Norma would undoubtedly greet her return with a long face, especially if she suspected where she'd been!

3 – Shades

After Maud's departure, while Clarrie settled in, Sarah put the final touches to the evening meal. She had tied an apron over her pale-green linen dress. She should really have changed but Sarah wanted to demonstrate that everything was ready even though Clarinda had been unusually early. Anyway, she was looking forward to discussing the events of the day and didn't want to waste time.

Over coffee later, she sympathised. The false start must have been extremely irritating but, privately, she had strong doubts about such an icy draught being possible on a hot day and was oddly disquieted about the boat arriving unnoticed. She pictured it, deserted, swaying at the end of its tether, and pondered; Clarinda's discomfort was due either to a physical threat that she sensed intuitively, or to something spiritually unusual. If caused by psychic disturbance, Sarah knew Clarinda might not accept it as such – she laughingly maintained that one eccentric in the family was enough and always dismissed her own sensitivity and possible clairvoyance.

Sarah roused herself to clear the table and Clarrie began to help, but they almost collided as Clarrie suddenly halted, to stare into the darkening garden. The eerie unease she'd perceived during the morning returned. She felt vulnerable. Was someone out there spying on them?

**

Unseen, the boy crouched miserably in the shadows, still disorientated. He'd been on a riverbank, frustrated when the woman ignored his cries for help and angry when she left. He was convinced that she was in this house but how had he followed her and why? He couldn't remember, yet for some reason beyond his grasp, he felt compelled to reach her.

His thoughts were in turmoil and his inability to cope infuriated him. Curtains suddenly swept across the windows hiding the warmly lit room, isolating him with his dark thoughts. The ground should have felt hard, damp and uncomfortable but, as weariness assailed him, he fell asleep … tomorrow, tomorrow would come. For now, he would bide his time.

4 – Sarah

Although Clarrie was obviously disturbed by her eerie experience that morning, she had trivialised it when describing it to her mother over dinner but Sarah wasn't deceived. She sensed underlying apprehension behind the light-hearted account. Because the excruciatingly low temperature was confined to just a few square yards, Sarah wondered if Clarinda had even considered that a supernatural presence might be the cause and considered tagging along on the next trip, to check the waterfront atmosphere herself but, aware that her presence might hinder her daughter's concentration, Sarah shrugged off her disquiet; her imagination was being over-active. Clarinda's good sense would be her own protection. Instead, she'd sort magazines – far more useful and long overdue. Besides, it was her turn to bake for Monday's bridge circle. Maud had remarked hopefully that Sarah's date and walnut drops were delicious; she couldn't disappoint her hostess.

Clarrie, inexplicably drawn to stare from the window, felt threatened and voiced her concern that she might have been followed from the river; surely she would have noticed. For a few minutes, they scrutinised the darkening garden together then, although observing nothing abnormal, they re-checked security, staring warily from every angle as growing twilight flattened the shadows. Eventually, Clarrie apologised. It had been an extraordinary day; her eyes and ears were usually more reliable. Sarah, too, felt uneasy as she went to bed, but she recognised the possibility that Clarinda's mood was catching and, as they were reasonably safe from any mortal threat, there was really nothing to worry about.

***

Neither had seen the stranger watching the house. He sensed that his waking periods were lengthening and wondered, vaguely, how long ago he'd been injured. His clearest recollection was of lying near a river and he clung to it, hoping that earlier memories would surface. With each emergence from that unfathomable void he'd grown more desperate for help, waving and calling whenever he saw people. Now, probably miles from there, he had even more to worry about.

How had he arrived in this garden and why?

The answer instantaneously came to him. An old lady had shaken him awake and pointed across the water to the woman – the woman with long hair, the one who had seemed to notice him …the one who was now inside the darkened house. The ancient reedy voice had floated above him as the lady talked with a child: a little girl. As if in a dream, he'd been consoled by her words, and trusted her instinctively.

She promised that the child would stay with him – he need never fear being alone again – but what use could such a baby be, he had thought dismally, putting a hand tentatively to his head, it was a doctor he needed. In his confusion, before sleep claimed him again, he barely registered that it felt whole and normal.

5 – Maud & Norma

Norma was offended. The salutation included her by name and the letter did end, "Hope you are both well", but the envelope was addressed only to Maud – why not also to her. Wasn't she supposed to open it? Maud was unsympathetic, always expecting to come first and get her own way because she was older by seven years. Even though they had now reached their fifties Norma fretted, Maud was still dictatorial and controlled both their lives, never allowing that Norma's wishes might differ from her own. It had been worse since Norma became interested in ESP. Maud would never scoff at anyone else for claiming an extra sense, but in her own sister? No way! She said Norma was being silly!

Why couldn't Maud acknowledge Norma's flashes of second sight? Last year, she had warned against investing in new shares but Maud did so anyway and within months, as Norma had predicted, their value fell. Maud was cuttingly sarcastic; they probably featured in a financial advice column that Norma remembered, albeit sub-consciously. Sometimes when the telephone rang she knew who it was and said so, but Maud just sniffed and muttered, "Intelligent guess". Only last week after wasting hours in a futile search for her address book Maud eventually asked Norma if she had seen it. Norma immediately visualised the book, wedged behind the writing desk and when they moved the furniture, the book fell to the floor, but did Maud thank her? No!

Irritated, Norma couldn't resist reminding Maud that only

minutes before the post arrived she had predicted news from abroad and, at Maud's reaction, she passed instantly from being upset to blind fury. As usual, Maud belittled her talent for predicting news or events. With a pitying look and a superior smile she'd pointed out, "Within days of my birthday, cards from Australia were to be expected. The fact that Alice has also written, from Canada, is pure coincidence! Even without it you would have claimed to be right."

Norma choked on her reply as Maud slit open the second envelope, also addressed only to her. Even sitting, Maud's slender build and height, inherited from their father, gave her a lofty grace that dwarfed her younger sister, filling her with envy. Norma bitterly resented taking after their mother, who only had to look at food for it to go to her hips!

Maud, her elegant head up-tilted slightly as she peered through the lower part of her bifocals, kept quoting parts of the letter aloud, without apparently noticing Norma's mounting irritation.

Alice, their childhood friend used to play more often with Norma but took her secrets to Maud, often for advice. This naturally resulted in her greater attachment to the revered older sister as they grew up. Hearing that Alice planned to remarry, Norma interrupted, suddenly lifted from her black mood. "I told you so," she cried. "Surely you remember? I knew she would. I dreamt about her standing outside the church with a bouquet. People were throwing rice!"

"Really," Maud sighed, "Alice is barely fifty-five and extremely attractive, she wasn't likely to remain alone for long." Drowning her sister's protests and riffling through the pages noisily, she said firmly, "When she divorced Sam, I could have predicted myself that she'd soon find someone else and I don't claim to be psychic!"

In a flash of temper Norma jumped up and started to leave the room but at the door she stopped and turned. "His name is Roland," she announced triumphantly, waiting.

Maud glanced down the page and saw that Norma was right. At first she was genuinely surprised but then answered with a knowing shake of her head, "Oh, come now, you really are pathetic, you saw it over my shoulder!"

Alone in her own room Norma tried to control the hot tears of frustration that forced their way from her closed eyes. Her small round face creased with misery and her usually sallow skin became flushed with unhealthy purple patches. She had never admitted it before but she detested Maud. When had her resentment soured to dislike, then hate? As a child she'd accepted Maud's superior attitude, she was the big sister, going on dates with boys. She understood, now, but would never forget Maud's irritation with her in their teens. Perhaps she had been a nuisance – eager to be included when not wanted – but no way did that excuse Maud's present meanness.

Maud had married in her early twenties but remained at home because her husband was a soldier serving abroad. He was killed in the Malayan Emergency and it was Norma's opinion that Maud had positively basked in the awful tragedy of her widowhood, milking the sympathy of friends. Norma suspected privately that she was relieved! She certainly hadn't been eager to marry again. It was years before she wore anything other than black and stopped dabbing her eyes sadly whenever the subject came up.

Norma, on the other hand, would have welcomed marriage and perhaps being a mother, but the right man never came along. As young as thirty she accepted that life had passed her by and could have adjusted to being alone – it was living with Maud that was driving her mad. If only Maud had married again and moved out before Ma and Papa died, Norma could have had the beautiful front bedroom, but without consultation Maud claimed it herself. She later maintained that she simply couldn't ask Norma to sleep there. Being so sensitive, their parent's ghosts would keep her awake at night!

Maud had then transformed her old bedroom, adjacent to Norma's, into a lounge to house Norma's books and television, which she personally considered an intrusion in the sitting room, insisting that Norma needed a haven that was entirely her own where she could relax quietly if she wanted peace. Norma recognised it as an excuse to banish the TV and encourage her to stay out of the way while Maud entertained downstairs.

They had several friends in common. The bridge-club members came to play twice every week – four tables. One of the sessions used to be held at Sarah Grey's before she sold up the family home and moved in with her daughter. Norma had loved going there. Sarah was fascinating. It was whispered that she was a medium, a genuine psychic, and Norma was sure Maud knew the truth even though she refused to discuss it.

Norma often tried to broach the subject with Sarah herself, eager to discuss her own experiences, but it was difficult to introduce the topic with others present, especially the Vicar's wife who took over, loudly, whenever anything touching on religious dogma was mentioned! Elsie aired her opinions as if they were unassailable facts and, brooking no argument, dismissed psychic phenomena out of hand ...the vicar would not approve.

Over coffee, during a break in play some weeks ago, Norma had managed to tell Sarah how enthralled she was by the supernatural, adding that she, too, could sometimes foretell events, although she'd never actually seen or heard a ghost. She'd hoped for an admission that Sarah could do both, but Sarah merely smiled politely and said that such senses often took years to develop so she need not give up hope. Maud stopped any further discussion by commenting how often one thought of someone then bumped into him or her in the street!

Why would Maud never concede that her predictions were more reliable than those casual impressions experienced by most people? It didn't matter how often Norma confronted her with the validity of the predictions, Maud flatly refused to believe in her, or them, and made a point of interfering whenever she wanted to talk to Sarah. It was sheer jealousy; Maud wanted to keep Sarah to herself. Norma determined that today would be different. Somehow she would contrive to have a private word with Sarah. As she came to this decision the doorbell chimed ...it was later than she thought!

6 – Sarah

The car braked to a halt outside the sisters' ivy-covered old house and Sarah realised guiltily that since the journey started she had been entirely wrapped up in her own thoughts. While waiting for her lift, earlier, after locking the back door, she explored the garden looking for signs of an intruder. Satisfied that all was well she began walking away but something made her glance back and she saw a child picking daisies on the grass: the spirit form of a little girl! As if she'd hoped to be seen, the child laughed delightedly and ran to take Sarah's hand. "You must come with me," she urged, pulling Sarah across the smooth lawn. Sarah looked down on the bright crown of fair curls, filled with wonder.

As always at such moments she felt enormously privileged to be granted such glimpses of life beyond death. A daisy-chain necklace broke from the child's delicate throat as she bounced with impatience at Sarah's slow gait. "Hurry, hurry," she pleaded.

A car horn shattered the peace and the vision.

Elsie, the Vicar's wife, had arrived. Sarah stooped to pick up the linked daisies and was overcome with sadness as they dematerialised in her hand but the child needed help and would undoubtedly come again.

7 – Norma

During the drive to Maud's house, Sarah's wonderment over her vision of the little girl and any likely connection with Clarinda's icy encounter on the riverbank had completely blotted out Elsie's interminable monologue. Thankfully, she mused, whether one replied or not, Elsie never noticed.

In spite of her dimpled smiles the child's aura was sad. There was urgency in her manner; she had wanted to show Sarah something, or take her somewhere, that much was obvious. Sarah guessed that she had almost certainly been wrong in assuming, when Sunday passed without incident, that Clarinda's foreboding was without foundation. There was nothing to be done now though, so she determined to enjoy the morning's bridge. She would, if she could avoid being trapped by Norma again.

Inside the house, Norma fidgeted with frustration. If only Sarah had come early she might have been able to talk to her while Maud set up the tables in the other room. Unfortunately she arrived last, and stayed close to Elsie, which, for some reason, increased Norma's intense irritation. Eventually, the small talk over, they all adjourned to the library to play. The room had hardly changed since it had been their father's study. Two opposite walls were lined from floor to ceiling with books, and low cabinets at each side of the fireplace held collections of old ornaments. In the recessed alcoves above them were the only additions to the room since the death of their parents: two oil paintings – portraits of herself and Maud – by Clarinda Hunter.

Although Sarah was proud to see her daughter's paintings so well displayed her gaze lingered more often on Maud's, finding that the portrayal of Norma made her feel vaguely uncomfortable. She had never really liked Norma and somehow the portrait revealed something deeply disturbing about her that was easier to ignore in life. Sarah never asked about her personal feelings for sitters but perhaps, inadvertently, Clarinda had captured intrusions from her own subconscious. Others admired both of the portraits without reservation ...some even likened Norma's strange smile to that of the Mona Lisa!

Norma had the dummy hand in the first round and at the adjacent table Sarah's partner also had the contract. No player likes to be left out of play and as they caught each other's eye sympathetically, in what was potentially a fleeting glance, they were both simultaneously distracted from the play.

Norma saw Sarah's expression intensify. Her normally smooth features were creased in a worried frown and as their eyes locked, Norma had what seemed to be a telepathic vision of Maud's face contorted with pain. They looked over the tables at each other – sharing the same dreadful image – then both stared at Maud, triumphantly tidying her tricks away, having made a slam.

The rest of the morning passed in a blur to Norma but when the party broke up she found that Sarah was, for once, anxious to talk to her! Accompanying her outside, while Maud was occupied with all the other departing guests, Norma was almost dizzy, anticipating Sarah's reaction when she described what she had seen. It was Norma's chance to prove herself to Sarah, but, before she could do so, Sarah spoke urgently, her voice tinged with alarm. "I know you'll think it a strange request, but please, I beg you – I feel this so strongly – you must keep Maud at home today!" Sarah refused to explain further, trusting that Maud's well-being would be supremely important to her sister, but Norma pressed for a reason.

Clutching Sarah's arm, Norma described what she herself had seen and for a few moments neither woman moved. Sarah studied Norma intently then came to a decision. "It seems that you really are receptive, so you should be willing to accept that she must be prevented from going out. Make any excuse because, if Maud drives today, I see her thrown violently against the steering wheel. Although I don't think she'll be badly injured, I can't be absolutely sure. It could end in tragedy."

Norma's mobile face registered mixed emotions. Her eyes widened and her mouth went slack. Sarah added hastily, "Don't worry, the situation can be avoided if she stays at home, but there's no more I can tell you." She was doubly insistent and more specific because she knew Maud always shopped on Monday afternoons. Sarah was relying on Norma to keep Maud safe because she was reluctant to advise her personally. Maud was stubborn and might insist that, being forewarned, she could avoid danger. The warning might then make her nervous and actually be the cause of a calamity.

As others joined them, Sarah hastily took her leave of Norma and departed with promises to have a real 'heart to heart' one day, soon, about ESP and the paranormal.

Norma was elated. At last everyone would accept her as a real psychic, like Sarah, or at least it would be enough to silence Maud. As the car pulled away, she planned her strategy. To start with, she wouldn't even try to keep Maud in; a bump on the head might do her good! Afterwards, she'd describe what she had foreseen and when Maud scoffed, as she was sure to, she'd announce that Sarah had also seen it.

Norma smirked as she pictured Maud's stupefaction. There was one glaring snag; she'd have to explain to Sarah her failure to pass the warning on. Norma sighed. It would have been such a satisfying revenge but Maud would have to be told after all. Anyway, it was gratifying that at least Sarah now believed her.

As she turned to walk back into the drive she saw the scene around her dissolve. The wide road was crowded with silent spectators and vehicles: funeral cars! A hearse waited at the sidewalk under a fragrant crown of flowers. She gasped with dismay – then the surroundings reverted to normal as the last guest came chattering happily from the house. Oh God! Maud really would die unless she intervened. Sarah, it seemed, hadn't been granted a full glimpse of the future – even Sarah, so experienced – but Norma knew beyond any doubt that what she had seen would actually happen. Then she corrected herself – it could only come true if she let Maud drive.

8 – Clarrie

When Sarah arrived home she saw the light flashing on the answering machine. After rewinding the tape she found two messages, both for her. The first announced the arrival of a book she had ordered. The second – she knew his voice immediately – was from Detective Chief Superintendent Holmes of the local CID. "Alec here," the rich deep tones announced. "We have a problem. You may not be able to help but I'd be grateful if you'd try. I can send a car for you. Please call back, extension one-five."

Several times in the past few years Sarah had assisted the police. They respected her wish for complete privacy and never advertised her involvement. She suspected that they would have been embarrassed had it been otherwise and were only too willing to use her when all normal avenues of investigation failed.

Their association began when she was shopping one day. Although her mind was concentrated on her list of most needed items and the best place to find them, she was impelled to stop at a newsagent's door. She found her eyes drawn to the local paper propped on a stand outside. Halfway down the front page was a photograph of someone with a coat thrown over his head and shoulders, being pushed into the back of a police van. He'd been arrested for robbing a post office. The crowded street and noisy traffic momentarily seemed to fade, as an elderly woman materialised before her and pointed to the prisoner. "In the name of God, help my boy! He is innocent," she pleaded.

Without knowing what she could do, if anything, Sarah went directly to the Police station. After an hour of getting nowhere, the desk sergeant had lost patience with her and his rising voice attracted the attention of a young man several feet away. Sarah turned at his approach and was relieved when he verified her name and asked her to wait. The man behind the desk was equally happy to hand over responsibility and indicated a row of seats where she might sit. Sarah was well aware that in revealing her mediumistic talents she was exposing herself to ridicule but she was an instrument being used by an unearthly power and had to follow her instincts. Not knowing where it might lead, she offered up a prayer for God's guidance and protection from evil. The risk was one she willingly took in order to bring help and comfort to those on both sides of the grave. Thus composed she waited quietly, not seeing her but sensing that the old lady was still with her.

Sarah was at last taken to meet Detective Chief Superintendent Alec Holmes of the local CID. Coming from behind his impressively large desk to greet her, he put her immediately at ease by saying, "The uniformed branch has to contend with many would-be helpful members of the public. On the whole they do a good job, weeding out time wasters." He pointed out that she had in fact been very evasive about how she could help, but admitted, "If you'd even hinted that your information came from beyond the veil you would most likely have been shown the door within five minutes!" He grinned. "Don't think I'm psychic too. My Detective Sergeant remembered you – apparently you helped an aunt of his last year, over some lost documents – he knew I'd want to meet you."

Alec Holmes said that he was greatly interested in the paranormal and had studied cases, particularly in Holland, where Psychics helped to solve crimes. Having seated her in a comfortable armchair beside the long occasional table, he lowered his large frame into another, ran a hand over his receding hairline and leaned back, waiting expectantly.

Sarah admitted her reluctance to advertise the fact that she was clairvoyant and also said that she had no idea how she could help, which had made it difficult when questioned about the source of her information. However, she knew that she had only to persevere to be guided in the right direction.

The Chief Superintendent smiled encouragingly and quickly established the reasons for her presence. The case that concerned Sarah was among his current files and he couldn't help feeling a tinge of excitement as he rang for coffee. He was quite confident that he could sort the chaff from the wheat and would listen with an open mind, in spite of the eyewitness who saw the robber discard his mask, gun and gloves in an alley. Another damning clue was the bus ticket that fell from his pocket at the shop counter when he pulled out the gun – later found to be a toy. The assistant saw the ticket flutter to the floor; it was issued on the route which passed through the neighbourhood of the man accused.

Still unsure what she could do, Sarah asked if she might examine the articles from the crime scene. Within minutes the file was brought in, together with associated evidence bags by a tall, dark-haired man in his early forties who was introduced as Alec's assistant, Detective Inspector Algy Green – green Algae to his men, but only out of earshot! Sarah liked him on sight and of course had no objection to his sitting in on the experiment.

She first picked up the toy and, although it was in a plastic bag, she was mentally transported to another scene. Concentrating, eyes closed, she saw a counter with other realistic looking guns for sale. Each was attached to a colourful card and small orange price stickers bore the name of the shop: BOYSTOYS. The two men were intrigued. Neither knew the name but they could certainly find it, if it existed. The rubber gloves were old and split. Sarah couldn't discern any useful impressions from them but the stocking, actually a section cut from a pair of tights, had last been in contact with a young female – she was absolutely sure. Others may have handled the stocking briefly but only the girl had used it.

As Sarah described a young woman with a distinctive purple birthmark on her forehead, she saw her companions exchanging glances with raised brows. Then she'd held the clipped bus ticket and, within seconds, gave them an accurate description of their principal witness, a middle-aged man who had never been inside the shop.

It was enough to make them think again, because the girl Sarah described was the daughter of the chief witness and almost identical in stature to the man they had in custody. It could well be that she'd dressed as a boy wearing her father's coat and purely by coincidence the ticket stub had supported his accusation. Further inquiries led quickly to the identification of the girl by the owner of the toyshop and the falsely accused man was cleared.

Alec and Algy had been valued friends of Sarah and Clarinda, in the background of their lives ever since and never hesitated to seek Sarah's suggestions when faced with a baffling case. Alec was married with grown-up children who lived somewhere abroad and he rarely discussed his private life. Algy's wife was in a long-stay psychiatric ward and didn't even know him when he visited her.

Clarinda and Algy, an amateur water-colourist, enjoyed an occasional dinner date. Neither sought more than friendship; perhaps that was why they always found it so easy to relax with each other. It had been months since they'd heard from Alec personally and, with a growing sense of excitement, Sarah wondered why he wanted her help.

Without delay she dialled to return his call.

9 – Norma

Walking down the drive with the last departing guest, Maud met Norma returning to the house and as soon as they were alone she voiced her exasperation. "I might have known you trailed after Sarah, waylaying her, pestering her with your silly second sight! You really do embarrass me." She paused for breath at the door and almost pushed Norma inside. "I wish you'd stop all that stupid nonsense – in fact, if you ever mention the subject again, I swear I will..."

Whatever she threatened to do was lost on Norma who went straight up to her room, white-faced, almost in tears. Maud rapped on her door later and told her to come down for lunch and not be silly. There was no answer. Maud knocked again in the early afternoon to say she was ready to go out, but Norma still maintained a tight-lipped silence. She was consumed with anger, her thoughts in turmoil. Maud's cruel words resounded in her ears.

It would serve her damn well right Norma thought, if she did let her kill herself but, in spite of everything, they were the same flesh and blood, so she relented. Leaving her room, she walked down the landing to the southern side of the house past Maud's bedroom. Through the open door she saw the sun streaming through the tall bay window. The room looked lovely: rose-coloured velvet curtaining: cream brocade tapestry and the inlaid walnut dressing table which had belonged to their grandmother.

She suddenly saw Maud as a usurper.

Norma pictured the dimness of her own room, hating it, but taking a firm grip on her emotions she hastened to fulfil her promise to Sarah. It was her duty. She really had no choice.

In the last few moments the sun had clouded over and from the kitchen window Maud was looking anxiously into the sky. It was darkening ominously. "I hope it isn't going to rain," she muttered, "I do so hate driving on wet roads." It was the perfect moment to persuade her that she should stay at home. After the tiff Maud would be amenable to a friendly overture; she could suggest updating the stamp collection together – Maud had been nagging her to help with it for weeks. As Norma opened her mouth to speak, Maud snapped at her. "If only you'd found time to make a decent shopping list last week I would not have to go out at all today! With your much-vaunted gift for seeing into the future one would expect you to avoid running out of things like soap powder!"

Watching Maud reverse from the garage, Norma was assailed by the enormity of what she was doing – letting fate take its course when she could so easily intervene – but she had tried to tell her …nobody could blame her! It was Maud's fault. Maud had upset her so much she couldn't think straight. Remorse struggled to surface.

At that moment, if Maud had not wound down the window and shouted, "Don't just stand there, do something useful. Shut the garage door," Norma would have stopped her from driving away but again Maud had forestalled her attempt to stop her. As the car accelerated away, Norma went back into the house and leaned weakly against the door, trembling. Was it with fear, shame, or excitement because, without Maud, she could look forward to a happier future? She didn't know.

The afternoon dragged on. Unable to concentrate on television or reading, Norma began to sort through her bureau. Soon the wastebasket overflowed with rubbish: an amazing accumulation of old receipts and letters. When it was tidy she turned her attention to her clothes. The thought that she would soon be moving into the front bedroom gave her the impetus to sort through them. There was little point in transferring things she no longer wore, so discards from the wardrobes and chest of drawers joined the mounting pile of rubbish. She fetched some bin bags, filled three and removed them to the landing noting that although it was not yet six-o-clock rain clouds made it dark outside.

She wondered how long it would be before someone came, to tell her about the 'terrible accident'. Would it perhaps be a telephone call? No, of course not; surely a policewoman would knock at the door. To keep occupied she started cleaning her newly tidied rooms. For another two hours Norma worked in a frenzy of polishing furniture, making the brass and mirrors shine.

10 – Maud

Ten miles away Maud was on her way home, worried because she was so late. She'd been delayed by a nasty accident on the main road as she left town an hour or two earlier. She was thoroughly shaken; she had almost crashed into the car ahead as it rammed into the back of a truck. It had been ages before the police and ambulance arrived. In trying to help the injured, her own clothes became streaked with blood. She could have left earlier but one poor woman was trapped behind her steering wheel and Maud stayed with her, holding her hand while firemen worked to free her from the other side of the smashed car.

Now she was worried about Norma who would be frantic, not knowing why she was late. Norma was still such a child in many ways, and so imaginative. She was probably a bundle of nerves by now, picturing her dead at the roadside! It was just as well she wasn't; Norma would be incapable of managing alone as her head was always in the clouds and unlikely to change. Maud resolved to be more tolerant of her in future. She wished she'd been able to telephone. Her vision kept blurring and the pain in her neck was getting worse. When her seat belt had snatched, the jerk threw her head forward. How it ached! Perhaps she should pull in and rest a while, she thought, but straining to see through the drizzle she saw the turn into her own road. She would soon be home. Less than a minute later the drive gates came into sight. To her relief they were open.

***

Norma's eyes went again to the clock. Maud was usually back long before this but, how stupid of her, of course Maud was late ...she wasn't coming back at all! Norma eyed the results of her afternoon's activity with satisfaction but she still had to clear the rubbish sacks from the landing. Early tomorrow morning the refuse collectors were due; she could take them all to the gate – anything to fill in time until the bad news came.

Outside, grey clouds reflected dismally on the wet road but at least the rain had almost stopped. Moving the heavy bags from upstairs and down the drive had involved Norma in several journeys and she was thankful that she had wheeled the heavy bin out earlier. She was exhausted as she propped the last bag against it with a sigh of relief. The sooner she got inside, out of the drizzle, the better. She would make herself a nice cup of tea and settle down to watch her favourite programme.

***

Through the smeared windscreen, as she approached the house, Maud thought she saw someone at the gate. She pressed the washer, momentarily making it worse. How she wished that she had replaced the old wipers! But, as the footpath was clear, she signalled and turned into the drive. Then she saw Norma and slammed on the brakes. Although she tried frantically to steer away, the wet wheels spun and the car drifted uncontrollably sideways, hitting her sister, flinging her violently to the ground.

The last thing Norma saw before she died was Maud's stricken face, exactly as she had seen it in her vision and she smiled. She really was psychic ...they would have to believe her now!

11 – The Boy

The boy woke again to find himself under tree branches silhouetted against a glowing sunset. There was still a gap in his memory between feeling compelled to stay near the young woman with long, flowing hair and understanding how he had done so. Nothing made sense. In a strange way he felt removed from his previous insurmountable problems, but he remembered the old lady with complete clarity. Where was she now? Would she bring help as she'd promised? The child wasn't here either – wasn't she supposed to stay with him? At least, he sighed, someone now knew of his plight. He rolled over, hugged his knees and dozed fitfully.

Although invisible to him, the little girl played at his side, singing nursery rhymes as she nursed a baby doll. Soothed, in spite of his fears, he drifted into oblivion. Wakening again in the greyness of dawn, he saw the house gradually shifting into focus and sensed that the child had been with him. He was somewhat reassured but couldn't understand why he hadn't been taken somewhere for medical attention – not that it really bothered him anymore; did it matter?

He was far more interested in the woman he'd followed from the river. There was no sign of movement in the house yet but he didn't doubt that she was still inside and felt impatient to confront her. Why had he been directed to her unless she was the key to making sense of the images chasing each other through his confused brain? In one, he curled on rough carpeting. The sound of an engine roared, not quite obscuring the frightened wails of a child. He tried to cling to the brief flash but failed, although the screams never quite left his head. Was he to blame for the child's distress? He couldn't accept that. But, if not, why was he so consumed by guilt, convinced that something vital remained undone? And how could the blonde woman possibly help when he couldn't explain his needs?

His overwhelming fear was that he had done something unforgivable and would be unable to make amends. When the delicate features of a dead infant, starkly white in the moonlight, formed in his mind's eye, he struggled to rise; the face, surrounded by blonde curls, was achingly familiar to him. It was inconceivable that he'd hurt her – surely not! The vision shimmered out of reach and the desperation that had compelled him to move passed as quickly as it had come. He listlessly abandoned the effort, fearful of what his returning memories might reveal, but his half-formed desire to leave the garden – to forget the woman he'd come to find – was quickly discarded.

There would be no peace for him until he discovered the truth.

11 – Alec

Detective Chief Superintendent Alec Holmes sighed with relief when he replaced the receiver after speaking to Sarah. He would never act on anything she told him without solid evidence to back it up, but she could always be relied upon for honest down to earth advice, even if it did originate from unearthly sources! He had once been as sceptical as the next bloke about messages from the dead, but had ceased to question that Sarah received valuable information from somewhere out of his own reaches. He'd have been a fool to ignore her existence and was confident that he was sensible enough to handle everything she passed on, according to its merit. It was definitely a bonus that he could value Sarah and her daughter as friends. They were good company.

Alec eyed the growing pile of information on his desk ...he needed to read and remember every scrap before Sarah arrived. From what she had said already he was beginning to fear that they might be dealing not with a kidnapping but with a murder – or two – or even both! After a couple of hours concentration Alec summoned his team in case there was anything to add to his files and, as they all knew her, he mentioned that Sarah was taking an interest. He hadn't been able to speak to her before lunch because it was her bridge morning, Alec said with an indulgent smile.

Detective Sergeant Terry White, who had arrived late for the meeting, said it was the second time her name had cropped up within the last half hour ...he had just come back from a traffic accident. It was a terrible tragedy, he told them. After killing her sister in their own driveway, the driver was naturally in a state of shock, but had managed to gasp out, "Please tell Sarah ...Sarah Grey."

12 – Maud

Maud was hospitalised immediately after the accident and had been discharged only that morning, in time to attend Norma's funeral. Afterwards, Sarah tried to comfort Maud who felt burdened with guilt at having been the cause of her sister's death. Realising that Norma had made no attempt to act on her warning, Sarah guessed shrewdly that, had the boot been on the other foot, Norma would not have grieved as much. Maud knew she would have to sort through Norma's belongings but the task was daunting – she dreaded even going into her rooms. Maud really couldn't face the ordeal alone and asked if Sarah could stay with her for a few days. Sarah took a taxi home, promising to return that evening and would remain until Maud was over the initial shock of her loss.

The timing suited Sarah. Clarinda would be able to go away painting for a few days and all the things she had to take care of herself could be dealt with by 'phone. Alec Holmes would be expecting her to call him again even though she had little to add to her previous impressions that would help him with his case. As soon as he'd told her of the missing child she wondered if it could be the infant she had already seen that very day and, when first shown the snapshot, she had thought it was. Holding it in her hand however, she was assailed by doubt and finally became convinced that the child in the photograph was still alive. The similarity was uncanny but they were definitely two different children.

Alec, inclined to trust Sarah's impressions and relieved not to be dealing with a murder, was redoubling all efforts to find Kate. To focus her thoughts he had allowed Sarah to handle the original photograph and a handkerchief, probably dropped by the three-year old, which was found in the road outside her home.

Sarah's initial feelings had crystallised and even if they didn't help, they would ease Alec's mind. Not only did she believe the child to be alive, but also sensed that her life was not in immediate danger and this resulted in an increasing sense of frustration, that Alec and the girl's family were the only people she was helping at the moment. Now, having returned to her friend's home, Sarah found that nothing she said seemed to alleviate Maud's acute depression and it was with considerable relief that they both agreed to have an early night. Tomorrow they might feel more able to cope with the sad task that lay ahead.

After breakfast the following morning they lingered over several cups of coffee, but eventually went up to Norma's rooms. As the door opened and Maud looked inside she gasped, astonished – she'd never seen it so tidy. The pictures had been removed, cleaned and stacked against the walls; the bed was stripped, and the contents of the bureau were neatly sorted. The wardrobes and drawers were even tidier than her own ...she was sure Norma must have thrown away all her oldest clothes.

Maud wept copiously. She said it was as if Norma had known she wouldn't need the rooms any more ...she really must have had the second sight she claimed! Sarah seized the chance to agree and gradually persuaded Maud that if Norma knew she was fated to die and had accepted it with such dignity she must do the same. She could now resume her life with the burden of guilt removed. Maud nodded quietly, gleaning some comfort from the thought.

A few days later, Maud drove Sarah home. She hadn't recovered completely but was considerably more relaxed and ready to make plans. She said that one of the first things she intending doing was moving out of the front bedroom into Norma's. After pausing to dab her eyes she explained, "Living in her room with all her books and things around me, will help me to feel closer to her in spirit. I'm sure she would approve – she was much wiser than I ever gave her credit for!" Maud sighed heavily. "If only I'd made more effort to understand her ...if only I'd known!"

13 – Sarah

Sarah spent the afternoon settling back in at home. After removing the light dust, which had inevitably dulled the polished furniture, she couldn't resist looking at the photographs she'd picked up for Clarinda. Those of the river were excellent. She was not at all surprised to note how faithfully the painting, even though unfinished, had caught the atmosphere of the hot summer's day. She was about to replace them in the packet when she remembered the cruiser. She hadn't seen it in any of the snaps. Another check through the whole collection of thirty-six and the negatives, assured her that none showed any sign of life, on or off the water.

It was enough to convince Sarah Clarinda must have had a psychic vision at the river. It was't surprising that the boat didn't appear in the snaps! A feeling of apprehension stole over her, tinged with anticipation. Was this yet another aspect of the mystery which already faced them? Clarinda's disturbed session at the river, the child in the garden … and was it a coincidence that Alec sought her help at this time? Sarah had no answers yet, but believed that they were being shown these things for a purpose. When the time was right they must be ready to help either the living or the dead.

14 – Clarrie

Clarrie had enjoyed the short break away from her usual routine but felt a little guilty knowing that the last few days must have been depressing for her mother. However, had it not been for Maud's needing company Clarrie would readily have abandoned her own plans rather than leave her mother alone. A strangely threatening presence still hovered over the house and whatever was the cause, she preferred that they deal with it together.

Nothing had actually happened. Nobody was spying on them – unless it was the spectral child! Neither could believe they were in physical danger but, sensing that something wasn't right, both were mentally alert, awaiting developments. As expected, the rush-hour traffic was heavy. If Clarrie hadn't remembered to ring up and ask her mother to collect the photographs she would have had to do without them; parking was impossible. With luck, she could work from the snaps on Saturday and go again to the river for the whole day on Sunday.

In spite of having been away, staying at a client's home to start work on a long-promised portrait, she wasn't far behind schedule. She would have preferred to leave the portrait for another week or two so that she could carry on painting the river scene. With an outdoor subject it was important to finish fairly quickly in case the weather changed, but the little boy's mother said it would be terribly disappointing if the painting was put off any longer as he must soon have all his baby curls cut off. His daddy insisted that he must look like a real boy when he started school in September! The child had been delightful and the portrait was going well. Now that it was under way and his curls captured for posterity she could work on it later in her studio and visit his home for a few days next month to finish it.

The weekend promised to be fine and bright again, so with an average amount of luck she'd be able to finish the river painting too. Only one thing worried her: the sense of being stalked. Were they under physical threat or was something unworldly menacing them? On the whole she was less afraid of the latter. Clarrie had great faith in her mother. Sarah was experienced and quite capable of protecting them both from spiritual danger, but faced with a real live villain she'd be as helpless as most other women. Until the situation changed they would keep a low profile and not stay in alone, especially at night.

15 – Beth

Sarah wasn't sure what time to expect Clarinda so she'd prepared a casserole, which was cooking slowly in the oven; they could eat early and have a restful evening. Even though it had apparently gone well, Clarinda would be tired after the concentrated effort she must have put into the portrait. Even well-behaved children were far from being good sitters!

Sarah would never admit it, but when she took a magazine and tea-tray into the garden to enjoy the late afternoon sun she had an ulterior motive. She was making herself available! The child had, after all, been happy to make contact before Sarah had been collected to go to Bridge on that fateful day. Elsie's arrival at such a crucial moment had been unfortunate. So Sarah was merely making it easy for the contact to be renewed, if the little girl needed her.

Many mediums specialise in reaching and recalling those who have 'passed on', virtually on demand, but Sarah avoided that temptation. She had a deep-seated conviction that any attempts at contact should come from the other side. She was equally reluctant to use the telephone frivolously; what gave her the right, just because she felt like a good gossip, to intrude on a friend's privacy at a possibly inconvenient time?

Years of experience had not beguiled her into taking her gift for granted. It brought with it a sense of responsibility: neither to exaggerate nor misinterpret glimpses of the after-life which she felt privileged to be granted. Half an hour passed and Sarah gradually became absorbed in the story she had started reading with only feigned interest. The hum of distant traffic didn't disturb the peace of the garden, where she stretched comfortably on a garden chair, shaded by an old cherry tree. Occasionally, bees droned by ...a light breeze sighed: whispered ...sang: lulling her to the brink of sleep.

Then her senses were suddenly alerted. She froze, holding her breath, and looked up slowly in order not to alarm her little visitor. As she saw her, Sarah gasped in wonder. The sinking sun, beyond, made a shining halo over her soft curls. The little body was a warm shadow within the creamy glow of her dress as it billowed gently, reflecting the last of the daylight. Oh! If only Clarinda could be granted such a vision − what a picture she would be inspired to paint! Sarah smiled encouragingly.

The child came to her eagerly with no hesitation, uttering excited cries. In a distinctly scolding tone and with a hint of a lisp she demanded, "Where have you been? I've waited simply ages! What's your name? I'm Beth ...Beth Maybury." Somewhat taken aback by the polite but imperious introduction, Sarah gravely gave her own name then continued the communication, eager to discover why Beth had come and how long had she been in the Spirit world.

The house was sheltered by woodland on each side and the rear garden − level for most of its length − ended in a steep downward slope. An extensive view of the surrounding country stretched like a map beyond the soft fringe of grass that blurred the edge of the distant scene. The grounds were fenced out of sight below and properties lower down the hill were totally hidden. There were no casual onlookers to observe her strange behaviour as Sarah strolled slowly around the flowerbeds and summerhouse. When she stopped occasionally with bent head, as though listening intently, there were no neighbours wondering ...to what?

***

Something disturbed the boy − a voice... was it the child again? No there were two voices! Raising himself, he looked across the garden. He saw a woman, older than the one he sought. She was also slim but not as tall, her hair was short but up-swept in waves of silver. Probably the young woman's mother, he thought. How strange: her voice carried clearly and the child answered, but the woman was coming towards him alone. He must be going out of his mind – hearing things! He shook with apprehension, but was powerless to run away.

The child's voice was familiar ...and he suddenly knew that the sweet singing, which had soothed and comforted him during the last few days – or was it weeks, or hours – he couldn't tell, had not been human! He was haunted! Scrambling up at last, he ran to the nearby trees but as he moved he felt lighter than air. The ground dissolved below his feet. He felt neither the roughness of the earth nor the sting of thin branches whipping his skin.

Again, hopelessly lost in a swirling grey mist, he sank to his knees praying more fervently than ever before, "Oh, God... Please, please help me!"

16 – Sarah & Clarrie

There was an air of sustained excitement about her mother that caused Clarrie to comment as she started unloading the car. Sarah admitted that she did have something interesting to tell her, but as it was after seven-o-clock it could keep until dinner was served: even a casserole would not wait forever! Clarrie wasted little time before rejoining Sarah downstairs and over their meal they discussed the visitation of the afternoon.

It had been as difficult to squeeze information from Beth as from any young child, but Sarah surmised that it was her Great-grandmother who had been waiting for her when she left this life, as Beth had first thought the lady was her Nana – 'Mummy's mummy'. Beth's description of her own passing was confusing (she said a fish hit her on the head) but it seemed she'd been looking into the water and fallen. Then, standing on the edge, she had seen herself, lying below the surface.

Before she became alarmed the "nice lady who was just like Nana" cuddled her and wanted to take her away but she refused to leave her mummy and daddy. Apparently the lady promised that when she changed her mind, she would come for her again.

Immediately after her death Beth was very perplexed. Her parents were crying so much they couldn't hear her trying to tell them she was all right. She soon grasped that they couldn't see her, but the old lady could, so she decided there must be something wrong with them. She didn't understand, but tiring of their grief and with a child's curiosity Beth sat looking at her poor drowned body. It was white and still. It no longer seemed like her, so she felt no concern for it.

After a while she looked around the house. Her parents weren't there and the front door was wide open. She was frightened to be alone at first, but went up to her nursery and soon forgot everything other than her toys. Sarah then arrived at the most interesting point of her tale; there was indeed a connection between the child and Clarrie's pursuer. Beth's great-granny had instructed her to look after him!

Clarrie listened, fascinated, and was as baffled as her mother as to why they should have become involved in the child's death. She sounded happy enough and clearly had someone to care for her. "How," Clarrie wondered aloud, "is Beth linked to the strange boy ...was he near, perhaps on the river bank when she drowned? Was it he who hit her? And where is he now anyway? Have you actually seen him yet?"

"It's so unfortunate," Sarah answered. "When we reached the place where Beth left him he wasn't there. The child stamped in frustration and said 'He did it again. He keeps wandering off: bad, bad boy!' I asked who he was, but Beth shook her head – I don't think she knows. He won't talk to her." Clarrie frowned in astonishment but didn't interrupt. "However, the old lady said if she insisted on staying near her parents she could be very useful". Sarah smiled, remembering the self-important note in the child's voice. "He needs a friend until he gets better, so Beth is trying to look after him."

After talking through the situation they finally agreed they weren't much better informed than before, but knew they must be on their guard until the boy revealed his presence and his purpose in lurking nearby. There was just a chance that he had been responsible for Beth's death – it seemed much more likely than that a fish hit her!

When they had cleared up after dinner, Clarrie realised it was far too late to do any painting but suddenly thought of the photographs Sarah had collected. Without comment Sarah handed them to her and waited. Eagerly, Clarrie looked for the river shots, the last on the reel. She recalled taking three or four frames and sure enough all were there. The last, the most important because of the boat, would have to be enlarged of course. But where was it? In amazement she peered at the negatives; the boat had gone!

She dismissed the fleeting thought that it had swung out of sight before the button was depressed; her eye never left the viewfinder and she would have taken more had the film not run out. In the first of the snaps a patch of mist hung over the water where, she was quite sure, there had been no mist. In the second, the foggy area was at the inlet where the boat had been moored. There was neither mist nor boat on the others although she had seen the boat plainly – it had definitely been there... How could she be mistaken?

Clarrie didn't like introducing yet one more worry when her mother already had so much on her mind, but there could be a connection. With growing stirrings of alarm, she looked up and as their eyes met Sarah spoke.

"It's all right dear. I've noted the absence of the cruiser. At the moment it's merely another item to add to our ever-growing list of mysteries. We can be sure it has some importance, so I think you should try to sketch it before your memory of it fades." Clarrie nodded slowly ...she would be working tonight after all!

17 – Alec

In his office, Alec had gathered the small CID team that headed the search for the child, Kate Mead. They again went over the notes made by Detective Sergeant Dee who interviewed her distraught mother while the road outside was being searched for clues:

Witness Ethel Mead.

By the time she reached the gate, the car she'd glimpsed briefly was round the bend out of sight.

She heard it screech to a halt and a woman shouting. On being questioned, she couldn't be sure it wasn't a man but it was high pitched. However, someone called out and Ozzy yelled something, presumably to the driver, but Mrs Mead didn't catch what he'd said.

The child started crying: sounded frightened. Ozzy again shouted loudly, "Hey, what do you think you are doing?" Then more angrily – "No, no you can't! Stop ...Stop!" Then the car engine roared.

She heard doors slamming, an anguished wail and a loud thud before the car drove away, tyres screaming on the hot road surface.

After realising that the boy was dead Mrs Mead went to pieces but, fortunately, two vehicles arrived together from opposite directions. The local delivery van driver took charge, placed warning signs and went for help, leaving her with the other motorist, an elderly woman. She insisted that Ethel should sit in her car, which she thoughtfully turned so that it faced away from the body, which was covered with a blanket from the van.

John Dee had been quick to answer the summons from the mobile unit. The first police on the scene sent a car to fetch Ethel's husband, Eddie, from a nearby farm where he worked as a dairyman. A cursory examination of the scene revealed only a screwed up handkerchief caught in a bush on the side of the road where Ozzy lay. It was a man's, but not a clue to the kidnapper – Mrs Mead recognised it and had burst into tears again, making further questioning impossible.

18 – Ethel

Ethel had been unable to control her sobbing as she remembered Kate's little fingers trying to secure the handkerchief on Rosebud's arm. The horror of it all played, like a looped film, over and over again in her head: she was walking to the gate; a car flashed by; brakes screeched and fear clutched her stomach as she heard Kate wail. Breathless with dread, Ethel ran to the ominously quiet scene, now etched forever in her memory. There was no sign of Kate. Ozzy was motionless, half on, and half off the verge, arms extended as though reaching for the vanished car. She'd needed only one look to know he was dead. Ozzy's dark brown eyes were wide and staring; above them, his head was completely caved in. There wasn't much blood but she knew no one could have survived such a heavy blow.

How long had she stood there? She could only guess: a minute perhaps. She screamed with frustration, not knowing what to do. How could she leave him alone? There were no nearby residents to hear her shout and she knew she shouldn't drag his body off the road. Through her tears, Ethel looked down at her lap where she clutched Kate's doll. She had found it lying in the road: what violence had made the poor child drop her precious Rosebud? Ethel shook with anguish. Whoever grabbed Kate was completely heartless and hadn't hesitated to maim or kill, in taking her. They must have known that the boy trying to protect her had been hit. What monsters, not to have cared whether he was alive or dead!

Why should her child be kidnapped? What would happen to

little Katy? They were ordinary people; no one could expect them to pay a ransom. It took all her self-control not to scream aloud her inner prayer... "God, protect my baby! Please bring her home, safe and sound."

19 – The Team

After the conference, all agreed that for the time being they could do little other than extend inquiries over a wider area. National publicity had resulted in a deluge of leads. All must be checked. It was time consuming and tedious but many of the men had kids of their own; no one would rest easy until the case was solved. Kate had been missing for almost three weeks. It was disquieting, but they clung to Sarah's belief that she was alive. Searches through fields and woods, dragging waterways and ponds had thankfully revealed no trace of her so all they could do was to proceed logically.

Alec would have liked to have the doll to show Sarah but the mother had clung to it desperately for solace. Now, he decided, other avenues being closed, he would take Sarah to the Mead's house. The dead boy's parents might also like to meet Sarah. It would be little help to the inquiry, but might comfort them. Not wanting to alarm the kidnappers that the case against them would include murder, Ozzy's death hadn't been widely reported. His family must feel even more miserable as, in spite of his sacrifice, he'd failed to save the child but at least it had been an instantaneous death. He hadn't suffered. Alec knew Sarah well enough to know that if, in any way, she could help them to accept his death she wouldn't begrudge her time.

Unbeknown to Alec, Sarah was already involved even more deeply in the destiny of Kate than he could have dared hope.

20 – Family Life

When Clarrie returned to the river on Sunday, all went smoothly. It was a pity she didn't have a photograph of the cruiser, but she painted it from memory, aided considerably by observing the other powerboats which occasionally puttered by. She was still mystified by its absence from the snaps. Sarah sympathised, but was not technically-minded so if it wasn't a ghostly apparition she was inclined to suspect the camera was at fault ...perhaps the viewfinder was defective!

Throughout the day Clarrie looked up hopefully every time she heard the throb of an engine; it might be the one she had seen before; she would have liked proof that it existed, but it didn't return. At the end of the afternoon, having packed her equipment away, she couldn't resist exploring the inlet to look at the far side of the opposite bank, where she had seen the cruiser. If anchored to a spike – she knew most boats carried one to drive into the ground when there was no reliable mooring – there would be no trace, but if tied to a branch there might be damaged bark to see.

Hoping she wouldn't end up in the water Clarrie ignored the physical discomfort and edged carefully through the sharp overhanging branches along the rough bank, to the other side of the narrow trough of water; there was no other access except by wading. Scrambling up to firmer ground Clarrie looked across to the spot where she had experienced such discomfort. Although the angle was acute and it was partly obscured by bushes, it was impossible to credit that it had been moored unseen when she first arrived. It could only have come, if at all, during her short drive along the road.

She sighed, disappointed, and turned to go, but suddenly her eyes were attracted to a tiny object twinkling in a low slanting beam from the sinking sun. Following the brief flashes of red reflected light she walked away from the bank to the edge of the wood. There, dangling from a low branch was a bracelet. The clasp was still fastened but one of the links was broken; the owner had probably not missed it as she brushed aside the undergrowth. Although no expert, Clarrie saw that the stones were glass; no reward for the finder of this little trinket, she smiled! It was very small, the youngster was probably upset to have lost it but, sadly, there was nothing she could do about that. Dropping it into her pocket she struggled back to the car; she had weightier things on her mind.

Now that her mother had made contact with the little girl, Beth, she was no longer frightened of the stranger in the garden. Sarah seemed sure that whoever he was, he needed help and meant them no harm. Even so, Clarrie considered abandoning her previous plans for a painting holiday in North Wales. Sarah, however, wouldn't hear of it, insisting that she was in no danger. After some persuasion she agreed to ask her old friend Polly to move in for three weeks. Polly used to have her own apartment at the Greys' old family house, until Sarah sold the property and moved in with Clarrie.

Polly no longer wanted the responsibility of housekeeping but she still worked for them on three mornings a week. Looking after the much smaller house was easy and it kept her in touch with the family. She said that living with her married daughter and grandchildren gave her the best of both worlds. Polly was seven years older than Sarah and they had known each other for thirty-five years, since Stephen had first taken Sarah to meet his family. While working part time to support her little girl, born only two months after her husband died, Polly graduated in domestic science and home economics so she was well qualified to move in and take over when their old housekeeper retired. It had been hard for her in those early years – she hadn't re-married, but in spite of everything she was unfailingly cheerful.

Sarah, then barely twenty-one years old, was a little wary of Stephen's parents who were not as demonstrative as her own. She was even slightly daunted by Polly who, although only a few inches above her own height, was broad shouldered and rather angular. First impressions were soon dispelled and Polly, who had liked Sarah on sight, went out of her way to smooth her entry into the family. She explained soon after they met why she was called Polly, although introduced as Gertrude Bailey. When she first joined the household as a daily maid, an ancient parrot lived in the morning room and soon learned to greet her and her only, as she did him – "Hello Polly"! Everyone else soon followed suit but she didn't mind; anything, she declared, was better that Gerty!

Sarah and Stephen married in 1958 and Clarinda was born two years later. When his mother died in 1971, all three moved back to the family home to be with his father and Polly happily stayed on to look after them. Stephen's father rejected all Sarah's assurances that there really was a life after death. Even in the face of overtly clear evidence he still scoffed, but since his own death had once come back with a wry apology! Polly on the other hand was a firm believer and sought Sarah's advice eagerly on any and every problem that cropped up, as if being highly accomplished in one field made her knowledgeable in all!

When invited to spend a few weeks with Sarah, Polly agreed happily to do so – it would be nice change. Even though the years had increased her girth she was still reasonably active but, she said, no matter how much-loved, grandchildren were a bit of a strain at times! Clarrie was satisfied. Having allowed until mid-September to complete both the river painting and the portrait, she was ahead of schedule and could spare time for a working trip. When she returned, both pictures would be dry, ready for her clients to view if she still felt happy with them.

Because the concentration required in painting a picture could blind one to its faults, Clarrie always liked to keep her work around for a while to be able to judge it impartially. The boat in the painting still worried her slightly. There was nothing actually wrong with it ...she couldn't quite pin down why she felt a stir of apprehension every time it caught her eye in passing. She shrugged off the feeling as she collected her equipment together and loaded the car for her trip.

Everything was ready. Polly had insisted on packing a picnic box (for emergencies) and put it on the floor by the front passenger seat, while Clarrie hastened to the studio for a final check that nothing was forgotten ...with luck she would be on her way long before lunchtime traffic jammed the roads. She glanced around the garden as she walked down the side to the kitchen door. It was quiet, but for a moment she thought she saw a furtive movement. No, nothing: she really needed a change of air!

21 – The Boy

Since first light, the boy had watched the house. He felt much better and wondered why – he still couldn't remember anything useful. When he first awoke he saw the little girl briefly and knew he was seeing a ghost but no longer felt any fear. He accepted that she'd been with him day and night but couldn't be sure how many. Time had no meaning any more. The fact that he hadn't eaten for a long time crossed his mind but, as he felt no hunger, it didn't matter. His anxiety to stay hidden no longer seemed relevant either. He needed help but could find it only if he walked to the house and asked.

As he stood, irresolute, Beth appeared beside him. She took his hand and walked with him down the garden. She pulled him down to look earnestly into his eyes. "Can you speak to me yet? Please don't go away again. That nice lady, Sarah, wants to know your name. What is it?" He still didn't know, but together they followed Clarrie into the house. He called to attract her attention but she walked on, unheeding. With some hesitation, but urged by Beth, he followed up the stairs. When Clarrie eventually turned and stared through him, apparently unaware of his presence, it slowly dawned on him that he too was dead! He accepted the fact calmly; at least he was not alone now, he had Beth.

The young woman was looking at a picture on an easel. He stood behind her and immediately recognised the river where he first saw her. His eyes rested on the boat: there was something familiar about it? The memory was almost within his grasp: a memory that brought back fear and helplessness. Beth, watching his face, saw that he was about to collapse again into the limbo she'd hoped he had left forever. She grew angry and shook his arm with all her strength. "Don't you dare leave me... Wake up! You must stay here!"

From far away, her pleas reached him and he forced himself back to her side. He gave her a quick hug of reassurance; it was no problem. He would not leave her again. Whatever lay ahead, he wouldn't have to face it alone.

22 – Home & Away

Clarrie's father was very much in her mind as she drove along the winding lanes he had loved. This was her first visit to Wales since his death, three years ago. Since boyhood he had been a dedicated painter of wild Welsh landscapes and his works were still on show in some of the local museums. Clarrie didn't expect ever to reach his expertise but she had enjoyed painting alongside him. Even after leaving home to marry she still joined him on his annual fortnight in the valleys. They used to drive on and on, until an aspect of the hills or light filled him with eagerness to set up his easel; then it was a race against time to capture the magic, before the sun strengthened or unwanted shadows fell.

Her husband, Tom, encouraged her to paint and would have accompanied her willingly although not inclined to pick up a brush himself. He admired everything she produced – without reservation, and always made hanging space in their home. He was also flatteringly sad when she sold something, leaving a temporary gap! When Tom died, barely a year after her father, Clarrie thought her own life finished, but Sarah, still not over her own grief, pulled herself together for both their sakes. She sold up her home and moved in to help, by running the house and cooking, leaving Clarrie free to paint. Polly continued working part-time and during the last two years life had settled into a routine comfortable for all three.

Sarah played bridge and served on a few local committees – determined to live as independently as possible. As well as their natural affinity, she and her daughter were good friends. In public it is necessary to maintain an equable disposition, but privately, in the early months of bereavement, Clarrie and her mother accepted each other's mood swings totally: no explanations needed. It was good therapy for them both.

For months after Tom's death Clarrie hadn't painted at all and Sarah reproached her, knowing that Stephen must be saddened by his daughter's lack of interest in something so special, which they had shared until his death. Clarrie was used to her mother's psychic flashes of wisdom, never quite sure whether they really were messages from the life hereafter or Sarah's method of getting her own way! But gradually, Clarrie started working again, painting near home or in her studio. Taking a painting holiday alone had been too big a step but, however painful, she had decided this year to take the plunge and retrace one of her father's old routes. In spite of her earlier misgivings it had been fun checking her gear and restocking with materials; they were prepared even if she wasn't! Sarah had not even offered to accompany her. She commented that the slow pace of a Welsh village must be unutterably boring – nothing to do but walk in the damp air and barely half the television programs in English – she would be driven crazy inside a week. She much preferred to admire the scenery in the comfort of her own sitting room, in oils on canvas!

Clarrie suspected her mother's rationale. It was more likely that she knew it would be more therapeutic for Clarrie to be alone with her memories. It was strange driving through the once familiar hills and vales without her father beside her. They rarely conversed at length but were so in tune with each other that a mere sigh of pleasure from one or the other was enough, as new prospects loomed into view. She'd never been the one to suggest a suitable subject but was rarely surprised by his sudden cry... "This is it"!

They never booked in advance, preferring to stop when fancy took them, which was what Clarrie intended doing too. For some miles she had been looking for a suitable lodging, rejecting two because she had visited them with him and might have been faced with painful questions. Seeing a sign to Dolgellau, where they had never stayed, she decided, after all, to divert. There was no reason why she shouldn't seek new aspects to enjoy and make her own. She had promised Sarah she wouldn't leave the beaten track – putting herself at risk either from accidental injury or attack by homicidal strangers – so Dolgellau might provide some ideal subjects.

The late afternoon sun gave little warmth but it flashed directly into her eyes through the tall trees lining the road, blinding her as she approached the old market town. Eager not to miss anything she slowed down and, as often as the traffic would allow, scanned the land on each side. A mountain started its rise on her left but on the right the view was more open. The few older houses, well spaced out, were not intrusive and she could see that beyond them was a valley, grooved by a fast moving river. She remembered her father calling it the 'Onion'. His pronunciation of the Welsh name probably left a lot to be desired, but it always made him chuckle when they drove through Bala.

Remembering, she smiled absently and was suddenly jolted sharply back to the present, turning her head in alarm! She could have sworn he was there beside her. His laughter hung in the air, still echoing over the hum of the engine. Clarrie chided herself for letting her imagination run away with her and recovered slightly, accepting that her mind was playing tricks.

Even so, Sarah, whose psychic ability was beyond doubt, asserted that loved ones often linger, to guide and protect. They don't stop loving us just because they have passed on. She accepted her mother's mystic talents but was glad she didn't take after her. Clarrie had to admit that she had sometimes experienced an odd awareness of the spiritual world but was convinced that, in her case, it was auto-suggestion because she knew it was possible!

Sarah understood her reluctance to accept that she too had the gift, but knew that if the spirit world wanted to work through Clarinda she would have no choice ...and events of the past few weeks made her suspect the time had come. Clarrie smiled, musing on her mother's propensity to speak of the dead as though still in the land of the living, but she had been an unfailing source of strength and comfort during the last few years so it was easy to accept her faith without reservation. Sarah's unorthodox religious convictions were at least private. If she owned a crystal ball and held séances it would be upsetting, but it hadn't come to that – yet!

In the miles she'd covered with her mind preoccupied Clarrie had missed several Bed & Breakfast signs. She was brought sharply back to the present, instinctively braking hard as she rounded a bend and was confronted by a car straddling the road. The driver was struggling to turn between the cemetery and a cottage driveway. A frail elderly woman, leaning heavily on a stout walking stick, watched anxiously from her garden, concerned no doubt for her newly painted gate! Catching Clarrie's eye she shook her head in exasperation. Clarrie was sympathetic. Visitors to the church obviously had nowhere to park and were probably a constant irritation to her.

Waiting for the driver to sort himself out, she lowered her window and could hear rushing water beyond the house. She allowed the car to creep forward and saw a small brook coursing under the road into the garden where it joined the larger waterway. The river sparkled as it tumbled out of sight over a bed of smooth grey stones. Distant springs falling down a ridge of mountains reflected diamond sparks of light. The ambience was hypnotic; her eyes glazed as her heavy lashes filtered the brilliance. The woman lowered her head to Clarrie's open window and spoke, "At last!"...If she hadn't, Clarrie might have fallen asleep. She hadn't realised how tired she was.

Once underway again, she was almost immediately in the town. The sun, now pale and low, gleamed softly on the dark stone houses that bordered the street. The yellow glow washed over small neat gardens and threw delicate shadows on the grass, like lace behind embroidered leaves. The artist in her responded to the atmosphere and she knew that memories of her father would not mar her enjoyment.

When filling up at the first petrol station she reached, she took the opportunity to ask about local hotels and the friendly pump attendant said she'd be sure to find a nice place on the Barmouth road. Even if she went to the coast it was only about ten miles ...no need to worry about everything being booked up at this time of the year!

Now in a heady mood of expectancy, she drove along the main thoroughfare, noting the variety of shops ...there was even one with oil paintings in the window which would perhaps sell materials if she ran short, and she must certainly visit those which displayed Welsh tweed while she was here. Sarah would be ecstatic with a skirt length or two. Driving out at the other side of town she couldn't help smiling again as she crossed the 'Onion' over a small bridge, and turned left towards Barmouth, confident of finding a place to stay.

Within a few miles, a small spring spouted onto the road and her eye was attracted to a narrow ribbon of light above it. She again felt slightly mesmerized by the sparkling water of a narrow stream as it caught the last rays of sunlight. Her eyes followed its course from the top of a low ridge and saw that it eventually ran alongside a narrow lane. Because the whole area was so beautiful and seemed likely to provide good subject matter she decided to save herself time tomorrow by exploring straight away. It could not be impossibly isolated and she wouldn't stray far from her route she promised herself as she turned off the main road.

The sun was so low that it was immediately dark under the canopy of trees bordering the road and with headlights on it was impossible to see whether the views were good or not. She immediately realised how silly she had been to divert tonight, when she had weeks ahead to explore. Unfortunately, there was nowhere to turn in the narrowing road, so she was forced to drive on.

Much to her relief the track ahead soon split into two, but as she drew nearer to the fork she saw that there were deep ditches on each side ...she dared not attempt a turn that would far exceed three points! Thoroughly annoyed with herself she weighed up the merits of each track. Which was the most used, offering the best hope of either turning space or swinging back to the main road? As she hesitated a light came on, breaking the gloom to her left. A light could mean habitation so, with luck, she'd be able to turn in someone's driveway. Before she moved another car drew up behind her with an impatient hoot. She couldn't go back anyway! In her driving mirror she saw yet another car join the queue and, with only a few twinges of uncertainty, drove forward towards the light. When she reached the source, the popularity of the lane was explained. It was a small hotel. What incredible luck, she thought: there would surely be a room to spare at this time of year. Aware of how tired she was, she fervently hoped so. A large sign set against the rough natural rock face proclaimed it to be 'The Rowen Hotel' and after locking her car she followed the other – obviously thirsty – customers.

Wide stone steps led up to a terrace where a rustic wooden porch covered the entrance to a bright, welcoming lounge. There were several cars already parked in the cleared woodland patch, so she wasn't surprised to find a crowd at the bar. An elderly woman, serving drinks, obviously knew all her patrons well, exchanging banter and greeting newcomers with a friendly nod. She stared with curiosity at Clarrie, a young stranger, female and alone, but smiled and gestured to a small table in a nook by the wide stone fireplace. Clarrie stood for a moment by the blazing log fire then, removing her coat, sat down. At first sight she liked all she saw. From outside, the place looked solid, square and rather ordinary – the welcoming lights being its main virtue but, inside, the atmosphere and the old-style furnishings were delightful. If she couldn't spend her whole holiday here, she would be extremely disappointed. As soon as she was free the bartender walked over to greet her and when asked about a room seemed as pleased as Clarrie that there was indeed one available. She said her brother-in-law would be down soon to organise signing in, bags and so on. "In the meantime," she offered, "Let me bring you a drink – on the house. Bit chilly out. Not a lot of visitors yere now. On holiday, is it?" she added in a tuneful Welsh lilt.

Confirming that she was on holiday, Clarrie explained that she had come to paint, hoping to capture the autumn colours. Her previous visits had all been earlier in the year. Mrs Tudor – "Call me Olwen," she invited – showed her the public telephone so that she could ring her mother, and then lost no time in telling her other customers, "We're to have an artist staying yere. Come a long way to paint our valley, she 'ave, from England, so mind your manners! Show her some Welsh hospitality!" The regulars welcomed Clarrie and vied for her favour eagerly. Not many strangers found the Rowen, being out of sight of the main road, and they usually liked it that way, but with great good humour they included her in their conversation, offering suggestions too about places worth painting. She was almost disappointed when at last Olwen called her to come and meet her brother-in-law, who would take her to her room ...but Clarrie's feelings underwent a startling change when she raised her eyes to meet those of Roger Derwent.

23 – Roger

Covertly, Roger had been watching Clarrie for some while. It was not only her grace and elegant clothes which aroused his interest; she was beautiful. He had known many good-looking women – most of them fell quickly under his spell, but he was wary of making commitments of any kind. He well knew, by experience, a pretty girl's absorbing interest was likely to be self-adornment and to that end, most were demanding and unscrupulous. One such involvement had put him off for life! He'd not easily be misled again.

Olwen's sister Megan had been a good for him. She ran the financial affairs of the hotel competently, while Olwen took care of the housekeeping and practicalities of daily life and in spite of frail health Megan had shared the bar-tending with Olwen until ten years ago, when Roger had arrived, seeking work. They both took to the handsome young man and within eighteen months he was literally one of the family. Marriage to Megan had been bearable. Being more mature she was devoted to him but not possessive. But next time, Roger thought, someone like this new guest would be perfect.

Roger held Clarrie's arm on the steps as they walked out to fetch her luggage. He was complimentary about her car and she found herself explaining; it had been her father's – mother didn't drive. What was wrong with her? Babbling like a half-wit to a stranger who was merely being a considerate host! Why shouldn't she drive a luxury car? For goodness sake ...she didn't have to efface herself! In truth, she suddenly felt very young and immature.

The nearness of this attractive man with his unnerving, deep brown eyes disturbed her poise. She signed the register in a daze – more aware of him, beside her, than the pen in her hand. Later, as he unlocked the room and gave her the key, their fingers touched. They both paused uncertainly for a moment, conscious of each other in a way quite unwarranted by their brief acquaintance. His eyes held hers searchingly as he wished her an enjoyable stay and informed her that she could order supper on the intercom from the menu on the desk, but there was no room service; meals were served in the dining room. He hoped she wasn't too tired to go down again ...that he would have the pleasure of seeing her later. Turning abruptly, he hurried away.

Once alone, Clarrie sat bemused, assessing the unexpected emotions that had assailed her since she first looked up at Olwen's call. The man had a powerful personal magnetism that drew her physically – the married man she reminded herself, who seemed equally aware of her. Roger must be married to Olwen's sister. If her husband and Roger were brothers her name would be Derwent too. She would find out tomorrow. If he still had this overwhelming effect on her and wasn't free to return anything more than holiday friendship she'd leave straight away. She'd had enough sorrow already and would not expose herself recklessly to possible heartbreak.

Eventually pulling herself together, she did a limited amount of unpacking in case she stayed only one night, already knowing that her resolve was weakening, but she decided against going down for dinner. A sense of self-preservation persuaded her that meeting him again in her present state of mind, might interfere with rational judgement! Before it grew too late she rang home. Her mother was out but Polly noted the number of the hotel so she could expect a call back early tomorrow.

Clarrie was disappointed. She had wanted to discuss her odd experience in the car. It seemed trivial now – probably only imagined anyway! Lying awake later, her brain was still whirling. She was utterly confused. Weariness after her long drive must have made her more vulnerable – so could she trust her present emotions? Did she want to? She hardly knew. Stupidly, the thought uppermost in her mind was that she was being unfaithful to Tom. After the accident a year prior to his death, her love for him never wavered, even though they could no longer enjoy a full physical relationship. He unselfishly advocated that she should seek fulfilment elsewhere until he saw how the mere suggestion horrified her. Far from resenting a new husband or lover he'd be glad for her, but the guilt remained – although tonight she was only turning from him in thought.

For hours Clarrie slept only fitfully. Drowsing, she pursued absurd strands of jumbled thought, which she thrust from her mind until she fell into a deep sleep. The night was still – no wind stirred the trees. The sibilant rush of water over the stones in the nearby brook lulled her, until, out of a dreamless void, Tom came to her. He stood looking down at her anxiously. Shaking his head sadly, he spoke – and she was instantly wide-awake. In her head she still heard his voice: "No, Darling, Oh no!" His presence had been incredibly real! Her dreams did not usually have such clarity. Asleep or awake, her mother coped with visions of the dead but, unlike Sarah, Clarrie couldn't accept the image as anything other than a product of her own sub-conscious.

Any likelihood of sleeping again was remote but she sank wearily into a light doze until the cheerful chorus of birds and the promise of a bright new day banished her pessimism of the night. She got out of bed, eager to see the view outside her window. When she arrived it had been too dark to discern anything other than the outline of a few tall trees – their branches reaching into a Payne's grey sky against far distant mountains. Now she saw pine-covered hills beyond the brook that edged the hotel garden. Some flowering shrubs, rockeries and a few deciduous trees adorned the lawns below. It was a beautiful new world. She intended to enjoy a well-deserved holiday and paint at least one masterpiece every week!

Her room was small but comfortable and as she stripped and showered in the neat en-suite cubicle she reflected that the Rowen was a lucky find. She had expected to stay at a more basic place – perhaps even having to share a bathroom, but fate had brought her here! As the thought struck her and an image of Roger intruded, she thrust it aside angrily; he had no place in her life. He was married and probably used to having females drooling over him. She would not add to the list. In any case, she'd been travel-weary last night: in a vulnerable state of mind.

She may have been a bit light-headed too, taking brandy on an empty stomach! No wonder her dreams were troubled! She would certainly not allow them to invade her waking hours. Even as she dismissed the vision of Tom she felt disloyal. The emotional shock of not only seeing him so vividly but also hearing his voice, had stunned her initially, but she now put the experience in perspective. His words were undoubtedly spawned by her subconscious mind but she had no reason to feel guilty. While he'd lived she gave him love and devotion ...she knew he wouldn't begrudge her a chance to be happy again if ever she found the right person. She dressed quickly, concentrating on her plans for the day. She would order a picnic lunch to take out and leave straight after breakfast. She would find a suitable place to set up her easel and paint until the light faded around four-o-clock. Then she would drive around a bit, exploring, before stopping somewhere for an early dinner. What she was really doing, she knew deep down, was avoiding using the Rowen any more than necessary. By avoiding Roger (and Mrs!) Derwent for a few days, she might be able to recover her equilibrium and settle down to work with less difficulty, but she brushed her hair longer than usual and took extra care with her make-up!

The dining room was no less attractive than the bar, with low beams and varnished wood. Wall lights were concealed behind parchment-coloured shades and old prints adorned the whitewashed walls, but the old stone fireplace where a cheerful fire blazed was the main feature. There were eight tables of similar size. Four were set for only two people so Clarrie guessed that they were for houseguests and sat at the one nearest to a window. A small posy of fresh flowers decorated each table; the dew on a rosebud briefly held a gleam of bright sunshine. If only the moment could be captured in oils, a perfect still-life painting. She wished she had brought her camera down; it would have been a memory to work on when she returned home. Perhaps tomorrow – at the same time – at the same table, another sunray would fall – on another dewdrop – on another rose? No, the magic moment had already gone ...the opportunity lost. Inevitably, her thoughts went to Roger. Was he destined to mean something in her life? A friendship or a romantic interlude: a new experience. Was this also a chance not to be missed?

While she mused, Roger stood behind her, quietly watching and admiring again this lovely creature. He could scarcely believe his luck, not only did she intend staying, she was unattached. Olwen said she had been widowed for a couple of years. He must be careful how he approached her. With her looks she must be used to fending off admirers! Anyway, before committing himself there were other things to discover. He was getting too old to make any more mistakes. He walked to her table making sure she heard him approach and asked if she had ordered breakfast. "I hope you had a comfortable night Mrs Hunter. You must have been exhausted – too tired to come down for an evening meal anyway! We'd hoped to see you again after the bar closed when we would have been able to devote more time to you."

How Clarrie managed to answer, in spite of her suddenly dry throat, and what she actually said, she couldn't recall afterwards. His nearness had the same disturbing effect as on the previous night! She tried to take in what he was saying as he smiled ruefully. "I hear you've ordered a picnic lunch. Are we to be deprived of your company all day?"

She explained that she had come to paint and conditions were so good she wanted to start immediately in case the weather changed. He asked if she knew the area and had a particular view in mind. Upon being informed that she had no set plans, he found a local map and suggested a possible route but didn't linger and she felt a twinge of disappointment when he left, wishing her a good day.

The girl who brought her breakfast had heard Roger's advice and couldn't resist commenting, "Trying to be helpful he is, but he 'aven't been yere long really. Born not two miles from this place I was!" She smiled shyly. "I could show you some beautiful spots that'd make marvellous pictures, if you feel up to a bit of climbing, that is!"

Promising to call on her for guidance if she couldn't find any worthwhile subjects where she was able to use her car – a lot of heavy equipment she explained, Clarrie tucked in to a substantial meal, which would satisfy her for several hours. Olwen must have been keeping an eye on her progress because as soon as Clarrie finished and began collecting her things together, she bustled in with a wicker basket: the picnic lunch.

"I hope you like pork pie and salad, my dear, and there's yoghurt and fresh fruit. Please say if you want anything changed, it would be no trouble at all, and very quick we could be. Oh! There's a flask of tea. Forgot, I did, to ask if you preferred coffee!"

"That sounds lovely, Olwen. Thank you," Clarrie assured the kindly older woman. It was funny; last night Olwen had not seemed as old. Clarrie wondered again about her sister, Mrs Derwent! She just couldn't leave for the day without discovering more about the woman she was already resenting although they hadn't met! "I'm quite impressed by your hotel," she went on, "It must be hard work providing such excellent service. Does Mrs Derwent also take an active part in the management?"

Olwen raised an eyebrow with a shrewd side-glance at Clarrie who, embarrassed, felt a flush rise to her cheeks. His sister-in-law must be amused by her clumsy attempt to inquire into Roger's private life. Just one more in a long line of besotted females! When she replied, however, Olwen's tone was friendly but sad. "My sister Megan was never strong, not from being a girl, but she ran the office side of the business 'til she married – then Roger helped her and took over when she died." Olwen sighed deeply at the memory. "Sad it was ...only had three years together. Of course, he knew when he married her it couldn't last, but he was marvellous – made her happier than she'd ever been. And he's never looked seriously at another woman since," she added, permitting herself a sly smile.

Clarrie expressed her condolences with such obviously

genuine sympathy that Olwen continued, "I remember when Megan was born. Seventeen years younger than me she was; we never thought she would live she was such a tiny scrap but the good Welsh air and the joy of a husband little more than half her age helped her to reach her fifty-sixth birthday, five years ago ...born and buried yere she was." Raising her hand to wipe away a tear, Olwen seemed so vulnerable, so alone, that Clarrie wished she hadn't revived such sad memories.

In an attempt to change the subject she asked, "Has the Rowen always been in your family? It is not a name I know, does it mean anything?"

"Bless you," laughed Olwen. "Named after the town my mother came from it is. After they married, when our Da brought her yere, he called it that to stop her feeling homesick! Only fifty miles away it is, but in those days people didn't travel far from where they were born." She dabbed eyes again, but her good humour was fully restored. "In those days it was a difficult place to run... No gas or electricity and carried drinking water from the mountain spring, we did. We still fetch spring water, but now we do it because it's the purest and healthiest there is. I never drink tap water at all."

Clarrie reflected that Olwen, in her late seventies, was a good recommendation for it! Olwen was pleased with Clarrie's favourable comment and explained, "The original male chauvinist was our Da! When he died in '69 he left us both a life interest as long as we lived in it, but my son Eric inherited the hotel. An architect he is, and can take all the credit for making the place modern and attractive. Olwen sighed heavily on the verge of tears again, "His father would have been proud of him but it wasn't to be, died in a pit accident he did, while Eric was still studying."

Clarrie found herself explaining about Tom's accident and their individual tragedies formed a common bond. Olwen took her hand in a strong, firm grip for a few moments as they stood quietly staring out over the well-kept lawn. It was as if speaking aloud of Tom and their woefully short but happy time together, in spite of re-living the sadness of his last months, had brought her to terms with her conflicting emotions. She'd done all that was humanly possible for him then, and must face the fact that he was gone. She could allow herself to be happy whether or not another man came into her life but if one did, she knew it couldn't be wrong in anyone's eyes, least of all Tom's. Olwen patted her arm and said, "There you go now my lovely, have a good day and we'll have something special for supper tonight, something to cheer you up!"

Knowing that Roger was a widower lifted her spirits. It didn't automatically follow that even though available he was destined to be anything special to her – she certainly wouldn't set out to attract him, but it did mean that she could relax and enjoy her stay, letting things take their own course.

It was not quite nine-o-clock when eventually, looking nothing like the 'Woman about Town' of yesterday, she walked down the steps to her car in trousers and sweater struggling with the picnic box and a raincoat on one side and a canvas rucksack swinging awkwardly on the other. It contained all she might possibly need during the day: paper tissues, toilet bag, magazines (for lunch break relaxation) and caramels. If a first aid kit hadn't been built into the car she would have thrown in sticking plasters and bandages! Her father used to accuse her of being the world's worst pessimist. As an ex-Girl Guide she called it being prepared!

Following Roger's advice she drove back into Dolgellau and headed for Machynlleth – not to go all the way, but to circle the mountain, Cader Idris, and return along the coast through Llwyngwril and Friog so that the sun would be behind her coming back, not in her eyes! Her father used to think of things like that. Roger had laughed when she told him their name for the river, pointing to it on the map ...the "Wnion" he said, pronounced 'Wun'.

Lost in thought, she hardly noticed the beauty of the passing hills and valleys. She kept reminding herself that she was seeking a subject to paint, but there were too many possibilities. She parked several times to assess likely angles where a dramatic grouping of trees or land sweep caught her eye, but to no purpose, so she drove on. When the lanes were not too narrow she explored the territory on each side, only rejecting some aspects because of her promise to Sarah... Why were the most beautiful spots always the loneliest? Clarrie realised she was being ridiculously unfair. The gloriously dramatic Cader Idris was in sight almost all the time, surely a suitable view and a convenient place to stop would coincide somewhere! Three hours later she decided it was a day only for planning, not painting, and stopped for her picnic. She had food, drink, something to read and a view of the sea now, between trees glowing with autumn gold... What more could she ask for? She was happy.

24 – Clarrie

On every side, all the way, the scenery was magnificent yet she was incapable of making a decision – or even a short-list of possible sites! A constant problem was the difficulty in deciding how much of any view's appeal was due to the topography of the land or the angle of the light. Her father used to paint two studies in succession – one canvas in the morning and another in the afternoon – rather than change location. Such niceties never troubled her then; she'd been pleased if her painting was even remotely like the subject! Now she strived for, if not perfection, at least something approaching the truth.

More than at any time when she'd actually painted with him, Clarrie felt capable of absorbing, understanding and acting on his words of guidance. His presence beside her in the car was almost tangible: the air fragrant with his special aroma of cigar smoke and after-shave. Refusing to question her senses, she allowed herself to enjoy the almost forgotten feeling of companionship. At times like this he had comforted her, "Don't fret my girl – we'll know it when we see it!" There was ample time: other places to see. A day enjoyed was never wasted. That route had been tried; tomorrow she would take another.

It was still sunny when she returned to the Rowen. Olwen would be surprised, having been told not to expect her until seven-o-clock at the earliest. Clarrie was eager to shower and change into something more civilised, rejecting firmly the thought that she would be embarrassed if Roger saw her in her present state, but she hesitated as she opened the car door to climb out. Her eyes went to the open map on the passenger seat ...the section uppermost was not the one she had been using. Settling back into the driving seat and picking it up without looking, as she had been doing all day, her route was impossible to read without re-folding. With the familiar section facing her, she re-placed it on the seat several times and even threw it, but never did it open as she had just found it. Mystified, she studied the new area displayed, thinking she might drive out that way next time, and immediately felt drawn to an empty space above Ffestiniog, about twenty miles north. The surrounding area was studded with villages but the part that held her gaze showed no roads or hamlets at all, just white paper. She felt a disquieting urge to find it. She had to know what was there. Taking the map with her so that she could study it later, Clarrie hurried inside.

After dinner, she relaxed in the residents' sitting room where she discovered a shelf full of magazines and paperbacks. The fireplace was smaller than the others but logs burned warmly and, nearby, a television set was tuned to the news in English. A video player stood below it with several film boxes. Clarrie marvelled again at the amount of thought that had gone into this small business. It deserved to succeed. When the news ended she considered going to the bar for a drink and some company, not of course hoping to meet anyone in particular but, before she moved, Roger came in and inquired after her comfort.

He wanted to know if she'd had any problems finding her way around and Clarrie discovered him to be an excellent listener as she went over her day's pleasures and frustrations. Suddenly wondering if she was keeping him she apologised but, instead of leaving her, he sat with a contented sigh. He'd just handed the bar over to Olwen so he was off duty. They conversed easily, discovering many interests in common, learning about each other and, when Olwen came in to say goodnight, were astonished to find that it was actually early morning – his Sunday off Roger said. If Clarrie would like a willing guide, he suggested driving her to Betws-y-Coed where there was a waterfall. She accepted with pleasure.

Clarrie lay in bed with almost childlike excitement as she

looked forward to the promised outing. Roger was very good company and clearly, he was equally happy to be with her. Had fate brought her here just to bring them together? She pondered ...then chided herself wryly; there was no reason yet to suspect Divine Guidance! No reason at all; she scorned her own silliness and slowly relaxed into a sound sleep.

She stirred at dawn feeling weirdly disorientated – almost as if she had not slept at all although she knew she had. Her sleep had been dreamless. She recollected nothing until she sensed herself waking, lighter than air, rising up ...up to the sky. It wasn't a frightening sensation as she hovered on high. It was exhilarating! She hung suspended, gazing down on the hotel among the trees ...the river gleamed faintly in the moonlight. Trailing behind her from the place where her body lay, a silver ribbon of light pulsated as though ensuring that she would not lose her way: her lifeline! She would never have moved of her own volition, but something beyond her own will pulled her away. Rushing air filled her ears and everything blurred until, just as mysteriously, she hovered again. The land now below her was as instantly recognisable as the road map she had studied a few hours earlier.

The unmarked area, which had claimed her attention so peculiarly, was directly underneath her, criss-crossed with farm lanes and tracks. There was a farmhouse and woodland nearby but at the centre of the scene was a small cottage. She desperately wanted to go down for a closer look but couldn't. The silvery thread grew taut – dragging her away abruptly through a dark echoing helix of wind, to her bed, where she became instantly awake. The experience had been incredibly vivid ...it was some time before she could shake off the feeling that she really had been on that strange flight.

Convinced at last, that her preoccupation with the map had invaded her dreams, she slept again but was even more keen to see what the road book did not reveal.

Sunday dawned bright and sunny. It was warm too, for the time of year, a lovely day for a drive. Roger rejected the idea of a picnic. Although it sounded like a busman's holiday he said there was a restaurant he wanted to check out, but Clarrie suspected he wanted her to feel pampered. Their route to the falls, going through Bala and returning via Ffestiniog, would take them close to what she now thought of as her mystery mile, and she was filled with anticipation. Surely she could persuade Roger to make the necessary diversion, but she would wait until they were near it before asking. If she explained her interest he'd think she was batty! A good reason for exploring would surely occur to her when the moment came.

The hours passed all too quickly as they exchanged their opinions easily. Roger commented happily that they agreed about all the important things – religion, food and politics – and had at least three weeks to sort out everything else! He laid stress on the 'at least' and glanced sideways at her with a boyish grin which made him seem irresistible. Clarrie glowed with contentment: tired and happy as they drove home. Strolling sometimes to admire the fantastic scenery and the good food savoured during the day seemed to have drained her of energy. She sat contentedly, listening to the tape he'd selected. The music, soft and romantic – swelling, only to die again – held her entranced ...the passing miles went unheeded.

"This is it! ..."

The cry rang out clearly over the music. Shocked, Clarrie sat up and looked sharply at Roger. He was equally startled by her abrupt movement and turned to look at her.

"If you jump about like that, you'll have us up a tree," he grinned. Then more seriously, seeing the expression on her face, he asked what was wrong.

Lost for a plausible explanation Clarrie merely shook her head and apologised, "A stab of cramp. Sorry."

When, in imagination, she'd heard her father's voice, they were actually on the stretch of road for which she was looking. It was uncanny ...thoroughly unnerving, but it increased her determination to carry out her plan. She asked tentatively if there was anything worth looking at down some of the side roads. "There was one which looked interesting about a quarter of a mile back," she told him, hoping there really was. At the time, she had been oblivious to the outside world ...in any case Roger stated quite flatly that there was nothing worth going back for. In comparison to what was yet to come, it was pretty dull stuff! He obviously had no intention of turning back, being keen to show her other splendid views before the daylight failed.

She couldn't blame him so, noting carefully where they were, she relaxed, making the most of their remaining time together. Tomorrow she would return alone. Clarrie stole a long look at his profile, feeling as if she had known him all her life. He looked a little like Tom, which possibly accounted for her instant attraction to him. Only time would tell if he could replace Tom, but she already knew that he stood a very good chance, if he felt the same way about her. She wondered what Sarah would think of him. Her mother approved of her re-marrying in principle; they had discussed the possibility although Clarrie insisted it was remote.

When Tom died Sarah had abandoned her plan to buy a riverside flat but if the need arose she'd go ahead with the scheme. The thought of living alone did not dismay her. What her mother would think of the voices and dreams she had been experiencing was more predictable. She had always believed that Clarrie was potentially psychic, but only by accepting the reality, was communication possible. Clarrie was reluctant to be used and more than a little frightened.

She had been conditioned to accept the afterlife as a fact – too many of her mother's contacts with it had afterwards proved valid – but was she as able as Sarah to protect herself from evil entities? She remembered being frightened of the dark when tiny and was allowed the comfort of a night-light, but imagination made monsters of the shadows. Instead of calling her silly, her mother taught her to deal with her fear by imagining herself inside an invisible egg, and told her to repeat her bedside prayers to prevent anything bad approaching. It had worked. It made her feel in control rather than at the mercy of the unknown, but would such a fanciful device work for a more mature adult? With an apprehensive shudder she hoped she would never need to find out!

Clarrie decided to telephone home again when they got back. Whether she could relate her dreams and admit to hearing voices without sounding ridiculous she didn't know, but she was eager for assurance that finding the Rowen had not been mere chance. She wanted to believe that she had been guided here to meet this singular man who would bring joy into her life again. She closed her mind resolutely to the subliminal image of Tom as he had appeared and spoken in her dream. She refused to allow the past to ruin the present ...advice given often by her mother.

She knew she could expect full support from Sarah whatever she decided. Clarrie re-considered all her uncanny experiences and, although not eager for repetitions, was much more fascinated than frightened. For the first time in her life she had an inkling of how her mother must feel. She also knew why, when it was avoidable, Sarah never revealed her powers. If people were happy with closed minds ...why risk their derision!

As they pulled into the car park Roger insisted that they must have dinner together to round off the day. It was almost dark and the illuminated signboard and entrance lights welcomed them so cheerfully that Clarrie was almost sorry when he said they would be eating out – fifteen miles out in fact. Helping her from the car, he held her arm gently and murmured, "I'll need an hour to freshen up. You still look marvellous!" He'd heard good reports of a restaurant out towards Welshpool, he told Clarrie, and was anxious to check on the opposition. What better excuse for going than to show off his new lady friend? He lifted a brow waiting for her to react and was rewarded by a raised eyebrow and a flutter of her long lashes as she left him to go to her room.

They were driving away again before she remembered her intention to ring home but with a mental shrug she decided it didn't really matter. It was not vital to make contact tonight. Clarrie refused to let even a faint stir of regret spoil her mood. In contrast to their non-stop verbal exchange of the morning and teasing banter throughout the day, the evening passed with a quiet serenity usually achieved only through years of intimacy. Clarrie could hardly remember when she had last felt so happy and contented.

Mai Griffin

25 – Roger

Roger was well pleased with the way things were going. Clarinda Hunter was every bit as interesting as she looked: intelligent without trying to be clever and quick to laugh without sounding hysterically eager to be amused. He hadn't expected to enjoy her company so much. The fact that she was also beautiful was an added bonus. Megan hadn't been ugly but when he married her it had been a calculated reaction against shallow prettiness. He knew it wasn't love but he sought security. At the time he knew it would probably last only a few years, owing to her poor health, but he'd made her happy: had kept his part of the bargain.

Across the candlelit table Clarrie's hair glinted gold as it fell in shining sweeps over her shoulders. A high-necked dress of russet-brown velvet gave her features an air of old-fashioned grace, emphasised by the antique Victorian brooch at her slender throat. When her deep violet eyes were not on him, he relaxed and enjoyed just gazing at her slim form and the glow of the low light on her smooth skin. He felt sure he had made a good impression on her too. Most gratifying of all, if he interested her, it was not because she thought him to be a wealthy hotel owner. She was obviously a woman of means, not a gold-digger like most he'd met in the last few years. He could scarcely believe his luck but must be careful not to rush things ...she had memories to subdue and would be scared off unless he was patient, but it was going to be damned difficult holding back! He had stagnated long enough; it was time he moved on.

They lingered as long as they decently could over liqueurs

and coffee, but eventually Roger tore himself away to retrieve her coat. His arm lingered round her when he drew the warm, silver-fox over her shoulders, luxuriating in their brief closeness. He released her reluctantly at last and they walked out into the night. Settling in the car Clarrie sensed a comfortable awareness around her where his arm had rested. Her doubts about whether it was right to accept his friendship – even love, if offered, had faded. She fervently hoped this relationship would deepen and grow. At last she was ready and eager to live life to the full again. There were still many gaps in her knowledge of him, but she felt no restraint now in questioning him about his early life, as he also probed for every detail of hers. There was nothing too insignificant to ask, or tell.

Roger confessed to having had little interest in school but his father cared even less, and actively encouraged his truancy. As licensee of a country pub he regarded him only as a source of free labour. Roger had been quite happy to work at home. Even though it was learning the trade the hard way – from cellar up, he laughed. It was more fun than geography and science! When he grew older and left school unqualified it was hard to see friends taking decent jobs, earning good salaries, while he had to rely on 'pocket money' handed out grudgingly.

"The old man and I felt no love for each other I'm afraid," sighed Roger. "I had no mother to consider; she died before I really knew her so on my twenty-first birthday I left home. If he had remembered how important a day it was for me I might have stayed, but something snapped that night. On top of everything, he flatly refused to put me on a decent regular wage. He said I 'owed' him because I was his son ...but I told him he owed me more: not only money in return for years of slavery but the support that most fathers give freely to a son. That was the last time we spoke."

Roger heard a quiet murmur of sympathy from Clarrie. He could have given other reasons for his decision to leave but they were unimportant now and he had no intention of talking about Susan who had set her cap at him while they were still at school and had made sure the other girls kept their distance. In spite of her angel face she possessed a fiery determination that was irresistible when it came to getting her own way. With a toss of her blonde curls, Susan continually taunted him for putting up with the treatment his father dished out.

At sixteen she complained that he couldn't afford to take her out like other boys, but ignored his advice to go and pester them and leave him in peace. At eighteen she became a necessary adjunct to his life. When he was twenty, fully aware of his own inadequacies, he feared losing Susan because he couldn't afford to keep her. She had no intention of waiting around forever and issued an ultimatum. She convinced him that he could easily get a job with good pay somewhere else, so he left. They left together! He would have done anything to please her, at the time, but marriage was no part of her plan. She refused to be tied down ...and what a damn good thing that had proved to be!

Clarrie hadn't spoken since he had fallen silent and he glanced at her anxiously as he took the final turn to the Rowen and parked under the spreading tree branches. Switching off the engine he studied her in silence. She was lost in thought, her beautiful eyes moist with un-shed tears and he knew they were for him. He touched her face, turned it to him, and gently kissed her parted lips. The emotional turmoil in which Clarrie had been since their first meeting, the awful sadness of his early life and the intense happiness of their day together were suddenly too much for her to endure; tears spilled from her lashes.

Reluctantly she pulled away from his embrace to find a handkerchief, but he took his own and dried her cheeks. He didn't attempt more intimacy, sensing that she was overwrought. After the long day she needed time to reflect on all that had passed between them. She would think more highly of him if he showed consideration and restraint.

It was well after midnight when they entered the softly lit hall and to their surprise Olwen came hurrying downstairs to greet them. "Heard the car, I did – not being asleep – so I came to have a word with you Mrs Hunter... Oh, dear! I hope I'm not interrupting." She hesitated and drew her housecoat more tightly around her. She felt slightly embarrassed. You never knew with young people today; they might not have been intending to say goodnight to each other!

Roger took Clarrie's hand in both his and thanked her for making his day so wonderful ...then turned away as she followed Olwen into the sitting room where the dampened fire still had a dying glow. Clarrie was mystified. What was so important that it couldn't wait until the morning? Almost bursting with excitement Olwen proceeded to tell her.

"Your mother, it was, on the telephone, just after you'd gone out. Gave me a message she did. It makes not an atom of sense to me, but writing I was, as she said it. Yere it is. But it's not what I want to talk about; I could've left this in your room!" Olwen thrust the paper at her and paused to catch her breath. "We had a lovely chat ...there's pleasant she is ...worried she was, you might be ill or something! I don't know why she should think that, but I told her you were fine and had gone out with a nice young man who I could vouch for personally!" Well pleased with her own wit she hugged herself, chuckling. "I said you made a handsome couple! Anyway, your mother said she was Sarah Grey. After she rang off I remembered you saying your father was an artist." Olwen paused as if for effect, and then asked, "Was his name Stephen?" Clarrie nodded, puzzled. Olwen beamed with pleasure. Leaning forward dramatically, she announced, "He was yere ...in the summer of 1957."

Olwen remembered him well – tall with fair, wavy hair. He was about halfway between the two sisters in age and was one of the first visitors after their parents made the family home into a guesthouse. Megan, about twenty years old, fell in love with the good-looking stranger who almost totally ignored her existence. He went out early and returned late every day, interested only in his painting. After he married, he laughingly declared, he wouldn't be able to take his easel on holiday. He didn't want to risk an early divorce! Halfway through his stay he twisted his ankle badly and had been unable to drive so they all got to know him better. For two weeks they looked after him, carrying his equipment in and out, setting him up so that he could work in the garden and taking food to him at decent intervals.

Clarrie sat in rapt silence ...totally gripped by this glimpse of her father's youth.

"As soon as he was able to drive comfortably, he left," Olwen said, "His wedding was only a month ahead otherwise he would have stayed on a while – liked it yere he did, and we liked him. His fall was really nasty. Apart from a swollen ankle he had a four-inch gash on his thigh. Ma dressed his wound twice a day – looked after him like a son she did – so he gave her this lovely parting gift by way of thanks." Olwen reached behind her chair and pulled out something, which she proudly held aloft for inspection.

It was an oil painting: the view from Clarrie's window upstairs.

Water cascaded over the stones in the brook exactly as it did now but there was no lawn. Rocky ground, visible between clumps of wild colourful shrubs, sloped down to the water's edge.

The scene had grandeur, more romance, than Clarrie had sensed and she didn't need to check the signature, it typified the special way her father saw the world about him.

He portrayed things in a way that heightened hitherto unseen beauty, without losing realism. She had wasted a whole day looking for a subject to paint ...if she had inherited his skill she might have achieved something as wonderful as this without leaving her room!

She had been forced to control her emotions earlier: now she failed. With this kind motherly woman, she was able to let the pent-up tears flow without embarrassment, while Olwen held her hand tightly without attempting to stop her.

She guessed that more than the picture was responsible for Clarrie's reaction to her story, but was content to offer comfort without asking questions. When Clarrie's sobs at last subsided to quiet intakes of breath, she thanked Olwen for sharing the memory with her.

She wanted to talk about her father again, there was much she was eager to ask but now she needed rest. Asking if the picture could hang in her room during her stay, and receiving permission, she took it upstairs, in a mental whirl. She was confused by the rapid succession of differing emotions in so short a span of time.

This latest revelation threw all her previous assumptions about why she might have been led to the Rowen into total confusion ...she simply couldn't take any more!

26 – Clarrie

Clarrie avoided looking at the painting again until she was ready for bed; she wanted to go to sleep with the picture in her mind's eye. She probed her memory but could not recall her father ever mentioning the Rowen or much about his youth at all. She knew of his scarred leg, which he said was suffered in the name of art. It was a reminder that the best angle is not always ten feet above ground level! Why had she not questioned him more? Perhaps children always assume they know everything worth knowing about their parents. Many queries sprang to mind, now that it was too late!

As she gazed at the painting in critical admiration she remembered the note that, according to Olwen, didn't make sense. Clarrie read it with a puzzled frown. It was no surprise that Sarah was in tune with her own confused state of mind but it was indeed a very odd message.

"Sorry I missed you. Don't know the question but by the time you read this you will have your answer. Take care."

Sighing, she switched off the lamp. The day's events gradually receded as though they involved someone else, in another world. The message: the picture: her father's knowing Olwen's family: his stay in this very room: all vied for a place in her weary head. "The question"... What question?

Comprehension came abruptly, jolting her back to wakefulness. She had asked, "Was I brought here to meet Roger?" The answer, she now knew, was "No"! If guided at all, it must have been by her father, anxious to retrace his journey of years ago.

Wide awake, listening to the rushing brook – her father's vision of it now superimposed over her own, she felt shaken yet again by her mother's facility for sensing her moods and being able to help with meaningful advice. Finding that she could no longer regard her growing attachment to Roger as heaven blessed, Clarrie held back from anticipating any long-term relationship. It might happen, but now she was considerably less certain.

When Olwen had handed her the painting to take to her room she said something that nagged at Clarrie's mind. She commented that it had always hung in Megan's room, which was now Roger's, but he wouldn't notice if she replaced it with another – he had no interest in art! Surely that couldn't be true. Roger seemed eager to discuss paintings they both admired and had even suggested a drive around some local galleries next Sunday. He was probably trying to impress her. Did it matter if he was, anyway? Wasn't it natural for men to bend truth a little when they sought approval from a woman? She should be flattered!

Gradually she relaxed and allowed herself to think of him ...the things he had said, and their many shared pleasures. She re-lived those last moments together in the car: the cool pressure of his lips on hers, and the almost forgotten sense of being cared for as he folded her closely in his strong arms. Unwinding luxuriously, as sleep overcame her she was content to accept each day as it came. Fretting over the future was pointless. She would enjoy the present to the full. Moonlight filtered through the gently blowing curtains and after a few deep sighs Clarrie's quiet breathing became inaudible over the sound of the brook. She sank into a deep peaceful sleep.

The nightmare began swiftly.

With terrifying speed, she felt sucked into space.

She hurtled through a vast, dark maw, with urgency and purpose, and was terrified until the fear evaporated with equal rapidity as she hovered, effortlessly, above the place she had seen in her earlier dream.

This time she looked down at the cottage and – as if wanting it made it happen, she sank lower, barely having time to register the dereliction before it disintegrated and re-appeared as it once must have been. The mature trees had shrunk; crumbling walls were transformed into firm structures and the roof, which had been a patchwork of moss, was whole and clean. A woman wandered around the garden, her arms full of freshly picked flowers.

Clarrie watched entranced as she went inside ...if only she could follow. But the cast shadows lengthened speedily until the scene became engulfed in night: a long-ago night. An unseen force pulled her away, as before, and she woke instantly with terrible surf-like, roaring in her ears. Fully awake, she accepted that any hope of regaining serenity lay in accepting the fact that, although in a different way from Sarah and to a lesser degree, she was also psychic. She must develop an understanding of the significance of her visions. Acceptance alone brought some measure of comfort but so far Clarrie had not been out of her depth ...if she were, would the egg and the prayer still work? Nevertheless, she knew the solution to the mystery could only be uncovered by finding the cottage and decided to search for it tomorrow even if it wasted the whole day; if it took the rest of her holiday she would locate it! With this firm resolve came release, and sleep.

Being anxious to leave the Rowen without meeting Roger and becoming deflected from her purpose, breakfast had been early and rushed, but it was another bright autumn day and Clarrie was brimming with excited anticipation. For a reason she couldn't yet comprehend she was being guided to a mysterious place with a past. She knew a little about it already; a young woman had lived there. Her confidence grew. More would be revealed and the reason for her involvement would eventually become clear. She could only follow her instincts, hopefully without faltering, however difficult the task.

On reaching the area where they had been the night before, when the ghostly voice spoke, Clarrie pulled the car over to the verge to consult the map, certain it was the right road, between

Dolwyddelan and Ffestiniog. The side road had to be on the next two mile stretch. Mozart's soaring music was calming as she drove slowly but, anticipation gradually changed to a cold sense of anticlimax. Reversing as soon as possible and retracing the route resulted in an immediate mood change so Clarrie was not at all surprised to find herself signalling a turn before actually seeing the junction, which was only revealed when she braked and swerved off the main road. The narrow lane was set back, almost obscured by overhanging tree branches. There was barely room for two cars to pass but hopefully no one was coming the other way. The narrowing track was now only one car width and Clarrie's heart sank as she imagined reversing the few hundred yards back to the junction! A ditch ran along the nearside and an unclipped hedge grew on the other, contact with either was better avoided ...she fervently regretted not leaving the car on the highway and walking.

Negotiating a blind bend a cattle bridge came into view, a few yards ahead. It covered the ditch and beyond was an open field. Thank heaven, she thought, somewhere to turn off. It would be possible to leave the car and proceed on foot, at least for a short distance, to assess the terrain. A few minutes' walk farther along the lane was reassuring – it would be safe to use the car – but again Clarrie experienced the cold sensation that reminded her of a favourite childhood game. This was definitely the wrong way! Turning back she was warm, then warmer until reaching the bridge and walking beyond it. The air seemed instantly cooler and Clarrie stopped, in a quandary: uncertain again.

There was nowhere else to go, nothing to see.

Her gaze was slowly drawn as if by a magnet to the hedge opposite. As an unexpected gust of wind ruffled the upper branches, glimpses of hilly ground, beyond, were revealed. Instinctively, Clarrie knew that what she sought was on the other side. Pushing apart the thinner branches, it proved easy to find the track, which, through lack of use, had become obscured and Clarrie's heart leapt with excitement as she stepped through and saw where it led.

A wire-tied fence ran along the narrow path and between the wooden slats she saw the old dwelling that was haunting her. On rising ground to the right, beyond a small hillock, was the thickly wooded area visible from the main road; trees shielded the cottage from prying eyes. With mixed dread and optimism Clarrie walked to the gate, which had jammed narrowly open, and saw that the gap was too small to squeeze through without damaging her clothes. She began to push it, but then hesitated ...why go in? With the undisturbed carpet of crisp autumn leaves shrouding the path and garden – the hills beyond providing a dramatic backdrop – it was a perfect picture.

A low bank opposite the gate levelled to a firm area where she could set up her easel: an ideal working position. The old dwelling filled the middle distance but, within its mass, was a wealth of interesting colour and detail. The shutters were rotted and stained ...some of the planks were split. The once whitewashed walls were pitted where rendering had fallen away and grey-black stains streaked down from a broken gutter. Climbing roses once supported by a wooden trellis had grown too heavy and pulled it down ...it swung crazily from the small porch.

Clarrie was mesmerised. The urge to capture it on canvas was compelling. It could be her best painting ever. In a vivid frame of wild growth and dry brown leaves, the old place nestled in brooding silence as though wanting to be left alone, its day ended.

26 – Sarah

Sarah was unusually disturbed. Within hours of Clarinda's leaving, her mood inexplicably changed from serene to anxious. Her husband, Stephen, had never appeared to her in spirit but his presence always felt near and knowing that he wasn't completely lost to her was comforting. Now Sarah sensed that Stephen was uneasy and trying to warn her, but of what?

In spite of the years since his death, she still wept inwardly for his loss, wishing she had spent more time with him. It was a futile notion: he enjoyed solitude when painting. In life, even without words, Sarah had always discerned Stephen's approval or disapproval. This awareness had not ceased with his passing. She knew that Clarinda's decision to re-visit Wales, undoubtedly hoping to recapture the essence of holidays spent painting with her father, had made him happy. What had changed?

All day she had been unable to put Clarinda out of mind. Apprehensive now, she wondered; was the mood communicated from Stephen? She tried to empty her mind of trivia, to be ready for any message he might wish to transmit, but without success. She was too personally involved: too close to the problem to be receptive to guidance.

Initially, after talking to Mrs Tudor, who sounded down to earth and sensible, Sarah had felt better but woke several times during the night, her thoughts immediately with Clarinda, clearly a telepathic link. Something unusual was happening but there seemed to be no good reason for panic. She had rung again an hour ago and been informed that Clarinda went off early for a day's painting, so how could there be anything to worry about? Sarah was aware that little Beth was still with her. Several times the child had been on the verge of coming through, but all the other things on Sarah's mind kept pushing her away. She made a mental apology and sighed deeply.

Polly bustled around with a duster, discussing what they would have for lunch. They were taking it in turns to cook and Polly liked to have her menu approved before preparing anything. Sarah barely listened, her mind was still pre-occupied. The monologue droned on, but Polly interrupted herself suddenly. "Dear me, how could I have forgotten? I wanted to ask you about the mess in the studio. When did it happen? I didn't hear you in there, although it's right next to my room."

Sarah stared at Polly in astonishment ...she hadn't been in the studio at all since Clarinda left. Aware that Polly would be worried if she said so, she asked a question of her own. "I'll clear it up before she comes home; do you know where she put her preliminary sketches of the river scene?"

"Oh, so that's why you tipped the drawer over! Those photos will take some sorting. I'll help if you like," Polly answered, satisfied. She reverted to the topic of food and Sarah could hardly wait for her to resume work in the kitchen so that she could go and see for herself.

At last she entered the studio, quietly closing the door behind her. The top drawer of the cabinet, where Clarinda stored reference material, was overturned on the floor, lodged on a pile of photographs. The second drawer was more than half pulled out: another fraction and it would have joined the other! Sarah was about to shut it when she noticed that the drawings uppermost were indeed those of the river, which, merely on the spur of the moment, she had just mentioned! What a strange coincidence ...but after all, it was the latest project. The drawings of the boat, drawn from memory, had been on top but leafing through the file Sarah couldn't find them. A quick search in the rest of the cabinet didn't bring them to light, so turning to a more urgent task, Sarah picked up the top drawer and started sorting the hundreds of photographs heaped beneath it.

She tackled the job methodically, keeping similar subjects together so that Clarinda wouldn't be too distressed by the muddle when faced by the chore of restoring them to their rightful places. Most were upside down, but fortunately, they were less jumbled than appeared at first glance. Even stranger, those facing up were all from the latest reel.

Long before reaching the bottom of the pile Sarah saw underneath it the missing sketches, which had been stored separately. Undoubtedly someone – probably Beth in a fit of frustration – was trying to tell her something! All but the river-related material was soon tidied away and Sarah sat staring at the finished painting, hoping her mood was sufficiently receptive to prompt answers to the questions flooding her mind. Breathing deeply, she was drifting into a light trance when a rap on the door brought her out of it. It was Polly, eager to help!

Repressing a sigh of frustration Sarah invited her in and waved towards the cabinet to show it was now in order.

Half turning to leave, Polly dangled a glittering object aloft and asked if she should put it on Clarinda's dressing table; she'd found it in the pocket of a painting smock and rescued it from the washing machine. Sarah gasped involuntarily and asked that it be left with her ...she knew who owned it and would deal with it herself. How it had come into Clarinda's possession was not important for the moment, but it was undoubtedly the pretty bracelet Sarah had seen Beth wearing.

To Sarah, psychometry was one of the most fascinating aspects of the paranormal and with the little wrist band, it might be possible to find out what was expected of her ...why her help was being sought.

After Polly had gone, Sarah settled down with more confidence, holding the trinket, shutting out everything but the sparkling red stones ...absorbing vibrations. As minutes passed, the room in which she sat faded from her consciousness. She was in a dark, damp place, surrounded by trees, near running water. She was floating: no, not floating: being carried! She looked down and saw a small arm – her arm – she was very little. It swung limply as she was borne along. Between the branches above, shafts of moonlight flowed over her ...a bright beam flashed fleetingly on the vivid red stones at her wrist as a dead twig hooked the chain and snapped it off. The man holding her stumbled at the force of the pull and almost fell. Briars tore the frill of her flimsy dress and scraped deeply into her leg. She felt no pain ...only the living feel pain!

Sarah had not been in a deep trance but when she emerged to find herself still sitting in the studio chair, she felt drained. She held the broken bracelet tightly. Without looking round, she knew Beth was waiting behind her ...and she was not alone.

The boy was with her – they were to meet at last.

27 – Alec

It was pointless ringing the hotel again until later but, with luck, Sarah thought she might reach Alec at the police station before lunch. She had no more to offer other than a growing conviction that Beth and Kate were linked – perhaps through the boy who had forgotten his name. If Alec had photographs of Ozzy, Sarah would know if he really was the brave young man who had died trying to rescue Kate from her kidnapper.

Both he and Beth were connected to the strip of riverbank where Clarinda must have found the bracelet. It was a pity she couldn't ask Clarinda exactly where, before ringing the police but, should a connection to the kidnapping be established, she would be able to focus more profitably on the mystery of the missing child's whereabouts. Could Beth have been a victim of the same kidnapper: her drowning no accident? Sarah planned to describe her to Alec and ask him to trace a Beth, or more likely Elizabeth Maybury, who had died within the past year or was perhaps still missing.

Collecting her thoughts, to avoid wasting Alec's valuable time, Sarah hastily made a few notes before picking up the telephone. What did she know for sure? Ozzy's death had been sudden and everything suggested that the death of the discarnate boy had been equally violent and unexpected. It was a long while before he realised he was actually dead. He was only aware, as he first emerged from a sleeping state, that his head was badly damaged. So terrified was he when he ran his hand over his forehead, that he immediately passed out again! Later, his head troubled him less than his loss of memory.

When mere seconds elapse between life and death, newly departed spirits are sometimes unaware that it's happening. More often than not, waiting loved ones help them to adjust but if, like the boy, they are consumed by a determination to complete something already started, they become earthbound. As the newly dead become less troubled they gradually release their hold on the physical world but if they remain obsessed, their problem unsolved, their spirits remain in limbo.

Ozzy had died instantly when the car hit his head. At the moment of death he'd been terrified for the child ...had tried to follow her. It was tempting to conclude that the boy with Beth was Ozzy, but she must stick to facts. If he was, then he linked the two children but there might be another connection between Beth and Kate. They were so alike. Had they attracted the attention of the same despicable individual?

Beth and her friend were excited by the boat – it was the first thing that held any significance for the young man since he found himself haunting the river bank – but he was adamant that it had not been there at all when Clarinda was painting so her glimpse of it was definitely clairvoyant. He'd seen it only once – had hidden on it and followed someone when it moored in darkness later. He said the painting of it was perfect except for the name; it was called Bobbylyn.

As these memories began to surface, Beth grew ever more ecstatic ...skipping around, laughing, and still wearing the bracelet. Sarah remarked how pretty it was and showed the actual one. Beth was indifferent to it. It was broken. How could it be hers – she wouldn't be able to wear it, would she? Sarah smiled ...a spirit could wear anything which, in life, had brought the most pleasure.

Careful probing revealed that, after leaving the boat, something so shocked the boy that he again lost his tenuous hold on consciousness. He thought it might have been the sight of Beth lying lifeless, because when he met her later she seemed familiar to him. After Sarah suggested it, he agreed that, at the time, he must also have been dead. Slowly, with resignation, the boy accepted his own death. He had died before boarding the boat; there had been no need to hide! It was far more than Sarah had expected to discover and she was sure he'd recall everything soon. He was calmer now that he didn't feel completely cut off from earthly help.

Luckily Alec was in and, having heard her report, said he would start two more lines of inquiry; one for Beth and one for the boat. Afterwards, if she didn't mind, he would drive straight over. He wanted to go through everything again and would bring more photographs with him. Sarah was very pleased and, after checking with Polly, invited him to lunch with them. The excitement of the two youngsters was contagious and their presence so strong that Sarah almost felt she should set two extra places at table – then she chided herself for being fanciful. Polly's nervous anticipation, having a guest at such short notice, was more than enough to suppress Sarah's earlier worries.

When Alec arrived Polly withdrew to finish preparing lunch and he immediately lifted a thick file from his bulging leather briefcase. Placing it on the coffee table in front of him he tapped it and remarked that it probably contained a lot of useless information but nothing could be discarded until the case was solved. "I'd be grateful if you thumb through it after you've seen the photographs, giving your impressions." Turning the cover of the formidable stack of paper he explained, "There's a chance you might notice something which links with what you may have discerned already but hesitated to say."

As soon as she saw Ozzy's picture, an informal snap with his brother, Sarah identified him as Beth's friend. There were several that Alec hastily turned over: official 'scene of the crime' photographs. Even in the brief glance she had been afforded, Sarah saw the agony in the boy's face and his sickeningly crushed skull. Alec nodded, satisfied with her identification, and expressed his hope that she would accompany him on a visit to Ozzy's parents. He knew that now, more than ever, she would want to meet them.

Sarah could think of no better way to restore his lost memory than to lead Ozzy home and agreed to go soon. While she looked through the mass of papers – countrywide reports from people who had definitely seen Kate, or were convinced a neighbour was the kidnapper, Alec examined Clarrie's photographs and sketches of the river where they were likely to find the body of Beth. Swayed by earlier examples of Sarah's ability, he even dared to wonder if she might lead them to the exact site of Beth's burial. He fervently prayed that they would find Kate before she met the same ghastly fate.

28 – Clarrie

It didn't take Clarrie long to assemble her easel and start work. Before nine she was painting feverishly, giving no thought to the strange way the cottage had been found or questioning what had driven her to seek it out. Had she sought an answer, she would have been satisfied that the way it inspired her. The glow of excitement as she anticipated the finished painting – was sufficient justification for a hundred nightmares.

After a few hours, as the day brightened and the sun climbed higher, the light distorted her perception of the scene. She was forced to stop. To continue painting would have ruined her previous work, so Clarrie ruefully started to return her equipment to the car. She retrieved four double-headed spacing pins from the boot together with a spare canvas to face and protect the wet painting and took them back to her easel.

Her father had always advised putting a painting out of sight for a few days before completion. Seeing it with fresh eyes highlighted both inadequacies and strengths. It also decreased the likelihood of overworking areas, often the cause of poor results... But Clarrie had been away only for minutes, yet she stared at the picture in amazement. How had she achieved this in one session? Her wild urge to paint it was burned into every brush-stroke. What she beheld encompassed all she had first seen and wanted to capture! It was good. Clarrie had never before felt so happy with her work and knew, incredibly, it was finished.

The sound of approaching footsteps caught her by surprise and her mother's plea to avoid isolation sprang to mind too late.

A man was clambering up the bank to stand beside her. Her heart began to beat so wildly that she felt he must be able to hear it! Unaware of Clarrie's fear he stood looking at the picture.

At last he spoke, admiringly, "Damn good Miss ...I reckon you've got a masterpiece here!"

"Well, thank-you," Clarrie managed to reply. "It must have been a charming place before it became a ruin. Do you know who lived here? How long is it since it was in use?"

The man seemed happy to stop and talk and she learned that he was the farmer who owned the property and the surrounding land. On his way home he had seen the parked car with an open boot and curiosity made him investigate. The track didn't lead anywhere other than the farmhouse and he said the car was unlike the kind usually abandoned in country lanes! Glad that all was well, he invited her to follow him to the farm for a 'cuppa' to meet his wife. "She dabbles a bit herself – nothing worth hanging up – but if I tell her I've let a real artist escape without her seeing what you've done, my life won't be worth living!"

Clarrie could hardly refuse and in any case her work was finished. She could waste the whole afternoon if she felt like it, so with his assistance she stowed the rest of her things in the boot and allowed him to lead the way. Gwen Williams, the farmer's wife, was delighted to have a visitor and welcomed her effusively into the warm kitchen which was filled with the mouth-watering aroma of roast lamb. Clarrie politely but reluctantly declined her immediate invitation to lunch.

Gwen's obvious disappointment and the fact that, when pressed, she admitted she was not actually expected anywhere else, settled the matter. She stayed. Everything was ready; they'd just have to wait a while for Gareth their son, a forester. "Disappointed Bill was," Gwen explained, "when Gareth had no liking for the sheep, but it's glad he is now we're growing timber on the slopes, lovely it looks too. Bill can practically manage the flocks himself, with only a couple of men."

Pausing for breath she caught sight of the picture, which her husband had brought from the car. "Oh my, there's beautiful! It's clever you are, at painting." She was obviously impressed. In awed tones she added, "Who'd have thought the old workman's cottage was such a picture! If I hadn't seen it with my own eyes I'd not have believed it... really glad I am, Bill brought you home!" As he started to carry it out again she protested loudly and made space for it on the Welsh dresser where it could stand and be admired during the meal. It was easy for Clarrie to re-introduce the topic of the cottage and its occupants. It was not worth repairing said Bill, because nobody would live there. "An old fellow who worked for my father when I was a lad had the place 'til he died about twelve years back. He never complained about ghosts, but then, he was deaf as a post!" Bill howled with laughter.

Gwen took up the tale. "A young couple lived there after that. We thought they were happy, but she was pregnant and he said she wanted to go back to their hometown to be married. Called on her, I did, a few times and she never mentioned any screaming. He never looked happy after she'd gone. I reckon he missed her badly, but he had to work out his notice. Sorry I was, not to have them back." Bill nudged her fondly commenting that it was the baby she'd wanted around!

"The next tenant," Gwen giggled, "heard nothing strange for a year but then this scream disturbed him every night for a week so we put him up here until another cottage came empty." They added up a total of eight successive occupants who'd been scared by the scream in the night.

"All insisted it was human," Bill affirmed, "inside, downstairs, and loud enough to wake them!"

Recalling her vision of the woman in the garden Clarrie had immediately jumped to the conclusion that it must be she who haunted the house until Gwen added that Gareth had heard it too and it was a man. Bringing the discussion to a close, Bill declared that if it was haunted at all, it was probably old Josh who'd had the place so long he thought he owned it. He always did like being alone!

Gareth's arrival sent Gwen racing to get the food on the table before he came down again to eat. Broad shouldered and tall, he looked like a Welsh Rugby forward. He turned out to be, in his spare time, a bird-watcher. He was also impressed by the painting and suggested that Clarrie might like to accompany him next time he went up Cader Idris. "It would mean an early start but mum could put you up overnight and I'll bet you've never seen anything so marvellous as the valley when the mist rises: sun shafting through to the villages below ...beautiful!"

Clarrie considered him closely. He was older than herself, probably five or six years younger than Roger but he had issued his invitation without guile and was so eager to act as guide that she heard herself accepting. It would mean missing a Sunday with Roger but Gareth also had only one day off a week. Her reaction surprised her but the opportunity to paint halfway up a mountain was too good to miss. She couldn't resist asking him about the haunting. "I hear you know first-hand about the screams. How did you come to hear them?"

"Not them," he replied. "It was only the one. I was off on one of my jaunts and not wanting to disturb everybody two hours before dawn I'd left my car up the track where you must have parked yours. I walked from here and took the short cut to the cottage. As I reached the gate, it happened. It was pretty scary and I stood, riveted to the spot. I didn't take my eyes off the place for several minutes. Nothing moved. No animal or bird I know sounds like that anyway." He shivered slightly, affected even by the memory. "Then I thought I ought to look, in case someone was really in trouble. It wasn't ink-black dark and getting lighter all the time so it didn't really take much courage. I was over the first shock! The house was locked up tight. There was nobody around. Real eerie but I still don't believe in ghosts!" In answer to Clarrie's query, he said he had no doubt, it was a man screaming: not in fear – more startled and angry.

Bill chortled again. "There you go! I told you so... Old Josh getting rid of intruders!"

29 – Roger

Clarrie stayed at the farm much later than she'd intended, pleased to have a firm date for the trip to the mountain. Volunteering to carry all her heaviest kit – no problem, Gareth said that since painting was as quiet a pastime as bird-watching, he'd happily stay close to keep an eye on her, all day – to please her mother of course! Everything had worked out perfectly; finding, painting and even discovering the history of the cottage. The existence of a resident ghost accounted for her being drawn to it and as Old Josh had nothing at all to do with her she could put the episode behind her. It was only her third day away from home; she still had seventeen left to enjoy! Although it was fairly late when she returned, Roger was still out. Olwen wasn't sure how long he would be – business meetings and evening drinks tended to merge – so after ordering dinner Clarrie telephoned home.

Once assured that her message had been received and understood, and all was well, Sarah launched into an account of the latest developments there. Clarrie was so enthralled, especially by confirmation that the boat did exist, that she barely touched on her own news, reporting only that she'd heard her father's voice. Sarah was thrilled, knowing that Clarinda must now accept this further proof of her own latent ability. "I realised that you are clairaudient, darling," she cried jubilantly, "You obviously heard Ozzy at the river. You couldn't see him, perhaps because of his own confused state, but you definitely saw the boat!" She paused briefly then continued more calmly. "I know the thought alarms you but if you accept it as a special gift and never abuse it, you can be sure of spiritual support and protection. Just relax now, enjoy Wales."

Immediately, she told Clarrie not to waste more money on the call, everything was fine at home and ten minutes later Clarrie returned to the dining room. Yesterday she'd been anxious, desperate for advice. Now, her problems had evaporated and she could afford to wait. She would savour the moment when she could give Sarah a full account, face to face. Even after a leisurely coffee Roger was still absent, so Clarrie decided to retire early and read in bed for a while, to wind down after what had been an exhausting day. She could not deny that she was disappointed by his absence; she'd been looking forward to showing him her painting. Olwen was quite enchanted by it and declared there was no doubt she was her father's daughter, no doubt at all!

With this heady praise Clarrie went to bed tired but happy. As she read, her attention continually wandered to the easel where the painting stood drying, glowing in the low light. It seemed to pulsate with life and she could almost imagine that a gentle wind moved through the tall trees. Unable to focus her mind on her book she soon switched off the light and, with a sigh of satisfaction, went to sleep almost straight away.

In the early morning hours she awoke – her whole body trembling, breathless and afraid. Most dreams fade on waking, this one gained clarity with full consciousness. Calming gradually, finding she was actually safe in her own bed, she reviewed her experience like a critic at a film when the outcome is still unknown. She had been outside the cottage again, only this time it was night. Inside, a woman was crying then screaming with terror. She had paused at the gate, perplexed; everyone else heard a man.

Curiosity overcame her fear and she went up the leaf-strewn path to try the door but it was locked. She couldn't enter. The cries grew more frantic and the dull thud of blows came from within. She had pushed through thorny bushes to reach a window and looked between the split wood shuttering. An oil lamp flickered in the poorly furnished room and through an archway she saw a stone-flagged kitchen, where another lamp threw huge shadows on the far wall. A man's arm rose and fell and the awful screams became rasping groans of agony.

Physically unable to assist the terrified woman, Clarrie had howled too, but their voices mingled ...her own cries went unheard. In frustration and fury, utterly incapable of intervening, she clasped her hands to her head crying to God for help and was immediately awake in her own room.

Striving for a firmer grip on reality, Clarrie left the bed, which now represented unbelievable horror rather than a restful haven, to splash her face with cold water. More composed, she sat down to assess her position. Quite unlike an ordinary nightmare, it had the same quality of reality as the dreamlike flights that had already proven visionary.

Clarrie allowed her mind to return to what she had no doubt, was a brutal, fatal assault on a helpless young woman. Frantic to save her, indifferent to the thorns which tore her gown and scraped her flesh, Clarrie had struggled back to the door; it was immovable. It was then her nerve had broken and when she cried for help she was instantly transported from that horrific enactment of a past crime.

Wearily, she stretched out again to rest. Before this ended she knew she would need reserves of strength as never before in the whole of her life. Sleep was out of the question and eventually she switched on the bedside light to check the time: only three-o-clock. How could she relax when she would inevitably lapse into the same dream ...helpless to intervene in what she knew to be bloody murder? She felt like ringing her mother – but in the middle of the night? No way! In any case, it was her problem. If she didn't solve it alone, how could she ever sleep peacefully again?

The wet painting had taken on a kind of glazed inner glow and she could not take her eyes from it, but something had changed! Gasping, she saw a crack of light edging a shutter; a lamp was glowing inside the room ...and then smiled wryly at her own stupidity. It was only reflected light bouncing off the bedroom's white wall onto the back of the picture. It gleamed through a thinly painted patch of canvas.

Having already made one false judgement, minutes passed before Clarrie would trust her eyes to accept another change. The carpet of thick leaves was scuffed with deep troughs as though someone had used the path. She must have smudged it on the way upstairs without noticing, and a smear of stark white flecked the bushes near the door. Her first reaction was vexation but, stooping to remove it with a tissue, Clarrie saw some tiny threads of cotton. Not believing what she instantly suspected, she twisted the sleeve of her nightgown. Part of the lace cuff was ripped off and tiny beads of blood had dried along a scar on her arm. Before she recovered from the shock, she saw too, that the gate was open much wider than she had painted it! Thoroughly disconcerted, she sat despairingly on the bed and stared into the painting. Slowly an idea came to her...

To put it into words, even in her head, would have resulted in rejection. It was too fantastic, but there was nothing to lose; nobody else need ever know how ridiculous she was being! Lifting out palette and paints without allowing time for second thoughts, anticipation of success lent speed to Clarrie's brush. When finished she rested on the bed, trying to relax: breathing deeply.

Soon, sensing the pull of that dark vacuity again, knowing it was more trance-like than normal sleep she had to fight to control her panic. The heady flight ended where she had expected, in the dark stillness of the cottage garden. Tracks she had made before stretched ahead to the now gaping-wide door. Re-painting it open had actually worked!

All was eerily quiet; not even the wind sighed. Cautiously, she stepped towards the silent house and, from the doorway, saw the tall figure of a man pushing with all his strength on the handle of a pick. He was levering old slabs from the hard earth floor. Lying beside him was a girl's body, savagely beaten.

Her wide, dead eyes stared straight at Clarrie who could not choke back a wail of utter dismay... Instantly the murderer whirled to face her. It was Roger!

30 – Sarah

Sarah had expected to feel more relaxed after speaking to Clarinda but instead she felt apprehensive: disturbed. Had she neglected something important, or merely overeaten! The meal had been horrendously rich. She was consequently appalled when Polly came in with what she called a light supper trolley ...they had finished dinner barely two hours ago. Polly was astonished when Sarah declined even a morsel. Sarah would have preferred to go to bed but it would have seemed churlish to leave Polly eating alone, so she sat and talked for a while.

Polly had heard enough during lunch to know she was trying to help the police with the Mead case and was eager to question her about it. Polly never gossiped and had always respected Sarah's wish to keep her psychic ability as private as possible. Polly would have been hurt had she been snubbed, so her spine tingled deliciously as Sarah humoured her. Since knowing Sarah, Polly had accepted that she lived surrounded by a world of invisible people, long dead, but to see them through Sarah's eyes brought them vividly close. Torn between hope and fear her gaze roamed constantly into the shadowy corners of the room... "Are they both here now, Ozzy and the little girl?" she whispered. "Could they appear for me, or move something that I could see?"

With an amused smile Sarah reminded her that Beth had already done something she could see: upset the drawers! Sarah would not dream of asking for a demonstration of the kind Polly wanted; those in the spirit world were not in the entertainment business. If they needed to prove their presence to further their own ends it was entirely different.

When Sarah saw the chastened look on Polly's face she quickly added that her sincere interest was really appreciated – nobody would ever dream of accusing her of attempting to ridicule Spiritualism! By the time Polly's appetite for both information and food was sated, Sarah was exhausted. She took a cup of hot chocolate up to bed with her but fell asleep before it was touched.

She hardly ever dreamed, or, if she did, had no residual memories the following morning so when she emerged suddenly, from the depths of sleep, with her head still full of images she was at first puzzled, then alarmed as some of the images took shape in her memory. There were shadows ...grotesque shapes, screaming wide mouths and in their midst a pinpoint of light. As she struggled to bring her impressions into focus, the light grew and brightened ...in it was the face of Clarinda.

Concentrating with every ounce of her power Sarah prayed for guidance. If her daughter was in peril, how could she help? Becoming calmer, she reminded herself that Clarinda wasn't stupid; she was probably in full control and capable of dealing with it alone – after all, the pure clarity of the light that radiated from her had banished the darkness. Inexperienced though she was, she must have absorbed considerable insight into spiritual channels ...had she not conditioned her, over the years, in case she ever developed as a medium?

Sarah's certainty grew that, if the need arose, Clarinda would instinctively do the right thing. Later they could compare notes and, with this in mind, she checked the time. It was exactly three-o-clock.

31 – Roger

At the Rowen, Roger's sleep was shallow and troubled. He had returned to the hotel before ten-thirty ...not all that late, expecting Clarrie still to be downstairs but the lounge, where he immediately looked for her, was unoccupied.

Olwen informed him that she had seemed tired and gone to bed early. He was chagrined. When they'd parted the night before he thought he had totally succeeded in breaking through her reserves. He had absented himself all day, deliberately avoiding her, imagining she would miss him. Tonight should have been a touching reunion! That was disturbing enough, but Olwen said she had painted a marvellous picture of an old cottage and spent the day with the family of the farmer who owned it – Williams! He knew it had to be Bill Williams, even though it was a common name in Wales.

If the prospect of marrying Megan and one day owning the hotel had not presented itself he would have been long gone from Wales, but too late, after all his sacrifices, he discovered her miserable old father had left the property to his grandson! He'd had to make the best of it. He was more than ready to move on now and the enchanting Mrs Hunter could be his chance, heiress to a fortune or not. She was well heeled enough to ease him along for years if nothing went wrong. For hours he lay awake: worrying, imagining Clarrie with the farmer and his wife ...but how could they possibly have said anything to connect him to the cottage? They had known him by his first name, Daniel.

Inevitably, his thoughts drifted back to Susan. She should

have married him in the beginning, when he wanted her, when she was the most important part of his life. Later, when he was considerably less besotted and planning to leave her, she stupidly got pregnant and expected him to be pleased. She actually started talking incessantly about their wedding! It was way too late – by then he was determined to escape her clutches. He had to agree to marry her; it provided a reasonable excuse for their departure, but he never intended to go through with it. No way would he have tied himself down to the miserable life they shared. A baby would have been the last straw.

Having saved her face locally, he'd hoped to dump her back home with her family but she flatly refused to go. She clung to him, suffocating his arguments with endless weeping. He felt only scorn for the pathetic creature she'd become and shut his ears to her declarations of undying devotion ...she knew he'd change his mind ...she would follow him anywhere in the universe ...to eternity!

God, she was pathetic! She had driven him to it!

32 – Clarrie

Roger's ululation of anger as he rushed towards her still vibrated in Clarrie's inner ear when she emerged from her deep trance. At last she had all the threads and the pattern they wove was one of total horror. She heard sobs, realised they were her own and stifled them with a supreme effort of will. It was painful to accept that a man she had admired and, she ruefully admitted, been willing, even eager to love was a monster! As she grew calmer she comprehended, at last, how and why she had become involved.

Accepting that fate – aided perhaps by her father – brought her here, to a place he had known in his youth, Roger could never have been part of any grand plan. Her father's memory could only encompass Olwen's family. She smiled grimly. There must have been Horror in Heaven when she fell for Roger! Now, unfortunately, she had an even bigger problem. What on earth should she do about him? How could she even face him again?

Pacing the room, Clarrie caught sight of her image in the mirror and saw what he must have seen on that long ago night ...she had been an apparition from the future. With her hair looped into its nightly knot and her long white gown billowing, hiding her slimness, she was totally unlike the daytime image he knew. It chilled her to realise that without spirit guidance he might eventually have seen her looking just like this. How fantastic! He would have recognised her and known that she had witnessed his crime all those years ago. What then? Would he have murdered her too? She could have been his next victim!

She would leave immediately of course. He'd think it incredible, but she didn't owe him an explanation, or anything! Should she persuade Bill to dig up the floor of the cottage? Surely Roger mustn't be allowed to get away with his gross, inhuman act?

Still gazing at her reflection she became gradually aware that she wasn't alone ...a young woman stood beside her. Shining blonde curls tumbled over her bare shoulders and she wore a full smock, which hung lightly over her slightly rounded form. Her slender, outstretched arms were full of roses. Offering the flowers to Clarrie she smiled and whispered,

"Thank you so much for leading me back to him ... for showing me the way. He's mine forever now ... the only boy I ever loved."

***

A few hours after dawn, a knock on her door disturbed Clarrie's troubled thoughts as she drifted in and out of a light slumber. She was apprehensive and on the point of rising anyway, to pack in readiness for an early departure, but was bewildered when Olwen came in with a breakfast tray.

Olwen put the tray aside, came to sit on the bed beside Clarrie and took her hand. Olwen's eyes were red with weeping and for a few minutes the power of speech deserted her. At last, she patted Clarrie's arm, "I know it will be a terrible shock dear, there's no way of breaking it gently... poor Roger had a stroke during the night! Probably around three or four-o-clock the doctor says. I'm afraid he died. The doctor said it was as if he'd had a tremendous shock ...staring, he was, as if he'd seen a ghost."

Her voice trailed away and they sat in silence for a while.

Rousing herself at last, Olwen said there was naturally a lot to do but Clarrie should stay upstairs; she must be upset. With her hand on the door-knob she turned in surprise and looked around, breathing in deeply ..."There's lovely, what a strong scent of roses!"

In lighter mood than she could have expected Clarrie took

up her brush and palette and, with a few deft strokes, restored the picture. As she had hoped, painting the door open physically, with her brush, had removed the last of her mental barriers too. Closed again, it could keep hidden forever the awful secret of the past. Already the terror was fading from her mind. Could it really have happened or had it all been a ghastly nightmare, conjured up from some dark recess in her own brain?

For a few moments she stood at the window remembering that her father too had loved this view then, well under control, she went downstairs to ring her mother.

***

Sarah had been awake, her thoughts with Clarinda, for hours after her disturbing visions. When she did slip into sleep it was dreamless and deep. Polly was surprised when, at eight-thirty, Sarah didn't come down as usual, then slightly worried as the hands of the clock crept to half-past-nine. At ten, she stood quietly at the bedroom door hesitant to knock but now feeling she should. To her relief she heard Sarah coming out of her bathroom and shouted to ask if everything was all right, offering to bring breakfast up on a tray.

For once Sarah would have welcomed a leisurely lie in, not having recovered completely from her troubled night, but she promised to be down within minutes and didn't want anything cooked. Sure that the crisis was over, Sarah expected a call from Wales soon and was consequently not at all surprised when the telephone rang as she walked downstairs towards it.

Before Clarinda could say too much, Sarah verified that there had been a traumatic happening at the time of her waking during the night. It was sufficient proof to Clarrie that even thinking of asking her mother for help had had the desired result. It was re-assuring evidence that when in trouble she was never really alone. Sarah didn't press for details and Clarrie was glad – there was too much to cover by telephone. It would be more comfortable and private when she returned. Sarah too, was glad to put off hearing the details; she didn't want to be distracted from the mystery surrounding Kate Mead.

It was clear that Clarinda was now set to enjoy her holiday so she brought the conversation to an end after asking two questions on Alec's behalf ...the exact location of the inlet where the phantom boat had moored and where the bracelet was found in relation to it. Unselfishly, Clarrie suggested returning to show him personally and Sarah said she would relay the offer to Alec, but hoped it wouldn't be necessary. While the details were still clear in her mind Sarah decided to ring Alec.

He was pleased to hear from her so soon and appreciated Clarinda's offer; it would avoid trampling the area too much 'on spec'; vital evidence might be disturbed. He had made an appointment with Ozzy's parents for tomorrow, Wednesday, if she could manage it? Sarah agreed; it was convenient and she would expect him around two-o-clock. Alec said they still had no information at all about Beth – quite a few Mayburys, two of them actually were named Elizabeth, but they were many years older than Beth.

After he rang off Sarah realised she had forgotten to ask about the boat! Never mind, he would tell her when they met. It was likely to be an interesting and, she hoped, a rewarding afternoon.

33 – The Reverend

After being so long on the telephone, Sarah saw that it was almost midday and decided to skip breakfast altogether. Coffee was all she really needed. Polly, after being informed of Sarah's plans, asked tentatively if she could be any help.

On reflection, Sarah decided it might indeed be a good idea to take Polly along on the visit to Ozzy's parents. The presence of a kindly older woman might reassure them if they were wary of the police and herself. Whether accepting her as a medium or not, Polly could vouch for her sincerity. ..."Yes," she smiled, "I shall be glad of your company." She wondered whether Ozzy's parents were disposed to believe in, or deride, the paranormal. Either way, the visit was vital for the boy – it would be a bonus if it also helped them.

Scarcely able to believe that she really was being included, Polly's rosy round face shone with pleasure. "I'll stay in the car until you're sure I can be useful. I'd love to watch you work, but I do understand that finding Kate is the most important consideration and I wouldn't want to do anything to hinder that."

The following day, as they sat waiting to be picked up, the doorbell rang. Neither had heard a car and indeed, their visitor was on foot. Sarah didn't recognise his voice as Polly showed him into the sitting room but as he smilingly turned to greet her, she saw his collar and realised that it was the local vicar, Elsie Kilroy's husband. They were obviously ready to go out, so he was full of apologies. "I really should have rung you first to make an appointment but, to be honest, I tried once last week and got your answering machine... Very disconcerting! It will be difficult enough, face to face, to explain my business. I also wanted to avoid suffering again from the pangs of guilt which always overtake me when I hang up without leaving a message!"

Sarah laughed, liking him immediately, and regretted that they would be whisked away by the CID at any moment! As she explained his eyes widened. He was noticeably impressed and said that it was in her capacity as a psychic that he wished to talk to her. Sarah couldn't resist saying she had gained the impression from Elsie that he thought it was all rubbish. She knew she was being wickedly provocative but was interested to see how he would react. She wasn't disappointed.

Drawing in his chin and looking over his glasses with raised brows he said in a confidential tone, "Elsie's father was also a vicar – very strong-minded, a good man in every sense of the word. I suspect she is sometimes a little confused and attributes to me, much of his wisdom!"

Sarah persuaded him to stay until the car arrived but he was reluctant even to hint at his reason for wanting to talk with her so she invited him for coffee the following morning; she had to shop in the afternoon. As he accepted, they heard the car arrive and left the house together. It was obvious that he and Alec knew each other and from the look on Alec's face Sarah guessed that he was slightly embarrassed.

"Why, hello, good morning to you Mr Holmes," called the vicar as Alec stepped out of the car. "As you don't come to church, you see I have to come out here to meet you!"

Alec admitted with a sheepish grin that it had been quite a while since he attended Sunday service. "I'll try to do better," he promised, "now that I know you'll be checking up on me and reporting me to my friends! Would a lift home put me back in your good book?"

His offer was declined with a broad smile and, once underway, Alec asked if she knew Ambrose Kilroy well and if she had much contact with the church. He was surprised to hear they had met only a few minutes ago. He was even more intrigued by the vicar's interest in psychic phenomena until he remembered an incident, six months ago.

A member of the congregation jumped up and ran out of church in the middle of the service, screaming that he was haunted! Polly's eager questioning amused Alec but he knew very little more – only that the man's sister-in-law had been killed by a hit and run driver. His wife went into a state of shock. It had been a terrible time for the poor man. His wife recovered fully within a short time but he obviously hadn't: probably because she blamed him for the accident.

Polly's appetite was thoroughly whetted so Alec had to continue. The fellow promised to collect his sister-in-law one night, after she had been to a meeting but, because he was late, she had caught a bus. Walking home from the bus stop she was knocked down and died instantly. Alec couldn't remember the details, but he'd felt very sorry for the man because of his wife's attitude.

With much tut-tutting, Polly shook her head sadly... "Poor man, how wicked of his wife to blame him!" Alec changed the subject quickly. He was more anxious to discuss the case he was working on at the moment.

Reaching the village at last they picked up the local constable, Harry Laker, well known to the Latham family. He had known Ozzy as a baby and had been looking forward to having him in the police force one day. The boy was very keen and they had discussed the qualifications he would need and the best way to plan a career. There was an older brother, married with three youngsters who had all adored their young uncle who often baby-sat for them, as he had for Tommy and Kate Mead. Harry said that Ozzy had been a responsible youngster and would have made a fine police officer.

Mr and Mrs Latham met them at the gate to their house – a neat semi-detached on an old housing estate. Mature trees lined the road and their own garden was a riot of colour. When Sarah immediately admired it, they relaxed a little, pointing out their favourite shrubs and flowers as they all walked back to the house.

By the time they settled, in the equally attractive rear garden, Polly and Annie were on first name terms and Annie's husband,

Jack, was also at ease with Sarah and Alec. Harry helped Jack to fix cold drinks for everyone.

As they bustled about, Sarah sat a little apart; tuning herself in to the home atmosphere of the boy she had never known in life, becoming more and more aware that he and Beth were also present. Ozzy stood behind his mother. As Sarah watched, he bent to put his arms around her and laid his cheek against her head, his eyes moist with emotion. Raising a hand to smooth her grey streaked hair she had, without realising, felt his touch. With her son's help, Sarah might find it easy to convince her of his continued existence after death. When the past was beyond recall Ozzy had been resigned to his changed state, but now it was different. With the rush of returning memories, he was beginning to mourn the loss of his parents as deeply as they mourned him. Sarah waited patiently until he felt able to initiate communication.

Polly asked if his parents also called him Ozzy and Annie explained that the middle names of both boys were after their two grandfathers. When the older boy, Frank William, was little, he was called Willy and hated it. He was nine years old when David Oswald came along and Frank made his point by calling his little brother Ozzy! "His father and I understood," said Annie, "and made an effort to call him Frank, but by that time the baby could say 'Ozzy' and sounded so cute that the name stuck. We expected him to object, as Frank had done, when he realised that he could! But he was such a sensible, quiet boy – very mature for his age. He once said…" Overcome with grief her voice trembled and failed her.

For a few moments Annie dabbed her eyes apologetically with the large handkerchief, which her husband had rushed to give her. Polly cried too, patting her hand in sympathy until she recovered. When at last everyone relaxed again, Ozzy left his mother, tried to hug his father and came to stand behind Sarah …Beth sat at her feet.

As though receiving his signal Annie spoke, "Jack and I have always been church-goers and know nothing at all about spiritualism and such! We've kept away from anything like that, it's all a bit frightening, but we've talked it over and think God will understand ...we are doing this in the hope that it will help you to find the little girl."

Alec nodded to Sarah and suggested that she might wish to talk with Annie and Jack inside where it would be quieter. Annie asked if Polly might come too and Sarah, agreeing that she could, followed them into the cool sitting room. Polly took Annie's hand again and whispered as they sat down, "Now you relax dear and remember what I told you. Sarah is no charlatan ...she is a very gifted psychic. It's been proved over and over, in the years I've known her and what's more important, she's a really good person and would never do anything to hurt anyone."

Sarah, slightly embarrassed, pretended not to hear. Jack, sitting on the other side of Annie on the green velvet chesterfield, stretched his long legs and squared his shoulders with a nervous cough. He fixed his gaze warily on Sarah, ready to stop the proceedings if she did anything to upset his wife.

"Before we go on," said Sarah, "let's say a short prayer. As you close your eyes, remember the creed you often say in church ...you do believe in Life after Death; sometimes we are allowed glimpses of it. We ask for help, comfort and guidance today and pray that the Lord will protect us from evil, in His name..."

Jack relaxed visibly. Annie nodded as she and Polly said 'Amen' together, quietly. Sarah, after taking a deep breath, shut her eyes for a few moments. When she opened them, she continued to talk in the same conversational tone as before.

"Annie, when we were in the garden you started to tell us why Ozzy was not eager to drop his nickname..." Annie looked surprised and started to resume where she'd left off, but Sarah waved a hand to silence her and continued. "Your son has been with us ever since we arrived and he says he remembers the occasion very clearly. You were in the hall. You had just taken a message for him on the telephone when he came into the house. You handed him the message pad ...you had written 'Ozzy' above the note."

Annie's jaw dropped in complete astonishment and Jack looked to her for confirmation ...she nodded dumbly as Sarah continued. "When you asked if he would rather be called David, he replied that he had loved your father; anything that made him closer to his Grandpa was okay by him!" Annie wept unashamedly as the words, which only her son could have known, convinced her. She no longer doubted that he really was with them in spirit.

Now that they both accepted the fact without reservation Sarah explained. Until being brought back to them today he hadn't even remembered his name. She described Ozzy's association with the river and Beth, and how she came to suspect that he was their son, and sought confirmation from the police. Sarah hoped, now that his memory seemed unimpaired, Ozzy would be able to tell them what had happened to the child.

Although their motivation for allowing Sarah to come was to find Kate, she knew they must wish to know more about the events surrounding their son's death ...so, before leaving, with Ozzy's co-operation, she would try to answer any personal questions they might wish to ask.

Sarah then suggested it was time to invite Alec and PC Laker to join them. They were also anxious to discover more about the tragedy and would make their own notes. Sarah went on to explain that she didn't often go into a deep trance but, if she did, she might not recall what was said so it was wise to have impartial observers. Alec pulled a chair up behind the settee for Harry Laker, who produced his notebook and started to write immediately, glancing at his watch to confirm the time and date. Alec then sat by the fire opposite Sarah, indicating his readiness to begin. As before, Sarah asked everyone for support in prayer and concentration. She asked them to picture the road before the accident; it might help Ozzy to recall everything more clearly.

To the small group gathered in that quiet village house it seemed that they were the centre of the universe, where something momentous was happening. They all felt uplifted – stirred by the amazing truth confronting them. Although each tried faithfully to hold the country lane in mind, other thoughts intruded as the minutes ticked by.

Polly, with complete faith in Sarah, waited with bated breath to hear revelations from beyond the grave, recalling many people who had been helped by Sarah in the past: their distrust, followed by complete astonishment when given proof of communication with the dead. With irritation, she reflected on how many of those people, when the shock of grief wore off, rejected the experience as impossible – obviously a kind of telepathy they reasoned! It was beyond her wit to understand why communion between two separate heads – miles apart – should be more acceptable!

Alec remembered instances all over the world where Psychics had helped solve cases, especially of missing persons and he had high hopes that valuable information would come out of this. Glancing at Laker he was satisfied to see his pen poised to write. Catching his eye, Harry patted his breast pocket, which held a tiny recorder. He adjusted the microphone clipped to his lapel; if anything did happen he was ready to prove it!

Harry hoped for what he considered privately would be a minor miracle. This Mrs Grey seemed sincere enough – he didn't think she was out and out weird, or a crook, but some folk were gullible enough to believe anything if it was what they wanted to hear. He pondered over what he'd overheard earlier. That business about the boy's nickname made him think. They'd never swallow it with their pints in the pub – if he was drunk or stupid enough to mention it!

Mr and Mrs Latham held hands and prayed. Jack was still wary but there was no doubt that only his wife and son had been privy to that conversation in the hall. He did remember she'd been touched and told him of it, but he'd discussed it with no one. In spite of himself he dared hope. He knew it wouldn't bring Ozzy back, but it would be some comfort if only he could be sure that his son had not suffered. He desperately needed to know what really happened that day...

Annie had dreaded meeting Sarah Grey. She had always thought spiritualists were gypsy-like, with flowing robes and dangling beads, clutching crystal balls. She had expected it to be a thorough waste of time and an embarrassing experience. Now she found herself not only liking Sarah but also completely convinced of her authenticity. Even if nothing else happened she would have a great many questions for the vicar next time he called! She stemmed her whirling thoughts and forced herself to picture the quiet stretch of road where her son had been so brutally struck down.

34 – Cyril

The small cruiser Sea Tease swayed gently at the jetty. Cyril Taft pottered about the deck, having just finished painting the new name on each side ...thinking happily that the play on his initials was rather clever. Anyway, nothing would have persuaded him to retain the name Bobbylyn! He had applied for Thames Authority permission to change it almost a year ago. He didn't believe it unlucky to give a boat a new name – at least he hadn't when he bought it. At the moment he wasn't so sure! A month after the purchase he was sent by his company to act as locum for a branch office supervisor who had been taken ill, so apart from a few weekends, hadn't been able to use the boat. Now the police wanted exact details of his movements between Wargrave, where he lived and moored the boat, and Liverpool, where he had been working until last week.

The plain clothed men, who had strolled casually down the riverbank to talk to him, chatted amicably for at least half an hour before introducing themselves. They wouldn't say why, but were highly suspicious to find him painting out the old name! If he had received permission for the change months ago, they said, it should have been re-painted straight away. Why hadn't he done it?

Cyril wondered what had he said while off-guard? Nothing significant surely: he had naturally assumed they were hotel guests walking off a heavy lunch – not knowing he was the sole object of their interest! It was alarming! But they had been no less friendly after telling him they were on an official inquiry!

He decided to ring the previous owner if the man didn't show up at the hotel marina today. Berry socialised with all the local bigwigs and might know what it was all about. He wanted to thank him anyway for the second spare tank and the extra keys which had been pushed through the vent while he was away.

Robert Berry had a new boat, a real beauty, about eight metres – a Nimbus diesel-engine job. It was moored at one of the longer jetties, nearer to the decorative gardens where guests sat to enjoy drinks in the fresh air. Cyril had given Berry's name to the police and pointed out his new cruiser but they seemed much more interested in his own craft. He knew they would check what he'd told them about his movements with his boss, but that didn't bother Cyril; he hadn't lied. Leaving the cabin to empty the vacuum cleaner he saw, on top of the trash in the waste bucket, the child's shoe, new and shiny ...so that was why one copper had nudged the other, but why hadn't they commented on it? Cyril would have said he found it on the deck ...you couldn't stop kids playing around deserted boats.

An hour later, when almost finished – he had only to get rid of the rubbish – Cyril saw the Berry family loading picnic baskets, obviously going for an early evening trip. They had friends with them so it might be difficult to talk, but he hurried to catch them before they pulled out. In his haste he spilled the trash and hastily crammed it back into the bucket but the small shoe fell out again, unnoticed, and the delay was enough to allow the Nimbus to leave its berth before he was within hailing distance.

Mrs Berry, a frail looking woman who giggled a lot, had already cast onto the jetty the springs – rope which normally held the vessel in place at its mooring, and she was coiling anchor rope in a most seaman-like manner. Heavy diesel exhaust fumes bubbled noisily through the water as the boat drew away. The deep gurgle made communication difficult, but as she waved in recognition Cyril cupped his hands and shouted, "Please ask your husband to ring me. It's very important!"

Evelyn acknowledged with a thumb up and disappeared into the cockpit where Bobby, a frown of deep concentration on his face, was steering the boat into mid-stream. Henry, the neighbour they were entertaining, sat on the starboard side gazing, enthralled, at the centrally mounted depth-finder hoping to sight a shoal of fish beneath them. His wife Jane was inside the cabin with the two children who were meeting for the first time. It would be marvellous, Evelyn thought, if Tabitha made a friend, she'd been so quiet and withdrawn lately. Evelyn liked the little girl and Jane, her new neighbour. It would be fun if they could go out together sometimes – shopping or a visit to the zoo with the children.

When Bobby relaxed at the wheel she relayed the message, then went down to open up the bar inside. As Evelyn poured beers for the men, Jane Burrows who had been watching with interest from the cabin window commented, "That chap looked a bit fraught – anything wrong?"

"Oh, I shouldn't think so," replied Evelyn with a giggle. "He's the man who bought our old boat. Look there it is – the blue one with the white roof. It hasn't sunk yet anyway, so his problem can't be too terrible!"

Jane held Tabby up to look at the moored craft and wondered if she missed the Bobbylyn, in spite of having this lovely new one. "Children can be so funny about things like that can't they?" The child shook herself free with a shake of her head and struggled to sit down again; grown-ups were strange and unpredictable. She was absolutely determined to stay close to Annabelle, her big new friend, who was more than five years old! ...It had been a long time since she felt so much at ease with anyone.

When they returned to the mooring three hours later it was almost dark. Henry, thanking them profusely for the really wonderful trip, started gathering his family and camera-gear together to disembark, but Bobby and Evelyn insisted that there was absolutely no need to hurry away. They had returned early merely because Bobby hated navigating with lights. Now safely moored, they could sit and have a leisurely drink.

The two couples had much in common. Jane said it was a shame they hadn't met earlier in the summer – the children could have enjoyed some day trips together. Bobby explained that shortly after moving house, Evelyn's mother was taken ill. He had driven them all up north – his wife had been far too upset to risk driving herself, and he came home alone the following day. Evelyn and Tabitha returned by train in the middle of August, a couple of weeks ago. Understandably, the child had been bewildered by the upheaval, but thank heaven the old lady was better now.

It was almost eleven-o-clock before the party ended. The two girls were fast asleep, curled together. Annabelle's arm was wound comfortingly around the little one's waist. She looked up drowsily as she heard Jane stepping down from the upper deck to use the small washroom.

When Tabitha, waking suddenly, realised they were to be separated she cried hysterically and was inconsolable. Evelyn declared with a worried frown that she couldn't understand it. "She is usually such an easy, amiable child to deal with. It must be moving house, and then taking her away again so quickly that has unsettled her."

The child's cries grew more frantic as Annabelle was pulled away and in desperation Bobby asked if they would allow Annabelle to spend the night with them; there was a spare divan in the nursery.

Annabelle looked eagerly at her parents for their agreement so it was settled; Jane would pick her up tomorrow.

Later, lying awake in the small hours, Bobby was at his wits' end. The child was troubled, retreating more and more into her shell, but he could do nothing without hurting his wife even more.

Evelyn persisted in her pathetic delusion that nothing had changed.

She had a long history of nervous instability – nothing to warrant hospitalisation but he didn't doubt that she was on the edge and it wouldn't take much to tip her delicate balance.

If he were instrumental in taking 'her little darling' away from her she would never forgive him.

He loved her too much to risk it. Surely, delaying a decision couldn't hurt the child but the wrong decision would definitely hurt Evelyn. There was no real urgency for him to do anything but wait and pray!

Halfway through the next morning, between meetings, he remembered to call Cyril Taft. He couldn't imagine what the fellow wanted. It had been months since they last spoke. After hearing of the police inquiry and telling Taft that he had no idea what they could be after, he was tempted to ring a contact of his in the local force, but on second thoughts, he cradled the 'phone and gathered his papers together.

Perhaps he would ring later; now he had work to do.

35 – Evelyn

After Jane had collected Annabelle, Evelyn went out into the garden. She sighed as she saw the tiny figure sitting dejectedly in the swinging chair. Tabitha was quieter this morning and after a tearful protest had resigned herself to the parting. An invitation to play with Annabelle on Sunday afternoon had helped. She used to be so independent and lively; now she was wary and withdrawn. She didn't even talk to her dolls any more. When Evelyn sang her favourite nursery rhymes and encouraged her to join in, she merely stared blankly: completely unresponsive. There was a strange haunted look in her beautiful violet eyes, which were paler now than when she was really well. Her very lack of communication made her seem smaller and more vulnerable. Even her curly hair had lost most of its bounce.

Evelyn knew it was entirely her fault and was consumed with guilt for being too busy to watch constantly. The poor baby was almost kidnapped a few weeks ago – no wonder she was disturbed. Just after leaving their old home too … and Nana had spoiled her shamefully – she could be missing all the attention. Trying to interest the child, Evelyn brought out all her favourite toys and put them on the smooth lawn. From the depths of the toy box she unearthed a golden haired doll, which she held sadly in her hands. Tabitha used to love this but had hardly played with it for months.

Slowly Evelyn realised that the child had come to stand near her. She was gazing at the doll, so Evelyn held it out to her and was overjoyed when Tabitha took it and hugged it to her closely. Teardrops welled in her eyes and rolled down her cheeks ...for the first time in weeks, she smiled.

When her husband returned home Evelyn greeted him with Tabitha in her arms. To his surprise the child looked almost happy. She still clutched the doll and carried it up to bed where she fell asleep almost immediately. What a change, after weeks of disturbed nights. Evelyn had made a special effort with the table setting – a few small sprigs of jasmine scented the air – and they enjoyed a quiet dinner. Later, they took coffee outside on the patio. The garden spotlights played on the fountain and they were as relaxed as they used to be, before leaving their old home. He had wondered if they would ever luxuriate in such moments again. Evelyn looked so contented now. He determined to do whatever it took, to keep her safe and happy. Safe and happy! That gave him an idea.

They had spent their honeymoon in Spain and loved it so much that before returning, they impulsively bought a tiny villa there ...so cheap in those days. Because of the house move they had missed their usual holiday on the Costa Blanca. His business was doing well and could run without him for months if need be: why not let it! There was no reason why they should not go immediately ...the peace and quiet might be all Evelyn needed to restore her to full health and sanity. No one was likely to disturb them there although, unusually for the district, it was on the telephone. Not so unusual was the fact that all the services were still registered in the name of the previous owner, even though the local bank dutifully paid all the service bills for him.

They had always delighted in keeping the villa a secret from everyone: their own little hideaway. It was the perfect solution and he didn't hesitate to act on it. They would be basking in the Mediterranean sunshine before next weekend.

He felt slightly embarrassed when he imagined facing Jane and Henry Burrows. After all the chat about the child being unsettled they were taking her away again ...and wouldn't say where!

During his lunch-break on Thursday he telephoned to tell

Evelyn that they had just three days to close up the house. She was absolutely ecstatic. She knew they must be going to Spain because of the things Bobby told her to pack, but he wanted to surprise her so she pretended to have no idea. If she didn't definitely know where, he thought, she couldn't tell anyone else could she? He wasn't even telling his staff – he would call the office once a week. This was to be a complete rest.

Evelyn couldn't imagine why he suddenly wanted to go away. They had only just about settled in and agreed that they didn't need a holiday break: it was exciting enough coming to a new place, meeting new people. Perhaps he too was worrying about Tabitha – that must be it! She hoped they really were going to their little Spanish villa. Maybe on this trip Tabitha would even learn to dive. She had thoroughly enjoyed the pool last year. Evelyn looked at the huge pile of little dresses. Some would be too small now. She called Tabitha to try them and, with amusement, relished her wide-eyed wonder when she saw them.

"Yes darling," Evelyn laughed, hugging her, "we are going to have a lovely holiday near the sea!" To Evelyn's surprise and delight almost all the clothes were wearable and nothing was too small. When the packing was finished except for the final toilet items, she lifted the phone, cancelled all deliveries until further notice, and then went downstairs humming happily to prepare the evening meal.

36 – Alec

Alec and his team were going over recent developments in the Mead case with an air of expectancy and controlled excitement. After seven weeks they at last felt close to a real breakthrough. Detective Sergeant Dee and his partner however, who traced the Bobbylyn through the River Authority records and interviewed Cyril Taft, were slightly downcast. Both had seen the discarded shoe and from their car, later, observed Taft tip his waste into the rubbish skip. They had searched way down into the mess but the shoe wasn't there. But anyway, did the lost shoe really matter? It had been new: white patent leather – certainly not Kate's. She had been wearing brown sandals.

Aware of Sarah Grey's involvement, something intrigued John Dee. The name of the boat in the painting was far too small to read but the artist had given it two parts beginning with S and T. Mrs Grey told them it was wrong and had given them the name Bobbylyn which proved correct, but wasn't it an amazing fact that it had now been changed to Sea Tease, as painted by young Mrs Hunter... Perhaps she was Psychic as well! Algy smiled to himself but didn't comment; he wouldn't be at all surprised!

John's partner Terry White, also a Detective Sergeant, had established that Taft's account of his movements was truthful but there was nothing to prove that he hadn't slipped back and used the boat on the day Kate disappeared. The Marina Manager logged all craft movements in and out. He relied on owners to fill in details about their destination and approximate return time.

The Bobbylyn had hardly been used since changing hands and certainly, according to the log, not within three weeks of the critical date. Mr Berry, he said, drove the boat in for Taft and had moored his own new cruiser at the marina since moving to Wargrave. Dee and White had seen, but not interviewed, Berry and wondered if there was any reason to do so. They decided to check him out, but not visit him for the moment.

The three members of the team who had not been at the Latham house with Sarah were anxious to hear in detail what transpired. Alec produced a copy of the tape, which they could play later, and said it was up to them whether they privately thought messages from the dead were possible, or figments of an over-active imagination, but everything Mrs Grey said was quite feasible. As confirmation was impossible he at least wanted to work on her version until a more likely one came up. He handed out copies of his notes but went over them aloud:

Ozzy was leading Kate back home when a brown foreign car came round the bend in the road at speed... Japanese, he thought, and his father said he was more likely to be right than not. He pulled Kate onto the path – well away from the verge, expecting it to drive straight on. Instead, the car screeched to a halt when it reached them and the driver, a woman, sprang out and rushed round the front of the car shouting. She attacked him and he released Kate's hand to defend himself whereupon the woman grabbed her. When he tried to take Kate back again he was pushed violently backwards and fell into the ditch. As had been verified by examining the area, he crawled out, ran into the road and was hit by the car.

The others, hard-headed professionals though they were, all leaned forward expectantly. In acknowledgement that he had reached the most amazing part of his account, Alec nodded his head slowly...

The woman pushed Kate into the passenger seat and pressed down the lock button; Ozzy could not open the door. Kate screamed, she was trying to get out ...the car started moving away. He grabbed at the handle of the rear door. It came ajar and the car swerved violently. He lost his grip on the door but kept running. It swung out and hit him.

"Yes gentlemen," Alec said, "it crushed his head, but he was determined to get into the car and, his death being instantaneous, he continued his desperate leap in spirit. He didn't realise that he had been killed! However, he can recall a violent pain in his head and imagined later that he had been stunned by the blow."

There was no interruption, other than some low whistles of astonishment, so Alec cleared his throat and continued:

When he 'came round', so to speak, he was lying in the back of the car in the dark with no idea where he was, or having any idea how he got there. He couldn't remember who he was but was extremely agitated, convinced that he had done something bad. He therefore thought he should stay hidden. At last he steeled himself to leave the car and investigate but was too late ...he heard someone coming. Apparently the car was in a garage and he saw that outside it was a clear, bright, moonlit night. He crouched low on the floor and was frightened when a rear door opened – someone, it proved to be a man, put something on the back seat and then drove the car out.

Again Alec paused and asked, "Any questions?"

Terry White who, throughout, had been making copious notes, flipped over a page of his note-pad and asked, "Did you get a description sir, of the woman who snatched the child?"

"Yes," Alec replied, a note of satisfaction in his voice. "She was about the same height as the boy, 5'8" – according to the autopsy report, tall for a woman: thirty-ish, thin, long fair hair, wearing something 'fancy' to quote Ozzy (or Sarah!), covered with a short overall."

"Not a very likely description for a possible kidnapper!" Algy Green said. Then added, "In a way it makes this – er..." For a moment he hesitated, stuck for a suitable phrase, "...this interview with the deceased, all the more credible." He continued by asking if there was a description of the house or surroundings, after the car left the garage.

Alec resumed. "Well, before he ducked out of sight he formed the impression that the garage was large, probably double." Checking his notes again Alec told them that as it drove away the car crunched over gravel before slowing down and turning, Ozzy thought, to the left. "So we are looking for a large house, probably detached, with a short drive to a good sized garage – oh yes – a lift-up door or doors. There is no information about the actual location because when he saw what was on the back seat he fainted with shock." Alec looked at the group of expectant faces. Before he told them more he wanted them to be quite clear that he firmly believed Kate to be still alive, held captive by the woman who had taken her. To explain his own conviction he told them about Sarah's first contact with the child Beth, and then took up the thread of the story again.

When Ozzy saw the dead body of a little blonde girl his mind connected it subconsciously with Kate and he was shocked out of what he thought was consciousness. When he came round he was outside the stationary car and the man, having removed the body, was carrying it away. Ozzy followed, across a field along a rough track that ended at a river. He couldn't understand why the man didn't see him, but he followed, along the riverbank until they reached a long line of boats. In the distance was a large building, which had lots of lights surrounding it. The boat the man boarded was about the third or fourth from the end. Having unlocked the cabin and put the body inside, he fiddled with some tubing from a fuel tank for a while so it was obviously an outboard engine. When he climbed round the narrow strip of decking to the front, to cast off, Ozzy went on board and into the cabin. There was a table with seats at each side and, again thinking he had to hide, he crouched underneath it and waited. The body was on a bench seat, opposite.

According to Mrs Grey, Alec explained, young Ozzy was then in a kind of limbo. He had passed so quickly from this world to the next that he had been unable to accept it. The violence of the few moments preceding his death left an impression that carried over, leaving him with a compulsion to finish what he had started, although he couldn't remember clearly what it was. At first, when he was struck, Ozzy said it was like being sucked through a dark tunnel, towards a tiny speck of light. The gloom began to lift but he resisted: turned; fought against it. He felt consumed with guilt, that there was something vital he still had to do in the blackness he was leaving behind. Later, he experienced alarming shifts between seeing dim shadow plays, as though dreaming, and seeing the world clearly but being ignored by everyone in it.

All he can recall of the journey over water is drifting a long way before the engine started. Knowing the man was at the wheel he took a closer look at the child and was puzzled. Why had he thought he recognised her? Who had he expected to see?

When the engine stopped he hid again, until the body was taken ashore. Although his memory had gone, his sense of right and wrong had not! He was horrified when the man left the body on the ground and went back to the boat. Ozzy knew the man must be a murderer – especially when he returned with a garden fork and spade. "I must say at this point," said Alec, "Ozzy was crouched low and saw only the tools as they hovered within inches of his face. The fork looked new – an orange striped label was still on the handle and the prongs were shiny black... Any questions?"

Again it was D S White, pen poised, who wanted to know if they had a description of the man, and was the boat actually the Bobbylyn, which they had already traced. Alec confirmed that it was the boat he and John Dee had seen at the marina – it was from Ozzy that they first heard of its existence! As for the man, the description wasn't much use: tallish, youngish, darkish ...it could fit millions! There had been a moon but there were drifting cloud patches so he assumed that during the brighter moments the boy wasn't in a position to see the man's face and unfortunately still thought he needed to stay concealed among the dark trees.

Alec was coming to the end of his notes.

Ozzy watched a grave being dug, then fled towards the sound of traffic. He attempted to wave down passing cars but most ignored him.

Alec took a deep breath. "Now this is quite amazing." He shook his head in wonderment and turned over a page...

Desperate to stop someone, he stood in the middle of the

road, waving, and at last a driver reacted. He swerved but braked too late to stop. Ozzy says he was terrified and leaped out of the way. The driver, an elderly man, continued braking and stopped within a few yards – he had not been driving fast.

The rest of the story, Alec told them, was from official sources.

"I've checked back to an incident report that I dismissed at the time. It was early in our search for Kate and we were keeping close tabs on any unusual happenings within the county. A man turned up at a police station a few miles from Henley – late one night just after the kidnapping. He'd braked hard, sure he'd seen a figure in his headlights but when he left the car and walked back, thinking he'd killed someone, he found nothing. He was thoroughly shaken and imagined somebody injured, unconscious, dying where they'd been thrown in the dark! Being a good citizen, he drove straight to the nearest station. They took his name and address and gave him some strong coffee while a car was sent out to investigate."

Alec explained that nothing significant had been found anywhere along the stretch he had described other than tyre tracks on the verge, after brake marks swerving off the highway, so it was concluded that nothing had happened. He was old and possibly tiring at the wheel. "Little did anyone think he'd seen a ghost!" Alec commented, "It should be a lesson to us all!"

He continued to explain, with reference to his notes, how Ozzy, having landed as he thought safely in the grass, was so scared by what he imagined was a close brush with death that he passed out again and it was daylight when he came round. Although, by then, he only vaguely remembered the girl and the grave, he still desperately wanted to contact somebody and was enraged by everyone's lack of concern. His continual failure to communicate filled him with despair.

"We have no idea how much time elapsed between the burial of the child's body and the day Mrs Hunter started her river painting." Alec pointed out, "Ozzy probably attached himself to her because although she didn't see him, at least she seemed to hear when he shouted, so he waited for her in her car."

He reminded them that, while waiting, Ozzy went into limbo again and later found that he was in the garden of her home. He waited for any comments but his audience was silent, so he continued. "We have yet another point to consider: the child Beth." He returned the notes to his briefcase with a sigh... "It seems reasonable to assume that it is her body that is buried near the river. We'll have to rely on Mrs Hunter to find the exact spot where she found the bracelet. I have her description of the area but I'd prefer to send a car to Wales and bring her back for a day; we can't expect her to drive herself."

They were all eager to get on with the inquiry. The young Detective Sergeants went over their assignments. Had Taft given permission for anyone to use the boat while he was away? Did anyone have access to his keys? Had a strange car – brown possibly foreign, been seen around the hotel or marina? Did anyone known there, drive one? Had Berry handed over all the keys with the boat? Would Taft necessarily know if he had not?

Neither of them had expected much to come of Sarah's efforts, but now they reminded each other with enthusiasm of all the instances where she'd been proved right. The boat had been found ...they could vouch for it being fourth from the end. The path beyond it petered out in a field – they needed to go and see how near it was to a road where the brown car might have parked – and there was no way Mrs Grey could have known about the chap who swerved to avoid a ghost!

They asked if Alec intended sending a forensic team to examine the boat and were told that had already been done. Alec regretted that they had been unable to trace a deceased Elizabeth Maybury. No one of that name was currently missing, reported dead, or drowned over the last twenty years. The research had gone much farther back than he'd requested, but he would discuss that aspect again with Mrs Grey. The more they could learn about Beth the nearer they might be to finding Kate.

Algy, who had been deep in thought, wondered aloud why the ghost of Beth was not able to tell them where the house was. At four years old she couldn't be expected to know anything about geography but most children were taught their address!

Her parents could then be traced. And why hadn't they reported her death – could they be dead too? Because he knew Clarrie Hunter well, he volunteered to fetch her from Wales personally; he would welcome the chance to discuss the case with her from the paranormal angle. Dee and White exchanged amused glances with raised eyebrows, but made no comment!

Alec agreed with all the planned action and brought the briefing to a close. At that moment his telephone rang. A post office official with vital information wanted an appointment with him as soon as possible. A few minutes conversation convinced Alec that the man was genuinely worried and was in possession of important evidence, which hadn't become known earlier because of a hectic period of local difficulty. When they were short-staffed, letters they were unable to deliver for any reason were put aside. Now they had all been sorted and there were two for 'Mr and Mrs Mead, Near Wallingford'. No more information was written on either envelope.

On opening the earlier one to return them to sender they found a photograph inside. One of the staff recognised the child as the missing Kate Mead. He wished to hand the mail to the police to avoid causing distress to the parents but wasn't sure that he should – would he be guilty of mishandling the Royal Mail? He was about to leave for his lunch break so a car was sent to collect him straight away.

Three anxious faces stared at Alec, eager to discover if they had heard correctly. Could this possibly be a ransom note at last? The envelope which had been opened was posted on Monday 23rd of July, three days after the kidnapping. The second, dated Monday August 27th was still sealed, thanks to the good sense of the postal employees, so the villain's fingerprints might be on the contents. It was thicker too – it could indeed contain the kidnapper's terms for the child's safe return.

They all silently hoped that the long delay in delivery, almost seven weeks, had not threatened the child's safety. Was this the break they'd been waiting for? It could it be a vital link to the person who had abducted poor little Kate.

37 – Ambrose

Polly had been especially solicitous since their visit to Ozzy's home. The long session proved to be a big drain on Sarah's strength. Alec had previously thought he might take her to Kate's home while in the area, but he could see she was too tired and, fortunately, had not promised to go.

The Meads knew the séance was taking place but Alec hadn't suggested that they might attend. It would have been painful for them and the additional strain on Sarah was unwarranted. They were obviously eager to meet Sarah so Annie Latham asked if she could pave the way for them, by describing her own encounter with Sarah. Alec agreed and they decided Annie could make arrangements for Sarah to go next Sunday, whereupon Annie invited Polly to tea if Sarah didn't need her.

On Thursday Sarah slept late again. Polly made no attempt to waken her until after ten-o-clock, taking a cup of tea up with her. To her surprise, Sarah was on her way down.

"You really shouldn't be doing this," Sarah protested. "You are here for company not to wait on me hand and foot!" She chided Polly gently. She was so good hearted and her feelings easily hurt, but she should take things a bit more easily at her age. "Anyway, have you forgotten – the Reverend Ambrose Kilroy is coming this morning. I must take some cakes from the freezer and grind the coffee."

"Now how could you think I would forget," retorted Polly with an injured air. "Everything is quite ready for the vicar. You just come and sit quietly until he arrives... Really!"

Sarah was glad to take her advice. She reflected that it was not only the strain of yesterday afternoon that had taken its toll, she had suffered through several disturbed nights worrying about Clarinda ...at least that was now over. When the doorbell rang she was almost asleep and, forced to concentrate, she fervently hoped that whatever he required of her wouldn't demand her immediate involvement, but Sarah was happy to be meeting the Reverend Kilroy properly. Unlike his wife Elsie, he seemed to have a sense of humour!

He settled comfortably in the other large fireside chair and Polly, after serving coffee, cakes and scones was leaving them, when he suddenly delved into a large shopping bag at his feet and produced a plastic box. "This is obviously 'coals to Newcastle' but Elsie sent these biscuits for you, Mrs Grey. She assures me that they are among your favourites – her own baking of course! I had mentioned that having seen your beautiful garden there was little point in bringing you flowers!"

"They must be shortbread with nuts! Yes?" Sarah laughed, peeping under the lid. She put one on her plate and handed the rest to Polly who then left them. "I eat more of them than I should at our bridge mornings. How kind of her. I won't say you shouldn't have, because they're so delicious – a real treat. Please call me Sarah," she added with a smile, "as Elsie does."

"Well, thank-you. I confess to thinking of you as such because Elsie often speaks of you. I dare say Ambrose would come easily to you too." Leaning forward he reached for his coffee and cleared his throat nervously. "I'm glad we can be informal. It will make it easier for me to explain the purpose of my visit." Sarah sipped her drink too and waited with patient curiosity, until he sat back, ready to speak. His smooth round face looked slightly pink.

After mopping his lips with a flourish of his whiter than white linen handkerchief, he began by affirming that although he had never had personal experience of the supernatural, he was willing to believe others had; indeed, the previous incumbent claimed to have seen many ghosts in the church, marvelling particularly at the monks. "They walked in single file, he told me, across the worn stone flags near the carved font and through the opposite wall where, he later discovered, there used to be a door out to the cloister garden. He said they did not walk at present ground level but several inches above it, where it must have been when they walked in life". Ambrose paused, folded his hands over his ample stomach appearing to be deeply engrossed with his own thoughts. Then asked, "Would these ghosts be different from the ones you see? They never spoke, either to him or to each other. Although he heard the rustle of their robes and sandals, they apparently didn't see or hear him."

"You are quite right. There are many types of ghost." Sarah answered. "Some are merely echoes from the past – their image somehow imprinted on places they inhabited." She said there was no reason to suppose that the spirits of such ghosts were earthbound. It's a bit like seeing the image of film stars, now dead; they act their part whether or not anyone is watching them – it hardly matters. "We can't be sure why they are sometimes visible; perhaps on an anniversary which had special meaning for them; or if atmospheric conditions are identical to those prevailing at a moment of stress. Perhaps extremely violent emotions make an impact on the fabric of the surroundings."

The Reverend Kilroy was fascinated as Sarah spoke of the many ghosts recorded by reliable witnesses over thousands of years. Ancient historians, before Christ's birth, often wrote of supernatural beings, ranging from relatives recently passed over and recognised, down to elemental earth spirits destined never to rise to a higher plane ...mindless entities which must never be encouraged into our world: they could be channels for evil. Every séance, she reminded him, begins with prayers to protect those taking part by attracting only good and helpful influences.

Ambrose agreed enthusiastically, "The Greeks believed, if I recall correctly, that Charon was not permitted to ferry the ghosts of unburied persons over the Styx! They wandered up and down the banks for hundreds of years before being allowed to cross. There are countless references to spirits in the bible of course."

As Sarah nodded he continued, "Matthew 14, verse 26, springs to mind; the Disciples saw Jesus walking on the water –

'They thought it had been a Spirit'. After his resurrection they again, 'Supposed he was a Spirit appearing in their midst'. I think it is significant that Jesus doesn't argue against the possibility, he merely points out that, 'a Spirit hath not flesh and bones as ye see me to have'. Most telling for me personally, as proof of the existence of ghosts is the fact that we have a special service of exorcism to get rid of them!" Ambrose added apologetically, "Of course I don't know half as much about the subject as you do, dear lady. Please continue. I'm absolutely fascinated."

Sarah smiled. At least she need have no worries about outright scepticism on his part. Unbelievers with open minds were no problem. The more belligerent, who only sought proof to back up their own pre-formed opinions, could obstruct attempts at contact with the 'other side'. "I'm really impressed by your enthusiasm Ambrose. You've obviously given the matter a great deal of thought, but are you also aware that some phantom appearances are of the living?" Sarah nodded as his face registered surprise. "They are usually telepathic communications due to the strong desire of the 'ghost' to visit or talk. It is as though the subconscious is less inhibited in reaching out than the analytical mind!" After a moment she added with a grin, "You started by saying you have never seen a ghost. How do you know?"

Ambrose raised his brows quizzically and tilted his head sceptically. He leaned back and then replied, "Surely, it is not an event easily missed!"

"Let me relate an experience of my own. Many years ago when our daughter was a baby, my husband and I were walking back to our car after a shopping trip in town." Sarah verified that Ambrose knew the street where they had parked, near a Roman Catholic infant school. Windows overlook the road and walls abut the main building on both sides, screening quadrangles for play and drill. Only two gates, one at each end corner of the property, provide access to the school – no street doors are in the main building.

Sarah continued. "For the whole length of the school, no parking was allowed, so the road was empty. I carried Clarinda

– Stephen was laden with heavy shopping as we walked side by side. We were within a few feet of the far gate when a nun came out and walked towards us. My husband strolled on but I dropped back and stood near the wall, to make way." Ambrose nodded his head sharply – guessing perhaps what Sarah was about to reveal, but didn't interrupt the narrative. "She acknowledged me with a smile, and I hurried to catch up with Stephen who had turned to wait for me. As I reached him I said, 'Didn't that nun have beautiful eyes?' 'What nun?' he asked. I turned and saw no sign of her ...we were alone!"

Ambrose was quick to appreciate the point. "There are times," he murmured, "when looking from the pulpit I imagine the pews to be filled with worshippers. Only as I bid them good-morning outside, later, am I aware that there are really very few." He sighed. "Perhaps my congregations are artificially swollen by those from another world!"

For a moment Sarah was concerned that he was laughing at her, but she saw that he was merely surmising that such a thing could actually happen! She went on to name several books which might interest him about scientific experiments into ESP ...now universally accepted as a fact and studied at higher academic levels. "So far, we have discussed only apparitions," she went on, "but some people are clairaudient. We are told that Joan of Arc heard voices – I fear that many others who do so are considered mad. Some are hospitalised because of similar experiences."

The idea obviously intrigued Ambrose but he looked doubtful.

"It is entirely right, I admit," said Sarah, "to confine those who are driven to madness, but who is to say that they were not ever in contact with another world? A sane individual hearing, or imagining, a voiced message would evaluate it, first of all for content. If informative, they would note and later check it – and the early involvement of a second party can substantiate the validity of the communication. If the message is an instruction to act – would such action help or injure?"

"It is certainly a novel concept to me," Ambrose murmured.

"The mentally healthy are able to deal with the experience," Sarah assured him. "Those unfortunate enough to be unstable are at risk from evil influences and better confined for their own safety. Perhaps the medieval practice of trying to drive out devils, though their methods were suspect, was not too reprehensible!"

"It would follow," Ambrose reflected, "that the inclusion of Para-psychologists on the staff of mental asylums would be a good move." He thanked Sarah as she poured more coffee.

Replenishing his plate with cake he commented, "These are quite delicious, I am eating far more than I should – I rely on you not to tell Elsie!" When they had both settled down again, he once more cleared his throat, less nervously than before.

Sarah knew that he was ready at last to give her the reason for his visit and looked at him expectantly. "Now, tell me, is a member of your flock haunted perhaps?" Sarah couldn't resist asking and her eyes sparkled as he looked astonished. He relaxed with a wry grin almost immediately, recalling seeing her with Alec: guessing who'd told her.

"Yes, I remember now... Superintendent Holmes was making one of his rare visits to church when the situation came to a head. It is difficult to know where to start really, because the reason for the fellow's delusion – or indeed his being haunted – stems from a tragedy which happened two years ago, for which I have only his version. His name is David Bane; there is no point in keeping it from you. His story is already widely known." Ambrose explained how ten years ago, aged thirty-eight, Bane married Bettina who had an unmarried twin sister, Barbara.

Bet and Babs as they were called affectionately, had never lived apart and Bane provided accommodation for Babs willingly, in his large family home. She had her own suite sharing only the kitchen. The arrangement suited all three – they were very happy. Bane didn't see much of Babs actually, because he rarely went into the kitchen – it was a house where domestics formerly ruled below stairs and he had never been encouraged to regard it as part of his home. Before some upper rooms were converted for Bet's twin, a large part of the house was shut off. A housekeeper cooked and he had all he needed to make coffee and snacks in the old nursery next to his dressing room.

Sarah could visualise the situation easily. The house sounded much like that of the Grey family, which she had known well. Stephen's father, born and brought up there, hardly ever entered that heart of domestic activity, the kitchen. When he did, it invariably ended in chaos: contents of cupboards disarranged, drawers muddled, cluttered work surfaces and the loss of his temper when faced with his own failure to do or find anything.

Ambrose stopped to peer anxiously at his pocket watch. He held the gold Hunter, obviously with great pride, at an angle to the light behind him and then looked beyond it to meet Sarah's gaze. She guessed he was about to speak of its history and forestalled him as his mouth began to open.

"Your Great Uncle Joseph is delighted to see his treasured time-piece still in use and keeping good time." His jaw quite literally dropped and Ambrose looked embarrassed as Sarah said, "Come now, confess. You were hoping, when you came this morning, for specific personal proof of life beyond the veil." Sarah then took pity on him, making him feel much better, by acknowledging that he was far too wise to expect or ask for it.

Ambrose mopped his brow in obvious relief as she declared, "Perhaps that's why my own subconscious held no barriers against the elderly gentleman who is standing beside you in spirit. He tells me that when you dropped the watch into your pocket you wished, as always when you carry it, that he could have known how fond you were of him and how desperately unhappy you are, not to have seen him during his final hours."

In seconds the Reverend's reaction changed to gasps of mixed sorrow and joy. Finally, blowing his nose and wiping unashamedly the tears welling in his eyes, he spoke. "When I heard he was ill I was about to depart on a seminar. It was important that I attend ...supremely so, I thought at the time! I'd be away for only two weeks I reasoned, and could visit him immediately on my return. One week later, when a telegram from my father informed me of Joseph's death, I packed up and returned immediately. Standing at his graveside I wondered, as do many in similar circumstances, what good was it being close to him then, when my presence would have meant so much more in life?"

He was obviously still guilt-ridden and it was a few moments before he spoke again. "My faith should have sustained me: it did to some extent. One hopes that on the day of judgement, when true feelings and motives come under scrutiny, thoughtless, hurtful acts won't count against us! Deep down we all crave that our sins should be forgiven right away. We live in an age of instant gratification, and being as guilty of that as others – to a small extent – I can hardly find words to express my gratitude to you for your revelation." There was no doubt in Sarah's mind that he had received the proof he sought. He scarcely needed to add, "I do believe that Joseph is here with us and I want him to know how much I regret my selfishness in putting my own interests first when he needed the comforting presence of his family."

"Don't worry ever again," Sarah said. "He knows how troubled you've been since that day and wants you to put those thoughts behind you. Be as happy as he is that he's rid of earthly pain. By the way, he wants you to see a doctor about your indigestion." As Ambrose' eyes widened in alarm, Sarah assured him, "The condition will be treated easily and you have nothing to fear, but anti-acid pills won't work!"

It was some while before the Reverend was ready to go back to the problem of David Bane. He confessed that coming to Sarah was more a last resort than in real belief that she could help. He had persuaded Mr Bane to see his doctor in case the problem was physical, and later to consult a psychiatrist to restore his mental balance. For months Bane underwent treatment and being a regular churchgoer Ambrose also saw him often.

At first Bane appeared to be deriving benefit from the sessions, declaring himself convinced it had been due entirely to an over-active imagination. In June his wife left him and now lodged with a friend but still attended church services. She was sick with worry and had requested help. She wanted Ambrose to do whatever he thought best. When he decided to consult Sarah it had been his intention merely to accompany Mrs Bane and allow her to tell the story her own way but, having an abnormal fear of the supernatural, she declined.

Apparently, when they were children, her twin had claimed to see ghosts. If true, it was the only way in which the two differed. Babs delighted in frightening Bet in the dark of night by describing the beings hovering over her. The game, gradually forgotten as they grew up, left Bet with a resolve to avoid the subject completely. When Babs was killed she was beside herself with grief – in no condition to cope with her husband's hallucinations.

She felt terrible now. She probably triggered the situation with her wild accusations that it was his fault because he'd forgotten his promise to pick Babs up on his way home; he didn't care for anything but his work; was he really in the office or drinking with a client? – And so on and on. She'd known he was already upset by her sister's death – they had always got along well – and her own thoughtless stupidity added unbearable guilt to his sorrow.

One Sunday morning as Ambrose looked down over the congregation he saw them, husband and wife, sitting apart. Perhaps one arrived late he thought. When it happened again he guessed they were avoiding each other.

After the service Ambrose drew Bane aside but the man constantly cast furtive glances back over his shoulder and from side to side, not once looking him in the eye, and had then hurried away without a word.

Mrs Bane watched him go but made no attempt to follow. When all the other worshippers had departed, Ambrose went back into the church and saw her waiting for him. Shafts of sunlight filtered down through the stained glass windows. Swirls of dust motes disturbed by shuffling feet danced upwards through the bright beams. She looked sad and vulnerable sitting quietly in the empty church. During the next hour she revealed all she had endured in the two years since her sister's tragic death. Weary frustration when she tried in vain to help her husband changed gradually to fear and finally to sheer terror which had driven her to leave him.

As Sarah listened, fascinated, she became convinced that the mystery of David Bane's delusions would be well worth investigating and assured Ambrose that, as soon as her present commitment to the Mead case allowed, she would ring him. In the meantime, she said, it would be of considerable help if Mrs Bane could select something personal which had belonged to her sister, place it in an envelope and allow Ambrose to bring it to her. A little psychometry was always a good first step.

37 – Alec

After lunch, Polly insisted that Sarah must rest in the garden. The sun was unusually warm for the first week in September; it would have been a pity to waste it. She promised to join her later after writing a few letters. When Alec telephoned it was therefore Polly who took the call. Hearing that Sarah had fallen asleep outside, he wouldn't allow her to be disturbed; he confirmed that they would all be going to the Latham house on Sunday and promised to ring again later.

The envelopes containing the snaps were on his desk. The first had been passed from hand to hand too often to be of use for fingerprinting. The contents of the second were carefully removed and it was found that the extra bulk was due to there being two snaps rather than one. There was no note and no ransom demand. Almost a month had elapsed between the posting of the first, in which the child had a wide-eyed, bewildered stare and the last two, in which Kate looked well; perhaps even a little plumper. He assured her parents when he rang them that undoubtedly she looked well cared for.

They understood that the police had to retain the photographs for examination and evidence but were satisfied with his promise to have them with him on Sunday. He pondered whether he should experiment, to see if they conveyed anything to Sarah before sending them to the lab, but he couldn't take the risk no matter how impressive she was. They would be replaced in the original envelope without undue handling – but the technicians should have first crack at them!

Alec was childishly disappointed, not being able to tell Sarah immediately of the latest development and that he was sending for Clarinda on Monday. He decided to take a chance on her being available and telephoned to book a lunch table for four. He wouldn't plan on going to the riverbank until early afternoon so there was no reason why mother and daughter shouldn't enjoy a meal with himself and Algy. Before then he must decide whether or not to publish Kate's pictures. The kidnapper might still intend to send a demand note; seeing them in all the newspapers and on television could create panic and result in Kate being harmed. His instinct was to withhold the information from the media until all other avenues dried up.

There were also several other investigations demanding attention; the quicker he could clear his desk the sooner he could concentrate on Beth again but all else paled anyway beside the enormity of a kidnapping. He pushed away the constant fear that even at this stage it might become a murder case.

38 – Sarah

Before Alec rang again Sarah heard from Clarinda about his plans for her day trip. Although they didn't know they would be lunching together, they were pleased to be meeting soon and hoped they would have a chance to talk before Algy took her back to Wales – so much had happened to them both since the start of her holiday.

Sarah, shutting her mind to the more gruesome aspects of what lay ahead, looked forward to meeting Kate Mead's parents on Sunday and seeing the snaps the kidnapper had sent. At last she would have a direct link with him, or her, a real contact to follow ...a breakthrough that might lead to finding the child soon and bringing her home.

Polly, taking her turn to prepare dinner, was busy in the kitchen, so after drawing the curtains against the darkening garden, Sarah sat quietly in the firelight, wondering if Beth and Ozzy would come through again, but minutes ticked by and her thoughts drifted first to Ambrose and David Bane, then to her daughter's amazing experience of which she had only the barest knowledge. Her own development as a clairvoyant had come at a much earlier age but she remembered all the mixed feelings of fear and exhilaration… Beth had been with her some time before Sarah gradually became aware of her and asked why she had come. Beth just smiled and held something out to show her – a baby doll with glossy gold hair. Cradling the toy in her arms, crooning a lullaby in a sweet clear voice, she slowly faded away.

***

After a quiet day at home Sarah was refreshed both physically and mentally. She and Polly had similar tastes in TV entertainment and finished the day by watching a film together. Polly sighed wistfully as they switched off and went upstairs. "I shall miss evenings like this when I go back home. Viewing there is almost impossible, and anyway it always seems geared to what the children want – and they stay up until all hours. Perhaps I should treat myself to a video player for my bedroom television, but it's only a black and white set, it wouldn't be the same; not much pleasure seeing exotic scenery without colour! I probably won't bother after all."

It was on the tip of Sarah's tongue to voice a wish that she could stay on, but it was, after all, Clarinda's house and one of the four bedrooms was her studio! She compromised by saying that she too was enjoying Polly's stay. She didn't add that she hadn't expected to, as she liked being alone sometimes. In fact, she was relieved to find that whenever she excused herself to spend a few hours in her own room, Polly occupied herself happily with no hint of reproach. Polly loved cooking. If she lived in she could do more baking and less heavy work. It wasn't right, expecting her to clean windows – and pushing the vacuum cleaner around was a back-breaking job. It was too much to expect Polly to cope for much longer but she would be hurt if they employed someone else.

They were both up early on Sunday morning because although not going out until the afternoon they had invited Alec for lunch. He arrived at twelve-fifteen and as Polly put the final touches to the meal he showed Sarah the three photographs. The two that had not been handled, even by the laboratory when they dusted them, were in the envelope again as he gave them to her. There had actually been a good partial print on one, but it didn't match any they had on file. Alec commented. "We didn't really expect to find any. It points to a non-professional villain and the absence of a ransom note is puzzling. I hope you get something through your channels to point us in the right direction! If not money – then what does the kidnapper want?"

For a few moments Sarah held the envelope and shut her eyes. Then she removed the photographs and held them, one on each open palm as she gazed at the small child. Alec hardly dared breathe and as Polly suddenly appeared in the doorway he instantly held up a warning hand to stop her speaking and causing a distraction. He beckoned and indicated that she should sit down. They both watched as Sarah started to tremble slightly and closed her eyes again. Eventually she spoke. "I feel a sense of bewilderment: not fear exactly – more a perception of loss. This is by no means a happy child but she is not fearful, there's no immediate reason to worry. She isn't harmed in any way."

There were two audible sighs of relief. "Beyond the room we see here – a laundry I think, I see a large garden and hear running water: a trickling sound like a brook. No, it is a fountain. I see it now in the middle of a small pool ...it is shaped like a – like... Oh no!" Her voice trailed away and her eyes, now open, were wide and troubled.

Polly went to her quickly, "For goodness sake, what did you see to frighten you so much. Is there any way I can help?"

Sarah shook her head and whispered, "The fountain, it was in the shape of a fish – a large leaping fish balanced on its tail, water spurting from its mouth."

Alec and Polly were bewildered; what could be so alarming about such a peaceful scene. They listened anxiously as Sarah, the photographs now enfolded between her closed hands, whispered, "It was not at the river, where Beth drowned, it was in the garden where Kate is being held. When she said a fish hit her I dismissed it as childish fancy ...what, or whoever had struck her it certainly couldn't be a fish! But now I understand; she was right, except that it was she who struck the fish! Leaning over too far, she must have fallen, banged her head on the stone tail and lost consciousness." Sarah gave up attempting to see more. She didn't want to witness the tragic accident. Knowing of it was enough.

Alec added another sheet of notes to his clipboard with a satisfied smile. There could not be many properties fitting the description he had now assembled, as long as the garden belonged to the house that Ozzy had seen ...surely now the end was in sight.

During lunch they discussed how much of their theory they should divulge to Kate's parents. Alec was in daily contact with them either personally by 'phone or through the local force and although he could report little official progress, Sarah's involvement gave them hope that Kate would return unscathed. Even so, if they heard that she was being held where another child had died it would cause them uncalled for anguish. It would be kinder to assure them that Sarah still sensed the child to be in no physical danger and had provided a fuller description of the place in which she was being held.

The unceasing efforts of the police – monitoring calls from the public, collating information, following up every lead, had created a bulky file, which Alec studied each night quietly at home. In spite of his conviction that Sarah was their best hope of finding Kate quickly, he was far too professional to abandon normal procedure. He was like a chariot driver with two separate teams pulling him along – thankful that they were both heading in the same direction and gratified when the findings of one confirmed those of the other. With Sarah's help, progress had been more rapid than immediately after the kidnapping, even with all their resources. He reproached himself for not inviting her to help earlier, but solid police work came first.

The weather was fine and dry when they set out, making the drive pleasurable, especially for Polly who had few opportunities to see the countryside from the luxury of a car. The serious reason for the outing was not lost on her, but supremely confident in Sarah's total control, Polly allowed herself to enjoy it. She was stimulated by the unusual and exciting turn her life had suddenly taken. She felt useful, knowing that her contribution to the ultimate success of the case, even though very small, was really appreciated.

Mapledurham was far behind and they were well underway before conversation lapsed. Sarah was disinclined to talk. She was garnering her mental strength in preparation for the afternoon with the Meads, wanting to provide as much support as possible without making rash promises. They must be allowed the luxury of hope which, she felt in her heart, was absolutely justified, but the situation could change. She had no power to influence future events.

When they skirted Wallingford and turned right towards Benson she knew they were almost there and felt a slight tightening in her throat. The worried parents would have built up high expectations of this meeting and she was human enough to be anxious not to fail them. As they neared Ewelme and turned towards the Latham house she felt the presence of both Ozzy and Beth and offered up a silent prayer of thanks. With their guidance, she was confident that all would go well.

Ever since hearing that they were looking for a brown car something had nagged at the back of Alec's mind. It was a loose end, which always veered from his grasp just as he felt he had the connection. Time and time again he had gone over the dozens of statements taken on that first day, but none held the reference he sought. It was extremely frustrating. As he halted at Watlington crossroads the answer came to him.

P.C. Laker interviewed the elderly woman who stopped to help Mrs Mead and had drawn a road map when he arrived at the scene, showing where each vehicle was, in relation to the body and each other. He'd sketched her car facing away from the body on the same side of the road as the kidnapper's car must have travelled, apparently going the same way. The van driver had stopped before reaching the accident spot. Both were shown on the same side of the thoroughfare! Yet Mrs Mead said that they arrived from opposite directions. He was so excited he almost pulled in immediately to telephone Laker – even if it was his Sunday off!

Laker was a friend of Jack Latham, who met them at his gate when they dropped Polly, so Alec asked if he had seen him lately.

Jack nodded, "I surely have! Funny you should ask because he says he wants a word with you! Bit shamefaced he seems to be, so I hope he won't be in trouble because he's a good man, one of the best. He's well liked in these parts. Anyway I said you'd likely be coming round later and he's calling in about five-thirty ...hope that's all right?"

Alec was delighted and said so, assuring Jack that he had no need to worry. He knew Laker's worth and in any case thought he knew what was upsetting him. He and Sarah drove on to the Meads' cottage a few hundred yards away; they could be sociable on the way back but now there was work to do. The car was rounding the bend where Ozzy had tried to save Kate, when Alec remarked that the kidnapper was still unaware that he had died. His death had been reported as a road accident; the connection with Kate's disappearance had been kept quiet. Even now, if word leaked out it could endanger the child. Already faced with a murder charge, her life might also be taken to cover up. They wouldn't, of course, discuss this with Mr or Mrs Mead.

39 – Ethel & Eddie

As the car drew up outside the house, nine-year-old Tommy was swinging on the creaking garden gate, talking to a slightly older boy. They both stared at Sarah as Alec held the car door open for her. Tommy, wide-eyed and with a nervous grin greeted her. "Hello. You're Mrs Sarah aren't you?" Elbowing his friend in the ribs, he sought instant confirmation for the boy's benefit: "The lady who talks to ghosts!"

Sarah laughed, somewhat taken aback and fleetingly lost for a suitable retort... "I would have thought you'd be more eager to discover if they spoke to me!" She then walked purposefully into the garden and was greeted by Eddie Mead, who apologised for the bad manners of his son. He ordered the boys to go off and play somewhere else. He ushered her inside to meet his wife and explained contritely, that although they had avoided talking in front of Tommy about Sarah, and the kind of things she did, the boy had nevertheless fathomed out what was going on, it was the way of children!

Ethel welcomed her nervously and looked relieved when Alec joined them. She left them with Eddie while she went to fetch a tea tray and bustled about serving everyone. "I know it's early," she admitted, "but after your drive I thought you'd like a cup of something. We'll have a proper tea later."

Clutching her own saucer so tightly that the cup rattled in its groove she eventually sat listening to the general conversation, making no attempt to join in. Whenever Sarah's eyes met hers she dropped her gaze quickly to her lap, but as she realised slowly that her guest was behaving normally and was not likely to fling herself about – possessed, she relaxed and smiled.

Alec had taken the envelopes containing the photographs from his briefcase and was waiting for everyone to settle down. Catching his eye Sarah took the initiative and announced that she had already seen and used them to practice a little psychometry. Seeing the puzzled glances exchanged by their hosts she explained that just as bloodhounds hone in to scents too elusive for ordinary senses to detect, a psychic can sometimes tune in to the invisible aura, which clings to inanimate objects. They retain an essence, which lingers. If close to an individual for any length of time – a favoured piece of jewellery for instance – the aura could cling forever, providing a link to them wherever they were.

She paused to assess her listeners' reaction and caught a quizzical look from Eddie ..."Forever?"

"Yes," she added, "even after their physical death. That's why, having examined the handkerchief your little girl dropped, I was quite convinced she's still alive."

Alec passed the snaps to the anxious parents, following Sarah's explanation with his own. "We have all the usual lines of investigation covered of course, but I asked Mrs Grey to help us because, as I told you, she has succeeded on earlier cases. Even while hoping for a short-cut, it seemed too much to ask when we had so little for her to go on." They both nodded, appreciating the problem. His next words brought astonished smiles to their faces ..."But now, through her amazing gift, we know almost everything about the place where Kate probably is except the exact location, and we have some valuable leads to follow. It is quite astounding!"

Eddie stared at the photographs of their lost child. He had moved to sit on the arm of Ethel's chair and put his arm round her as she gazed dumbly at the little face, which seemed poised either to smile or cry. Eventually he gave her a quick hug and whispered, "These prove beyond a doubt that she was well a few weeks ago ...just look at that lovely frock she's wearing and her shining hair. Someone is taking good care of her, as Mrs Grey told us." Turning to Alec he asked, "It's as though she was taken by someone who likes her and perhaps intends to keep her! Otherwise, wouldn't they have demanded money or something? And if that's the case, why in God's name did they send us these pictures? It is so contradictory!"

While they talked, Beth was in communion with Sarah who recalled her own vision of the garden and mentally asked if the child knew it. Beth bit her lip in frustration – it was too difficult to 'member', but she did 'member' her other garden! Sarah's pulse raced as she asked where it was, the other one. She was immediately rewarded with a parrot-like chant:

"My name ith Beth. I live in Biar Cottage, Watewy Lane."

"What a clever girl! Did you leave it to live in another house?" Sarah asked hopefully. Beth frowned and nodded...

"Yeth," she lisped, "a big big houth with pwetty fish but I don't go there now. Mummy doethn't want me!"

Sarah was stunned and sought to protest, but Beth shook her head and said she didn't care; she had Ozzy and Granny. She pointed to a built-in cupboard beside the fireplace and Sarah knew before Ethel opened it, although she did not say so, the doll was in there.

As Mrs Mead rose and went to the cupboard, Sarah leaned over to Alec, took his pen and indicated that she wished to write something. He pointed to the bottom of his notepad and she scribbled quickly: Biar (Briar?) Cottage, Watery (Waterway?) Lane. Alec frowned, puzzled, so she added: Beth's former address!

How he managed to sit through the next hour or two he afterwards couldn't have said. He wanted to put a search in motion to compile a list of Watery/ Waterway Lanes, but there might be yet more startling revelations so he forced himself to concentrate. The Meads were eager to hear what Sarah had to tell them about the photographs, particularly her impressions of the person who sent them.

She said, "I feel they were from a gentle person facing inner turmoil – torn two ways. I'm sure these were sent to comfort you; to tell you not to worry. My impression is that they were from a man who will do everything within his power to make sure that she comes home safely." Sarah paused as Ethel gasped,

"What do you mean – within his power? His must have an accomplice who thinks differently and may not even know that he took the pictures!"

Alec raised a hand to calm her. "I have considered that," he assured her, "and in order not to alarm anyone else involved, the matter will be kept away from the media. The photographs won't be published, either on TV or in the newspapers, so try not to think about that aspect."

Her husband took Ethel's hand with a worried frown but she told him not to fret. She knew they had every reason to hope Kate would be rescued soon. A few days after the kidnapping they had suffered the ordeal of a television appeal for her safe return and Ethel wondered aloud ...was it because he had seen it that the first photo was sent at the end of July? It supported the theory that he was not entirely heartless.

When she took the doll from Ethel, Sarah felt close to the tiny child who had loved it above all her other playthings. As the others talked, their voices rose and fell soothingly and gradually she shut them out entirely, allowing her mind to drift, trying to picture Kate, wherever she was. Gradually she succeeded. It was as if a film of Ozzy's tragic death was being re-run but, in the replay, had become distorted. All was larger than life and even more bewildering because she was seeing it through the eyes of a three-year-old. A woman, shouting, was pulling her away ...she was lifted and pushed into a car, crying. An arm pressed her into the seat ...treetops rushed by as the car hurtled along. The scene faded and she felt less fearful. She was looking out over a garden, from a room that seemed big and white. Sarah, in a light trance, eyes closed, breathed slowly and deeply. 'Rosebud' was cradled in her arms.

It was several minutes before the others, realising she was no longer listening to them, fell silent and waited for her to speak. Sarah disassociated herself from the child. It was her own analytical sense she needed. She saw the garden pool with the fish fountain and, aware that everyone was now watching, anxious to share her experience, began to speak aloud of her vision. "It's the garden I saw earlier. I'm looking at it from a first floor window: the window of Kate's room." They were all puzzled when she suddenly broke off and said, as though to an unseen presence, "Yes dear, I guessed! It is really your room ...I am so sorry. She has your dolly too but you mustn't mind – no, of course you don't, you understand now, don't you?"

Minutes passed in silence, until Sarah resumed her description of the room. "It is very pretty with white furniture and white, flower-sprigged wallpaper. I see Kate sitting in a small wicker chair nursing a doll exactly like this one. There is an open suitcase on the bed and a small pile of clothing. Someone is either packing or unpacking, I can't tell, it is fading away now..."

No one dared break the silence as Sarah slowly opened her eyes. Nobody wanted to dwell on the implications. Unpacking or packing! ...To go where?

40 – Kate

Following her visit to the Meads', as always after such sessions, Sarah was mentally exhausted. In spite of the unspoken fear that if not found quickly Kate might be moved, just as a picture of her surroundings was emerging, they left her parents in a hopeful mood. Handling the doll supported what they already surmised but had also increased Sarah's concern for Beth, who was beginning to understand what must have happened on the day of her death.

The house revealed to Sarah in her vision felt like a loving home, not a criminal hideout. The other individual involved was very close – probably married – to the man who had sent the snaps. Sarah was convinced that he hadn't seized Kate himself so it followed that his wife had done so. The man's attitude, in condoning her crime, was shocking but not difficult to understand. He must know they couldn't keep Kate, but if he loved his wife, the woman in the brown car, how could he face handing her over to the police. Beth must be their own little girl, whose drowning had unhinged the poor woman. There was no point in labouring the point with Alec; he already possessed all checkable facts.

Polly again insisted on giving Sarah breakfast in bed and, as Alec wasn't due to pick her up until mid-day, Sarah gave in with a minimum of protest and was persuaded to lie in. Apart from the stimulation of seeing Clarinda and hearing in detail of her recent experiences it was likely to be a difficult day. After lunch the investigation would, hopefully, take a big step forward.

Sarah was appalled to think of poor little Beth being buried furtively. It was an inexplicable feature, which tormented her in her assessment of the situation; it could only have been her father who had gone out that same night and hidden her in a lonely grave. It was gruesome. Sarah thought of the body as something quite apart from the beautiful child who had seldom been far from her during the past few weeks and, while relaxing, mentally re-constructed the incredible chain.

Ozzy, linked to Beth through Kate, had found help by attaching himself to Clarinda. He might have failed because, unable to paint at her chosen spot, she drove away – intent on moving a few miles along river – but something prompted her to turn onto the second track, even before she saw it! Beth's great-granny, concerned for Ozzy, told Beth to stay with him. She must have been aware of Clarinda's psychic potential; could she have known that Kate needed help too? Granny entered the scene at the moment of Beth's drowning. Beth's mother, the likely kidnapper, was her grandchild and that might have created her desire to put things right. Sarah's own involvement had been Granny's object from the first: the wondrous, mysterious ways in which the world of Spirit worked never ceased to amaze! Sarah gradually fell asleep, unaware of the old lady who stood watching, smiling gently with satisfaction.

41 – Clarrie

Algy started driving to Wales before dawn on Monday morning. He'd planned to leave at six but woke up at four. Unable to get back to sleep he decided it was less tiring to leave even earlier, avoiding the heavy morning traffic. At Welshpool he treated himself to a large breakfast. He wasn't due until nine-thirty but with luck, if Clarrie was ready, they could be on the return journey by then. It was the first time he'd taken that route to the coast since the road improvements and he was enjoying the run. In the event, he reached Dolgellau in less time than he had allowed, found the Rowen, and was even able to have coffee with Clarrie who was just finishing breakfast. There was time too to see the work she had so far completed during her holiday.

Clarrie was delighted that Algy had elected to drive her. He was a valued critic who never hesitated to give her his honest opinion, although he always stressed that he was absolutely untutored in oil painting. His watercolours were attractive but he was an amateur, his pictures lacked authority. Clarrie always encouraged him – if he let himself relax and gained confidence, his work could be saleable.

He was full of praise for the cottage painting and suggested that they take it, with anything else she had finished, to make space in her own car later for more canvasses, which she could buy locally. As they drove back, Algy was amazed to hear how it had come to be painted. While not doubting Clarrie's sincerity he nevertheless questioned her exhaustively. It was a good story whether she had dreamt it or not! On the whole, Algy ended up accepting it as fact. He recommended saying nothing about it at all to the farmer, as Roger was now dead, but the idea of a body lying unclaimed under the stone flags obviously caused him a great deal of professional concern. He then brought Clarrie up to date on the kidnapping case and how her mother was solving it, ruefully admitting that she was continually a step or two ahead of official efforts. Algy shook his head in wonder. "You are a truly remarkable pair."

With a slightly hesitant air he asked, "Tell me, how did your father and your husband react to 'messages from beyond'? How did they cope? There would be no sneaking off for a quiet drink at the local without one of you knowing!"

"I cannot imagine anyone on the other side of the veil considering it worth snitching on that kind of activity," Clarrie laughed. "There is no easy explanation for how it happens. My personal experiences have actually been very few. I was really alarmed by what just happened to me. I kept recalling things my mother has said in the past – about coping with the strangeness of allowing oneself to be 'used' while still seeking protection from spiritual danger. I think she must have been preparing me all my life, just in case I took after her."

"Yes, but how did your father feel when Sarah saw and spoke to people he couldn't see? I'd have been scared stiff!"

Clarrie appreciated that Algy's attitude was that of most people and answered him seriously. She admitted that never having experienced anything faintly unearthly himself, her father was at first extremely sceptical, but he came to terms with the fact that Sarah was psychic long before they married. "He was a great support and trusted her good sense not to get involved with fringe religious activity. That really would have alarmed him I'm sure. My own husband was absolutely overawed by my mother's strange talents. He jokingly hoped that I wouldn't turn into a witch too!"

"And did he ever find out that you had?"

As Clarrie broke into peals of laughter Algy almost choked with embarrassment. "Good grief – sorry, I didn't mean – I mean, I wasn't calling you a witch!"

"Even if I am!" she teased him.

Much to his relief Clarrie changed the subject and inquired after his wife. Everyone accepted that her psychiatric condition was hopeless but, even though she didn't recognise him, Algy visited her regularly. He was still devoted to her, never giving up hope that she would recover and was always eager to discuss any minuscule signs of improvement he saw, or imagined. Not having ever met her, Clarrie suspected Algy might consider it an intrusion if she offered to visit his wife, but he liked to recall their early days together and Clarrie was a good listener.

The powerful sports car was the pride of his life and, as he handled it impressively, she thoroughly enjoyed the drive. When they pulled into the car park Alec and Sarah were walking into the hotel and, seeing them, they paused to wait. "Good Timing," Alec greeted. He was anxious to inform Algy of yesterday's events and said the cottage had already been traced. "Dee and White are checking it out. They'll join us here later."

While the men talked business Clarrie and Sarah were fully occupied; there was much to ask and tell. Eventually, when they sat down to lunch, they were all in an optimistic mood. Subconsciously they were shutting out the grim purpose of the meeting.

42 – The Bobbylyn

Detective Sergeants Dee and White stared apprehensively at the old thatched cottage. Earlier that morning, before being instructed to organise a search for Briar Cottage, they had already obtained the address of the former owner of Bobbylyn – now Sea Tease – from the River Authority, and even located it. The first lead had been through the kidnapping: Ozzy and the boat. The second was apparently through a dead child!

In spite of the sunshine, they were both chilled by the thought.

There was clearly a connection between the dead child and the kidnapped one; they must exercise great care now if their own inquiry was not also to end in death. Because they had not had to waste time searching for the cottage, the day was still young which, under the circumstances, was just as well ...they now recalled the marina manager's casual comment that Berry had moved to Wargrave!

The new occupant was able to tell them the approximate location of the Berrys' new home so they returned to their car and contacted D.C. Jean Steadman back at base. She soon came up with the address. The name of the house was Southways. Under the circumstances they were reluctant to go there without precise instructions and it would be profitable to gather background information on the family beforehand, so they decided to split up. Two large policemen on a doorstep might cause considerable alarm in this quiet Wallingford backwater ...one friendly man would seem less formal and find it much easier to encourage people to talk.

It was quite obvious when they compared notes later that the family was well liked and had been good neighbours.

Bob and Eve as they were generally known were devoted to each other and to their daughter, who was a bright outgoing child – extremely well mannered and exceptionally lovely... 'a little beauty queen', several claimed. She was their second child, the first baby died. Bob worked hard at his business and as it expanded they did more entertaining. Eve loved the cottage but it was too small and the kitchen inconveniently old fashioned, so they moved on.

The Bobbylyn had been moored near Wallingford Bridge and the boat-yard was the next place they checked. Their visit did nothing to change the picture of a normal loving family. Berry paid his bills promptly and never created mooring problems with other owners. His car then was white – a Mercedes. From Wallingford they drove straight to the Hotel Marina where Berry moored his new boat – Wide Awake. It was a pleasant morning and as the distance from river to road would have to be checked anyway, they decided it would be wiser to do so straight away, before it rained!

On arrival they walked along the line of boats to the field at the end where they could still hear traffic quite clearly. It was extremely unlikely that the track to the road would yield any useful clues to the child's murderer, should there actually prove to be one! They would have to wait for Mrs Hunter's visit this afternoon for confirmation of that. It wasn't quite mid-day however, so they set off fairly slowly, one at each side of the track. They walked on the rough stubble, their keen eyes traversing the central strip looking for anything incongruous. If anything significant had been dropped there, they'd find it!

By the time they reached the road they had a small collection of rubbish: a rusty buckle, some plastic bags and a broken milk bottle. They needed no expert to tell them they had found nothing important but, just in case, were reluctant to drop everything in the bin. They used the largest of the bags as a container and with guilty looks up and down the road to make sure they were unobserved they hid it in the dry ditch weighted with a stone.

It proved easy to push through the hedge at that point and at the other side was a lay-by where the brown car might have pulled in. The driver, with his gruesome burden, could have been away and out of sight in seconds.

All that remained now was to establish a connection between the cruiser and the brown car – that was all! John examined the ground where the vehicle must have parked while Terry fetched their transport. Nothing much: a crushed drink can and sweet-wrappings that he let lie – someone disposing of a body would be unlikely to stop for a picnic! Anyway, they couldn't have been there for more than a few days.

Enquiries at the marina proved fruitless. If such a car frequented the hotel car park it did so with a very low profile. Having had no high expectations they weren't unduly depressed as they drove off. A tour up and down – half a mile each way, dashed any hope that the field and riverbank could be observed from a nearby dwelling, so they went to the office to write up their reports.

With luck there would still be time to grab a quick lunch before meeting the senior members of the team for what they both hoped would be a more illuminating afternoon.

43 – Robert

The Iberian Airways jet descended slowly through thinly scattered clouds, which did nothing to veil the hills below. Robert Berry drew a deep breath of satisfaction ...arriving in Spain was always thrilling whether in sunshine or at night when the lights of the Costa outlined the Mediterranean like jewelled chains. He was glad they'd taken the earlier, lunchtime, flight to Valencia, although he usually preferred to arrive at Alicante airport, which would have meant a shorter drive to Jávea, but ten minutes after midnight wasn't a good time to start a fifty-mile trip.

He blanked future problems from his mind, determined that the next few weeks would be perfect for Evelyn. He hardly expected the holiday alone to cure her delusions, but whatever happened she would have some happy memories to wipe out the sad.

The moist heat enveloped them as they stepped from the 'plane into the heavily flower-scented air ...instantly calming his nerves. Pushing the luggage trolley out of the customs hall later he couldn't help wondering, as he always did, at the lack of formality. No effort had been made to stamp their passports and two officials in attendance smilingly nodded them through. As he looked back he saw that a young boy had in fact been stopped. Custom officials were solemnly watching as he opened a huge cardboard box; it had after all been luck, avoiding delay. Evelyn clutched Tabitha's hand tightly as they crossed the road to the car park where Jaime would be waiting for them.

When they bought the villa they had inherited Jaime. He and his wife lived close by and had looked after the place since it was built. Marie kept it clean during their absence and on arrival they always found beds made up, the refrigerator stocked, bowls of fruit and vases filled with fresh flowers. Jaime cared for the pool and garden. The fee for their joint service was negligible but they collected all the produce from the fruit trees and vines. Not only had the place been bought fully furnished – a little Seat was included in the sale, but because of its Spanish registration, Berry, a non-resident, had been nervous about owning it. He had solved the problem by giving it to Jaime who kept it running and was happy to drive them to and from the airport. They always had the use of it during holidays, avoiding the expense of car hire.

Jaime saw them coming and waved to attract attention. Like most Spaniards he adored youngsters and as soon as the child came within reach he lifted her in spite of her alarm and swung her at arms length, laughingly telling her she was as beautiful as ever. Evelyn was radiantly happy at his greeting – Berry looked on anxiously, wondering what Jaime really thought.

When alone Jaime used the coast roads but he knew Robert preferred the motorway even though very little quicker. Time seemed important to the British who thought it worth the toll to arrive sooner, even if only by ten minutes! Although Jaime spoke a little English, the exchange of pleasantries over, he pushed a Flamenco music tape into the carrier and nullified the need to converse.

Berry mentally planned their holiday while, behind him, Evelyn played happily with Tabitha. There were so many things they had planned to do one day. Previous visits had always inevitably ended in loud laments; the days had gone too quickly ...there had been no time to explore the surrounding towns and villages. The exit to Gandia flashed by reminding him that at least they must visit the Ducal Palace: home of Francisco de Borja y Aragon, fourth Duke of Gandia.

In contrast to the infamous Borgias, he was a good man who did a lot for the church. He'd given his wealth and life to spread the Gospel in Europe. People said the palace was really magnificent. Then there was Denia castle, even nearer home; in all the years they had visited Spain they had never explored far. The whole coast was of historic interest. This time they wouldn't waste a minute: time was running out. Berry was determined to live each moment to the full. He was unlikely to have the chance again.

They left the motorway near Denia and Berry handed over a thousand-peseta note for the toll. Jaime thrust the change back as he roared away quickly to beat the car in the next lane. Berry smiled indulgently. Why did he bother – the roads weren't at all crowded by British standards!

Within minutes they were driving around lower slopes of the mountain, the Montgo, on the south side near Jesus Pobre, and finally turning into their own driveway. The bushes were a riot of colour – too many oleanders really, Berry thought, they grew like weeds. Bourgainvillea competed with pale mauve and orange bignonia to cover the walls and roof of the open naya with heavy blossom. Waves of perfume from the lavender competed with the basil in the herb garden ...he stood breathing deeply, savouring every second. The houses lower down the slope didn't obstruct their view of the valley and distant mountains and the sheer beauty of it all made him wonder, as it always did, why they had not come more often.

Marie bustled to meet them with a stream of Spanish. There was no need to understand the language to appreciate how pleased she was to see them again. The child, overwhelmed by the sudden commotion, burst into tears! Jaime exchanged a few words with Marie in their native tongue and explained, "My wife, she is upset that the little one has forgotten her, and that she has made her cry ...she says please to forgive her." They were surprised and troubled by the anguished wails.

Berry was glad of the excuse to usher his family inside quickly and assured Marie that the tears were due to over-tiredness and excitement – no need for concern. Unpacking didn't take long and they were soon stretched out on the patio enjoying the last few hours of afternoon sunshine. To Evelyn's surprise, Tabitha refused to join her in the pool or even to paddle on the wide steps where it was shallow. The water temperature, according to the thermometer dangling below the surface, was 27oC. Last year, she commented, the child had practically lived in the water although it was two degrees cooler. Turning away she said, "Come along, Beth darling, we'll go inside now. We'll both swim tomorrow when it will be hot and sunny."

"Stop calling her Beth!" Robert snapped suddenly. Seeing her draw back in alarm, his tone softened. "Please, I keep telling you, it's time she used her proper name." He walked over and drew Evelyn to him gently. "Look at her my darling. Really look, and think. When did you last hear her call herself Beth? And can you not see how much she has changed? Doesn't she seem altogether less talkative in these last few weeks: less happy? When did you last hear her sing?"

Evelyn shook herself free and backed away from him ..."I don't know what you mean. Children change as they grow older. She hasn't been well since that boy tried to take her away. He is to blame ...I'll never forgive him!"

"Yes, Darling, children grow older – not younger! Please think about what I've said. Be happy with her, love her – she is a beautiful child but don't call her Beth... it upsets me more than I can say." He walked away dejectedly. He had to get through to her – to make her understand, yet dreaded the moment when full realisation came.

There was little time to put things right but he must ease Evelyn away from her obsession with the child – show her how much he loved and needed her. He'd do everything in his power to cushion the shock, when she remembered. Her condition was forcing him to suppress his own grief when they should have been grieving together. Tomorrow they could picnic on the Arenal beach, then drive along the sea-front to the port to see the fishing boats before shopping in the Pueblo, the romantic old town with its cool, narrow streets. He was determined they would enjoy their sojourn in Spain and waste not one moment regretting what was past or dreading the future.

Evelyn, untouched by his inner turmoil, had settled the child in bed and returned to relax by the pool. She flipped the pages of a magazine idly, her gaze rising more often to the spectacular vista surrounding them. She reached for her husband's hand tentatively. The sun dropped lower with no noticeable cooling of the atmosphere, the clear blue sky became pale, and then warmed as tongues of orange licked the few streaks of cloud which clung to the mountain.

By the time the heavens were a fiery red the humidity was high and they were more than ready to go inside where ceiling fans whirred to move the air. While his wife worked happily in the kitchen, humming as she prepared supper, Robert Berry sat writing a letter. Ever since finding the strange child on poor Beth's bed he had felt sick with guilt. The child was asleep; probably exhausted after her terror and he had dreaded her reaction on waking. His immediate concern was for Evelyn but as the hours passed he came to realise how seriously disturbed his wife was. Having erased Beth's drowning from her mind, the child in the nursery, to her, was Beth.

Their first baby had died in his sleep at three months old – one of those tragic, mysterious cot deaths, and he'd thought Evelyn would never recover from the shock. She had gone to feed the baby one morning and an hour later was still nursing him, unable to believe that he was lifeless. To lift the baby from her arms the doctor sedated her and she had undergone two years of therapy. After Beth's birth she again became the woman he had loved and married; he couldn't face her reverting to a neurotic shadow.

He could do nothing for Beth so he was desperately trying to save his wife's sanity by allowing her to live her dream. Surely, he prayed, she would gradually come to understand what had happened. He must protect her from the consequences of her actions for a little longer. There was no going back but the terrible thing he had done that night haunted him ceaselessly. Seeing Kate's parents on TV had shocked him. He needed to keep Kate but was anxious to let her parents know she was all right, so the next day he took and posted a Polaroid snap. He wanted time to think. Having lived in the new house for only a week no one had seen enough of Beth to know her, but Kate's family was almost local; someone might recognise her before he was ready to part with her. Evelyn's mother hadn't seen Beth for over a year so it was worth the risk of taking them both to visit her for a while.

When they returned, Evelyn had still not recalled anything about Beth's accident and Berry was frantic to find a way out of the situation. He sent more photographs to the Meads to ease his conscience – they would see how well their little girl was and not worry too much, or so he deluded himself. This trip to Spain was his final chance to penetrate Evelyn's mental shield. Not only must she face the loss of her second child but she would have an added burden of guilt for what she had done to Kate's family.

Writing to describe the events of that day, Beth's birthday, wouldn't excuse his actions but it would explain. If he didn't do so immediately those poor people would continue to suffer. He could justify, at least to himself, his decision to put Kate beyond their reach for a few more weeks – extending their ordeal – but he wanted them to know she was safe and would be home again soon, unharmed. Taking the cap off his pen, he started to write:

Monday Sept. 10th

Dear Mr & Mrs Mead,

Before describing the awful events of Friday July 20th I want to assure you that Kate is well and will be returned to you safely. For reasons that will become clear later, I have been reluctant to contact the police. I can't expect you to forgive me but hope you will at least understand how it all came about.

44 – Clarrie

It was a fine afternoon; warm for mid-September ...late holidaymakers were still sailing and cruising up and down the river. Two police cars followed Alec as he drove Sarah and Clarrie to find the place where, three weeks after Kate was kidnapped, she first set up her easel to paint. Cautioning him as they approached, she showed him the turn where she had left the road to park the second time, then pointed ahead a little, to the slightly wider opening in the trees where she had first stopped. An overgrown track was barely visible. After allowing them both to alight Alec pulled away and halted ten yards farther along. Algy parked close behind, White and Dee were with him, and they all walked back to consult with the uniformed police officers emerging from the other cars. There was no point in disrupting traffic on either road or river yet but if, as Alec hoped, they found what they expected, no time would be wasted; everything they needed was in place. Informing the local force of his suspicions had been a matter of courtesy but Alec hadn't taken them into his confidence fully and they regarded the two women with obvious curiosity. They would clearly have liked to follow when Alec and Algy accompanied the ladies through the woodland leaving Dee and White to ensure their privacy.

Someone said, "Isn't this where that bloke said he'd run down a young boy? Could be his body we're looking for!"

Clarrie stopped as she reached the place that provided a good view of the opposite bank and the sweeping bend of the river. The undermined bank gave the willows even more cause for weeping into the water. After a moment's thought she pointed to the bushes growing on the other side of the inlet. Walking back a few yards they were able to skirt the water and reach the place where she had found the bracelet. To Clarrie, the air now felt completely normal. She found it difficult to imagine how it could have been so cold and uncomfortable.

Alec looked expectantly at Sarah who gave a helpless shrug. It was unlikely that their spirit guides would have allowed them to come so far only to desert them now, at this crucial moment. "Being mere mortals," she said, "we can only be patient and pray for help. We can't make demands or expect too much, but must always be ready to receive gratefully whatever is freely offered." The faces of the two men registered disappointment and frustration so Sarah suggested they should walk back to their colleagues leaving her alone with Clarinda for a while. They went reluctantly, leaving mother and daughter standing silently in the pale sunshine: each quietly absorbed in private thought.

Clarrie recalled her acute discomfort as she had grown colder and colder, feeling that she was being watched. Sarah thought of the lovely child in the garden and of poor Ozzy who had been a lost wandering soul. He had been here and called to Clarinda, wondering why she couldn't hear him. He had come with Beth, who had waited with him, his little protector, until he came to accept his own passing from this life to the next. His part in this drama had been played ...Sarah prayed that he had found peace at last.

Alec paced slowly back and forth. He hadn't lost faith in Sarah but he kicked himself for taking her for granted. How could he have expected her to turn her powers on and off at his will? He looked at his watch and wondered whether he should walk back and call the whole thing off; Sarah must be embarrassed – but he steeled himself to wait. When she wanted to give up she'd return and until she did, he was reluctant to risk interrupting her meditation.

45 – Beth

It was Clarrie who reacted first to the subtle change in atmosphere. She began to shake as if chilled and gripped her mother's hand. They waited, both sure now that they would be shown what they sought. Sarah turned suddenly and pulled Clarrie towards the edge of the wooded strip of land, which bordered both road and river. They stumbled through the tangle of bushes for a few yards, coming to a sudden halt when Sarah stopped and asked quietly, "Can you see her, showing us where she lies?"

"No," Clarrie whispered, "I see nothing." She wished she could, but was relieved to feel perceptibly warmer. The cold knot of discomfort that first drew her to that quiet glade had served the purpose and was now completely gone.

They returned to sit in the car while Alec organised the unearthing of the shallow grave. The river police arrived to prevent boaters from mooring near the inlet and to transport the pathetically small body away to the mortuary.

Before it was removed Alec asked if Sarah felt up to identifying it as the child she had come to know as Beth. He said he wouldn't have suggested it but he thought she would be interested to see how the infant had been buried. Agreeing to look, Sarah nevertheless refused Clarrie's tentative offer to go with her. There was nothing to be gained from subjecting her to the ordeal.

Sarah was grateful for Alec's supporting arm as she gazed down at the white, still face she had known only smiling and happy. The little body had been enfolded in a thick blanket and wrapped in heavy black plastic which had protected it from serious intrusion – it may have been used for that very purpose. Her hands were folded carefully over her chest. Beneath her hands was a small leather bound book.

"We haven't disturbed anything yet, but the photographers have finished. Would removing and examining it serve any useful purpose?" Alec asked hesitantly. His meaning was obvious, so Sarah lifted the book away gently. Under the puzzled gaze of several policemen she held it silently for a few moments, not even opening it. After replacing it on the body she turned away and said to Alec,

"I'll wait in the car. Please be gentle with her."

Clarrie looked anxiously at her mother as they met again. All this had been a great strain and she felt guilty because she had been away from home instead of being on hand to support Sarah. "Look, I have to return to Wales to collect my car and luggage but I'll come straight back. If only you had told me what was happening, I might have been able to help."

"Good Heaven's, child, I wouldn't dream of allowing you to give up your holiday! There is absolutely no need," Sarah assured her with a smile. "I haven't been alone, after all. Polly is a great comfort and very supportive. She would be happy to live-in with us again, by the way. There is less space than we had in the old house, I know, but what do you think? She could share the cooking and do light work in exchange for her room ...we could find a daily for the heavier chores. Of course we would be permanently deprived of the guest room so it needs careful thought." Clarrie was a little taken aback initially but almost immediately decided it was a good idea. She and her mother would be freer to come and go as they wished, not having to worry about leaving the other alone and they need not give up the guest room; she could sleep on her studio couch. It was large enough and she sometimes worked half the night anyway!

"Polly can have my bedroom," Clarrie decided. "I'll move the free standing wardrobes out, then there will be space for an armchair and television." She grinned, seeing her mother's astonishment at her lightning agreement, and said, "Ask her tonight, but please don't start moving any of my stuff, I'd rather do that myself."

By the time Alec joined them Sarah was ready to speak of Beth again.

The way the body had been protected and the placing of the bible made it evident that she had been buried lovingly. As Sarah had held the small volume she sensed very strongly that whoever had buried her would come back for her; she hadn't been abandoned.

Sarah was overcome with sadness as she described how Beth indicated the grave.

Reaching it, the child took her hand shyly and whispered, 'Bye-bye, Tharah. Tell Daddy I love him.'

"It's so sad that she spoke only of her father. She feels un-mourned by her mother. We can guess why. Kate has taken her place and, being only a baby herself, Beth doesn't understand that the poor woman must be mentally sick to do such a thing." Sarah took a deep breath and added, "I'll miss her, but our task is finished, unless I can help her parents eventually." Tomorrow, decided Sarah, she would ring Ambrose Kilroy. His problem would take her mind off Kate – it might be an interesting challenge. It couldn't possibly be as harrowing! She would welcome it as light relief after all this ...or so she thought!

Algy and Clarrie departed for Wales with little delay and Alec took Sarah home. He was quietly jubilant and obviously optimistic that the case would soon be closed. "By the way," he asked Sarah, "did you notice, that she was wearing only one shoe? It's a pity that the other, spotted on Taft's boat, was never found, it would have proved conclusively that the Bobbylyn was used to transport the child's body."

He looked hopefully at Sarah. He really had come to expect miracles of her and instantly chided himself mentally. Sarah however, to his surprise, looked flustered and tapped her head. "I really don't know what's wrong with me sometimes! Didn't I say? I don't think it was thrown into the trash at all. It's probably lying somewhere near the path!"

Alec glanced at his watch. If he left straight away, he said, he'd be able to take a look himself before it was too dark to see; if he didn't find it, he'd send someone to make a thorough search later. Almost running to his car, he promised to keep her abreast of further developments.

After his hurried departure Sarah and Polly talked well into the small hours.

Polly wanted to hear all that had happened and expressed disappointment that Clarinda hadn't been able to come home for an hour or two. "Still, I suppose if she had, it would have been too long a day for that Detective Inspector who went to fetch her."

"Algy? Oh yes," agreed Sarah, "He started driving before dawn and must be exhausted. Alec told him to stay at the Rowen overnight and take his time driving back but he's so keen on his job ...I wouldn't mind betting he leaves the hotel at crack of dawn tomorrow!"

Polly brought in the tea trolley with a light snack and Sarah told her that before they talked of anything else there was something personal she wanted to ask. "It was Clarinda's idea, so you don't have to wonder about her reaction." Polly nodded warily, patently bewildered – there was nothing about her personal life they didn't already know. Sarah continued, smiling, "She would be very happy for you to move in on a permanent basis. We all get on very well and she'd feel freer to come and go if I'm not here alone."

Polly's look of incredulity changed to delight as the words sank in. "I can hardly believe it," she gasped, "It's what I would have prayed for, if I'd thought there was half a chance! I'll be on hand to work, but I won't accept a penny wages – and I'll cook too!"

"Just a minute," interrupted Sarah. "We'll agree that you can do light housework and share the cooking but for heavier jobs we'll find someone else – just a few hours a week."

Polly mopped the tears rolling down her cheeks with the edge of her apron, quite overcome with the prospect. Suddenly, pulling herself together she stated, "Then I'll pay my niece to help us – and that's my last offer!"

Breaking into peals of laughter, Sarah wiped her eyes too. Tears withheld all day, finally had an excuse to flow …to her great relief.

46 – The Police

Outside the Berry family's new home Dee and White parked their car and walked to the drive gate. An attractive landscaped garden fronted the detached house – far more impressive than the one from which they had moved. Flowering shrubs and an ivy-covered trellis shielded the rear of the property from view. The drive and garage fitted exactly Mrs Grey's (or should they say Ozzy's?) description of the place to which he was transported. They knew the Chief's latest theory, which had hardened yesterday with the discovery of the child's body. Their inquiries around Briar Cottage supported it.

Berry's daughter's name was Tabitha May and it was understandable that Mrs Grey had mistakenly joined May to Berry. She was a marvel to have put them on the right track in every other way. After all, in spite of her esoteric connections, she was only human! Finally though, it came down to solid police work. Today they were looking for information about four-year-old Tabitha. It was highly likely that the body found near the river was hers so they couldn't risk alerting Berry. Yesterday they hadn't hesitated to introduce themselves officially; today they must be more cautious. Today they were under-cover!

They had equipped themselves with flyers offering the best prices for second-hand furniture – composed and photocopied in the office that morning. Starting about a quarter of a mile away they had already visited several homes on their approach to the house, Southways, with no luck; either no one answered the door or the Berry family was unknown.

Probably, because the properties were well spaced out, there was little interest in the newcomers! The nearest house on the other side was separated from Southways by a small field. There they met Jane Burrows. She was polite enough to read through the leaflet they gave her and said it was possible her husband would accept an offer for an old table in the garage – perhaps they would care to see it? They accepted her invitation and went with her. Fortunately, it was clearly unsuitable for anything other than a workbench so they didn't have to bid for it.

It was comparatively easy to draw Mrs Burrows into speculation about who in the village might have anything of interest to sell. She said most of the older residents had already had their household treasures valued by the local antique dealer so if they expected to buy cheap and make huge profits they'd be disappointed. They protested their professional integrity and said, after calling next door, they would give up.

"Oh really," Jane said. "I know you'll certainly have no luck there – they've only just moved in and all their stuff is new! Anyway, they went on holiday yesterday, so there's no point in wasting your time," she advised, strolling back with them to the gate.

John Dee shook hands and thanked her. Seeing a swing near the garage he said casually, "This is a lovely area but it must be pretty lonely for the kids. There can't be many around here!"

"Oh, we only have one child and it's true, she was short of friends until Southways changed hands – they have a nice little girl. We've only just met them but the kids get on very well. It's such a shame they've gone away so soon." Jane lamented as she latched the gate. "I could hardly believe my ears when they came for tea on Sunday and told us... Only last Wednesday they blamed the child's nervous state on too much moving around!"

Knowing she would see them going back to Southways they told her they would put a leaflet in the letter box and after exchanging a few more pleasantries, she left them at last. Terry shook his head in disgust and commented on the ease with which they had discovered the place was full of new stuff – probably expensive – and that it would be standing empty for a few weeks! He said, "With friends like that you couldn't risk going even as far as the back gate!"

Now they knew that a child, introduced to the Burrows as Tabitha, had been seen within the last few days. They wished they could have shown Kate's photograph but it was too risky at this stage. As Southways was unoccupied it should be easy to look around the house and garden. If they found a fishpond there they'd report at once to HQ.

Ringing at the front door brought no response so they walked to the back of the house.

A well-cut lawn edged a patio area that was partly shaded by a large cherry tree. Following the crazy paving between the flowerbeds they found what they sought – an ornamental pond teeming with colourful fish. In the middle was a fountain: a carved, stone fish with a splayed fantail. Turning to look at the house they noted that it didn't look empty; a vase of fresh flowers stood in one of the windows.

Suddenly a voice startled them.

"Good morning gents. Can I help you?"

Approaching from the bottom of the property, where he'd been tending vegetables, was an elderly man – without doubt the gardener. Brimming with self-importance, and with very little prompting, he informed them that the family left early yesterday morning and would be away for a few weeks – he didn't know where. "You ask Betty – lives in the village, she does. She'll be coming in every few days to keep an eye on things ...the flowers are her way of making the place look like as if they're in! Clever girl, Betty," he grinned, gap-toothed, tapping the side of his nose. "She might know where they are, if it's anything real urgent.""Bloody incredible!" exploded Terry as they walked off. "So much for clever Betty's attempt to make the place safe!... The old guy never even asked what we were doing on private property!"

They were lucky when they got through to the office. Alec took their report personally and agreed it was now pointless attempting to conceal their identity. He deliberately avoided the subject of getting a look inside the house; they had no search warrant. He cunningly suggested interviewing Betty and 'seeing what turned up'! They might let her see Kate's picture too if they could do so without explanation.

47 – Betty

The cottage where Betty lived with her parents was easy to find. Together they approached the front door. When told they were CID officers Betty was at first alarmed, then intrigued. She eagerly invited them inside into a neat, little-used parlour. Her mother brought them coffee but, becoming conscious of the pause in conversation and pointed looks, she reluctantly departed. John Dee raised an eyebrow at Terry who leaned across and closed the door after her.

Without divulging the purpose of the inquiry they learned in the first few minutes that Betty had no idea where the family was, other than that it must be somewhere warm, because of the type of clothing they'd taken; she had ironed a heap of summer dresses. She couldn't remember Berry's office number but could go to the house with them and look at the 'phone book – his secretary would surely know more than she did.

Agreeing that it would be a good idea, they could hardly believe their luck. They would be able to see inside the place without arousing suspicion, at Betty's invitation! Drinking tea and eating their way through the scones, it was easy to turn to more general, seemingly innocent topics. Mr Berry drove a white car. She thought it was German – it had a ring on its nose! The only child she had seen around, apart from Tabitha, was Annabelle Burrows who'd slept there one night. Tabitha, a quiet nervous child, was away at her Grandmother's with Mrs Berry when Betty started working there. "He took me on just after they went," Betty said. "I must say, it struck me as a funny thing to do, going off leaving the poor man to cope all on his own, just after moving in; plain mean I thought, but really she's quite nice."

She broke off to offer them more tea and they tried not to show their impatience. Settling again at last, she continued, "He's okay too, but he looks real miserable most of the time. I think they're happily married, but you never really know what goes on between other people do you?"

Eventually, they drove to the house and Betty pointed out Burrows' place. She said it was possible that they knew the Berry family plans because it was the day after they'd all been out together that the trip was first mentioned. Bert, the gardener was weeding at the front when they arrived and Betty waved to him with a nonchalant air as she unlocked the front door and ushered them in. The telephone book on the hall table gave them not only the number of the office but several others, which Terry White copied into his note-pad. It was a brand new book so he looked in the cupboard for another, which might have more entries. He found only directories, but a slip of paper fell out. On it was scribbled a Reading number which he also noted, in case it had any significance.

While Terry was occupied, Betty was giggling happily at John's pleasantries. He admired the gleaming, dust-free furniture and congratulated her on the way she kept it – adding that it must be a real pleasure to look after such a place; it was impressive, what he could see of it. Was it all as stylish as this entrance hall he wondered? Naturally, she couldn't resist giving him a conducted tour! As they passed Terry, John winked and grinned broadly. Upstairs was a principal bedroom and a large guest room, both with bathrooms en-suite. A shared bathroom linked another large bedroom and a nursery. Everything was immaculate. The nursery was exactly as he had imagined it from Mrs Grey's description – lots of white: curtains, wallpaper and matching bedspread, all sprigged with tiny flowers. John wiped his brow shakily. It was more than a bit spooky.

Several silver frames on a landing table held photographs. An elderly woman holding a baby and two more of the same woman with, most likely, the same child at about twelve months and two years old. Seeing his interest, Betty said they were all of Tabitha with Mrs Berry's mother. One frame stood empty; logically it should have held another of Granny with a three year old. Picking it up he took from his pocket the photograph of Kate and held them together. The other three were also Polaroid – probably from the same camera. Betty's eyes widened, in astonishment.

"Oh, what a lovely photograph of Tabitha, it's really perfect for that frame." She frowned. "Mr Berry took the other for his wallet he's sure to want this to complete the set. Where did you get it?"

"It's a long story," John smiled grimly, "Don't you worry your pretty little head about it and don't by the way, mention this business to anyone. If Mr Berry himself contacts you, do not, on any account, tell him we've spoken to you or even hint that we've been in the village. Carry on exactly as instructed but when they return telephone us immediately, in case we haven't found him ourselves by then."

"Good Heavens! Is he a criminal? I can't believe it. When my Mum and Dad hear this they'll never let me come back to work here!"

"Betty," he said sharply, "I told you not to discuss the matter with anyone! That definitely includes your parents." He looked stern – then attempted to put her mind at rest. "We wouldn't ask you to carry on normally if you were likely to be in danger. However, if you come one day and find them here, complain of a toothache, go home and ring us immediately." Seeing in her expression a mixture of curiosity and fear, he gave her a friendly grin and continued cheerfully, "When we've wound up the case I promise we'll come round for more of your mother's cakes and tell you the whole tale. Take my word for it, it's worth waiting for, but only if you're a good girl and hold your tongue!"

"Yes, right then, I'll do it! I'll be a kind of special agent won't I? What else do you want me to do? Tell me what you're looking for, perhaps I can help." Her fear forgotten, Betty was eager to be involved so he asked what Mrs Berry drove.

Betty confirmed that it was a brown car, bought locally – she actually knew the previous owner. It was downstairs, she could show them if they liked!

They were extremely happy to be shown, so she took them through the utility room to the adjacent garage. On the way they identified the wall against which Kate's picture was taken. Betty was excited. "Why, yes of course I remember now … it was the day Mrs Berry and Tabitha came back from their trip." Betty frowned. "I saw him bringing her in here with the camera. I wondered why he didn't take her outside, it was a lovely sunny day, but it came out well didn't it?"

As they entered the garage they saw the rack of garden tools. Most were fairly new and neither of the two young detectives was surprised to see a fork with remnants of an orange striped label on it. The car was in good condition. The only damage was a shallow dent in the nearside back door panel. It was Japanese: a Toyota five-door. Raising the one at the rear they found nothing other than a few crisp leaves and crumbs of dry earth. While Dee distracted Betty, White scooped samples into an envelope. They had more than sufficient reason to believe that Berry and his wife snatched Kate and had taken her away with them and were eager now to inform the Super. Leaving Betty to lock up, they moved fast; the sooner Berry was found the better ...if only they had come a day earlier!

Immediately after Dee and White reported, Alec issued instructions for tracing Berry's car but it wasn't to be stopped or the driver alarmed by being followed. "If they've left the country in it we should be able to trace it. If they are still on the mainland it has to be parked somewhere." He congratulated them on their morning's work and was particularly pleased to have the Toyota's number. On reading the files for the umpteenth time, Alec eventually found the reference to the woman driver who had turned her car round before Dixon arrived and made his sketch.

The Constable, interviewing her at the accident scene, noted a remark about a brown car nearly hitting her at the end of the lane. He had assumed she was travelling in the wrong direction for it to be of any importance, although afterwards, back at the station, he checked road reports relating to the area for the day. The car she described featured in none of them so he had not included it in his final report. His account of what she saw started from her reaching the distressed mother screaming for help. It was only when he learned they were looking for a brown foreign car that Dixon realised his mistake and was mortified. He looked up the complete statement he'd taken at the time. The woman not only described the car, she remembered a partial number, which he had given to Alec at the Latham's. Alec saw now with satisfaction that it tallied with the registration on the car owned, and no doubt driven, by Berry's wife on Friday July 20th.

***

On Wednesday morning Alec telephoned Sarah to tell her he'd found the lost shoe and, as promised, he relayed everything that was discovered at Southways the previous day.

So that the rest of the team could concentrate on finding Robert Berry's car, he had himself telephoned the few people on Berry's contact list.

Only Mrs Berry's mother knew they'd gone away and even she didn't know where they could be reached. She said they often went to the continent for holidays – they always came back brown and the holiday snaps were sunny with palm trees!

"I'd love to see them," Alec told Sarah, "but we can't risk alerting Berry if he telephones her. We'll try to manage without his mother-in-law's assistance for the moment."

Alec was annoyed that Berry's office had been no help either. "When he's away, he doesn't leave a number to be reached, he prefers to ring them. They were not told, of course, that it was a police inquiry!"

After ringing off he remembered the extra number from the loose slip. Checking White's report he dialled it and waited patiently. After several rings a female voice answered, "Sun Days Travel may I help you?" Alec confined his inquiry to how he could find their agency and rang off. Algy could call there when he got back from Wales. The voice was young: young women were always eager to impress Algy! If there was anything to find out, he was definitely the man most likely to! Had they made a hotel reservation?

Even as the question crossed his mind Alec knew it was too much to hope!

48 – Sarah

Shortly after Alec's call, the Reverend Ambrose Kilroy arrived for coffee, radiating the fragrance of peppermints – which he consumed constantly having given up cigars. He was relieved to hear of Sarah's readiness to become involved with David Bane's problem. Since his last visit he had approached Mrs Bane who willingly provided him with a gold chain that Babs always wore, even when other necklaces were added. By handing it over she considered herself absolved from personal contact with Sarah.

Ambrose had accepted it wrapped in an envelope and avoided handling it again by placing it beyond reach, on top of his wardrobe ...he said he was sure the daily woman never dusted above eye level and his wife, Elsie, had no reason to make the climb! Perhaps he was being unduly cautious he admitted, but he was worried that casual contact with another person might spoil the vibrations. Sarah, hiding a smile, solemnly assured him that he had done the right thing. Polly tactfully prepared to leave them although she was unable to resist hovering for a few moments to tell him she was now living in – it was less likely that he'd have to talk to the dreaded answering machine again!

Ambrose expressed concern that he hadn't seen Bane recently. The poor man had stopped attending Church services abruptly and, according to neighbours, hardly left the house although he hovered at the windows. There were few deliveries from local shops now that his housekeeper had left him entirely to himself. She went away because his behaviour frightened her so much. He accused her of spying on him: screamed at her to leave him alone.

"Usually, only those with something to hide accuse others of spying," commented Sarah. "From what you said before, I thought he was suffering a persecution, not a guilt complex!"

"I really don't know what to think. Perhaps you'll get some of the answers from this," Ambrose said, handing her the packet carefully, glad to be doing so at last. Sarah tipped the chain from the envelope onto her open palm and gazed at it silently before shutting her eyes. Ambrose didn't need to be asked to pray for guidance, or for the soul they were hoping to contact ...he also closed his eyes until she spoke.

"Barbara was a happy fun-loving girl: very popular. She was more extrovert than her sister Bettina, I think. It must have surprised people when the quieter twin married first. I can understand why her sister welcomed Barbara to live with them. There was no trace of envy in their relationship. If trouble arose later, it's difficult to believe she was the cause. It is really puzzling. Why, I wonder, should David Bane feel threatened by Barbara, alive or dead?" Sarah opened her eyes abruptly and shuddered. "Was she wearing this when she was killed? Never mind, I'm sure she was."

Sarah's eyelids fell again, heavily, as she empathised with the dead woman. "I'm walking – feeling tired! It's dark." Sarah began to breathe more quickly. "Not much light from the street lamps: sounds of distant traffic. This road is very lonely ...must hurry to get home! An engine starting with a roar – a car hurtling toward me! No headlights." Her voice rose in a wail of fear "Can't see the driver ...Oh! Oooh ...RED CARPET!"

"Carpet?" Ambrose couldn't stop blurting it out.

"Good Heavens, I did say carpet didn't I?" Sarah, startled back to the present, stared down at the gleaming golden chain as it dribbled through her fingers. "Yes, amazing: Barbara's last conscious thought was of a carpet!"

"Why in God's name! Oh, do forgive me Sarah! But why at such a moment of terror would she be worrying about a carpet? One has to consider choosing and buying floor covering when furnishing a home, but she had no reason to think of such things in the ordinary way. Could she have been trying to tell you that the floor mat in the car caused the accident? Perhaps it was badly worn."

"I don't think so," Sarah answered, "because I have not actually been in contact with Barbara. My impressions came entirely from this chain. If she hadn't been wearing it, those last seconds of her life would never have come to me."

Ambrose was impressed. "The ways of the Lord are indeed mysterious! If Mrs Bane had selected a different item we couldn't have learned anything so revealing. Even though we cannot yet understand, I have faith. We wouldn't have been guided thus far dear lady, only to be abandoned!"

"I like your reasoning," Sarah laughed. "I think our next step will be to take advantage of my favourite policeman and examine the accident reports, together with any follow-up data." There wasn't anything significant that Ambrose could add to what he'd told her originally but Sarah encouraged him to divulge everything he knew about Bane, who was an only child of extremely strict parents.

His domineering father, a man of strong religious convictions, demanded unquestioning obedience and expected all in the household to observe his ruling on every matter. The mother was rumoured to be afraid of upsetting him and, to prevent her son doing so, didn't hesitate to chastise the boy physically with a cane. David's father punished him with words and loss of privileges... His mother maintained that a beating was over and done with more quickly and was more of a deterrent.

David's close friends were few, but those he had spoke well of him. It was inconceivable that he harboured a grudge against his parents because he stayed at home long after he was old enough to leave. After his father's death he continued to care for his mother who died of a heart attack a year before he married Bettina.

Nothing in his boyhood home changed until his bride moved in but when Bet wanted to re-decorate and replace furniture he made no objections. Only his parents' rooms were left un-touched and a few of the older things he wished to keep were moved upstairs to the wing they once occupied. David had no weird ideas about not using the rooms. His father's dressing room became a study and the parental bedroom was available for guests. When his young wife asked if Barbara could move in with them he readily agreed. Later, when asked if Babs could have a little extra space he said she could use his mother's drawing room – her private retreat where she'd spent many hours.

None of this made him sound other than a well-balanced, sane individual, willing to do anything to make his wife, and her twin, happy and comfortable. Whatever changed him from a contented man to a monster happened only after the death of his sister-in-law. Was it remotely possible that he had been closer to her than anyone suspected? Why otherwise should he have been so distraught? Sarah wanted more than ever to talk to Bettina.

Appetising aromas, too much for the extractor fan, began emanating from the kitchen, prompting Ambrose to check his watch. As he rose to go Sarah urged, "Please try to convince Mrs Bane that she should meet me. I'll happily visit her if she is totally averse to coming here." He shook his head doubtfully but promised to let her know immediately if he succeeded.

49 – Polly

Sarah went to help Polly serve lunch and discovered that she remembered Mrs Bane senior. "I never met her but Master Stephen's mother, your mother-in-law, knew her," Polly said. "She could always be relied upon for liberal contributions to local charities. Not many house-owners with gardens large enough for church parties were willing to let strangers tramp through them. The Greys did – it made a lot of work. I once commented unwisely that the Banes didn't and was informed that they always parted generously with money!"

In answer to a specific query, as she arranged strips of crackling over the sliced roast pork, Polly said she had never heard that their son was ill-treated but in the old days lots of people thought sparing the rod spoiled the child! Sarah was inclined to agree that he seemed to have been normal until recently, but how could one tell: some scars hid deep wounds.

There was no more she could do for Ambrose at the moment so Sarah concentrated fully on the domestic scene. In deference to Clarinda's desire to direct Polly's move from the guest room personally, they confined their efforts solely to planning. Sarah said if Polly would like to bring her favourite armchair, there would be plenty of room for it in the one Clarinda was vacating as long as the built in wardrobe was enough for her clothes.

Almost as if she had been given a new lease of life Polly was bursting with more ambitious ideas and asked, her eyes sparkling, "Would you believe I still have a valid driving license? I always renewed it, even though we didn't own a car!"

She explained that in her twenties, during the London Blitz, she drove an ambulance. "When your parents-in-law first employed me I often used the family car, but never had one of my own – didn't need one, living near town. Here, it's a tidy walk from the bus stop especially with heavy shopping!"

Sarah's enthusiasm grew as Polly listed all reasons why she should buy a second-hand runabout and eventually interrupted the flow. "I think it's a marvellous idea with a few provisos. Take me shopping sometimes, give me the odd lift, and let me pay half so that I can enjoy sharing it."

"Why, you know I'll do all that anyway, without you helping me to buy it ... I have savings, you know!" Polly was affronted, but eventually understood that Sarah would feel more inclined to ask, when she wanted to go out, if she contributed to the cost.

Thursday and Friday passed uneventfully. At first it had been a relief to blank out the trauma of the last few weeks, but Sarah's mood changed. She was growing anxious about the search for Kate, whose image seemed to be receding rather than coming closer. Sarah wasn't at all convinced that things were going well. She tried to banish her fears and forced herself to wait for Alec to contact her, expecting to hear his voice every time the telephone rang.

At noon on Saturday, when quite resigned to a frustrating weekend, his call came. "If you'll be at home this afternoon I have something to show you," he said, looking at the letter in his hand. It was an extraordinary letter from Robert Berry. Alec had already contacted Kate's parents to relay the content and would take it later for them to read properly. Before it joined the file he thought Sarah deserved to see it too. As well as worrying over Kate's fate, he understood her concern for Beth: Tabitha May. He wondered if, as Sarah read it, the message it contained would reach Beth through her. But Beth was dead and wasn't she too young anyway, to understand how and why her mother had forgotten her? It was too much for him.

In spite of Sarah's having repeatedly been proved right – could her success actually be due to some other phenomenon:

ESP, telepathy: surely both were inexplicable anyway! He felt ashamed that such thoughts should come to him but like many who acknowledged Life after Death, something deep down in his fibre, in the absence of personal experience, questioned the existence of visible and audible Spirits. Putting reservations aside, Sarah was an interesting woman and he was pleased to hear she would be able to see him at such short notice.

Since deciding to buy a car Polly avidly read all the garage advertisements and 'For Sale' columns. She was constantly buried beneath sheets from local evening papers, having retrieved a bundle that had been tied up, awaiting collection. Hearing that Alec was on his way, she carried the whole stack into the kitchen. He would expect to speak to Sarah privately, and in any case she wanted to cut out some of the more interesting items; it would be less messy using the Formica table.

Clarrie rang to ask how Sarah was bearing up. She had painted so many pictures she wondered if she should return home before there was too much for the car to hold! Being assured by Polly that all was well, Clarrie decided with obvious relief to adhere to the previous arrangement and return next Friday evening. She would relax and enjoy Wales for her last week: walk, shop and take photographs to work from during the winter.

When the doorbell rang Sarah was in the middle of telling Polly that Clarinda was so pleased they were buying a car that she'd decided that her contribution would be to provide a suitable shelter for it. She'd have a carport built alongside the garage. They were to contact Mr Green, a builder who had worked for her before; he was extremely reliable. After greeting Alec, Polly returned to the papers with even more enthusiasm while waiting for the kettle to boil. She hadn't expected to be so happy, ever again.

50 – Alec

Alec dealt with the less pleasant things first. The earth and moss from Mrs Berry's car unquestionably came from Beth's grave and the water in her lungs matched the pond water. The evidence was sufficient for an arrest and search warrant, but as they didn't need to go in the house again it was better to avoid alerting the neighbours. He thought, in all probability, they were being unnecessarily cautious because from the tone of his letter it seemed Robert Berry would co-operate fully in returning Kate.

It was such an unusual case, which Alec had been forced to handle with restraint from the beginning ...how could it end in an orthodox fashion! Anyway, by minimising the distress to Berry's wife, he hoped, the less alarmed the child was likely to be. Having explained, he handed an envelope to Sarah. It was addressed to Detective Chief Superintendent A. Holmes and marked 'Personal'. Inside was a letter written to the Meads and a shorter note, to Alec:

Sir,

I know I face imprisonment for my part in this affair but wish to plead for my wife. She is sick and is unaware that she has done anything wrong. I hope you will treat her with compassion.

I would also like your help in retrieving the body of my own child and giving her a decent Christian burial. We will be at home on the afternoon of Monday Oct. 4th.

R Berry

Sarah handed it back to Alec without comment. Taking a deep breath she then opened and read the letter.

Monday Sept. 10th

Dear Mr & Mrs Mead,

Before describing the events of Friday July 20th I assure you that Kate is well and will be returned safely. For reasons that will become clear, I was reluctant to contact the police. I can't expect you to forgive me but hope you will at least understand how this situation came about.

My wife and I had a beautiful little girl, Tabitha, who was four years old on that day. I was coming home early – we planned a special tea and a trip out for her to choose a gift. Her mother, putting a few final touches to the meal, was probably watching her from the kitchen. Beth must have been looking at the fish in the pond as she waited for me to arrive. I can only assume that she slipped and fell. When I walked into the house it was to see my wife running, screaming, across the garden. I followed and lifted Beth onto the path. She could have been under water only a matter of minutes but I could not revive her. While I tried, my wife ran away – I thought to telephone for help, but I heard her drive off and wrongly assumed that the telephone was out of order – it was a new connection and had been giving trouble. I carried Beth to the patio and laid her on a garden seat, then found that the phone was working – so why had my wife driven away, and where? I'm afraid I lost my head. Guessing that the shock had unhinged her, I feared for her life. I could do nothing for my child and remembered that when our first baby died Evelyn used to sit for hours in an old church near the cottage where we used to live. In desperation, when she wasn't there, I eventually returned home where she greeted me as if I'd just come home from the office. Excitedly, she told me about saving Beth, now safely asleep in bed. I went to look and saw a little girl so like my own that even to me she seemed miraculously restored to us. Apparently, on her flight, my wife saw the child who was so like our own that the horror of the last hour was wiped from her mind. She still firmly believes she went looking for Tabitha and rescued her from a boy who had taken her from our own garden.

It was comforting to shut out reality for a while, but after my wife fell asleep I forced myself to carry poor little Beth from the patio to take her to hospital or somewhere. I couldn't think straight, but I knew there would be trouble. I hadn't sent for a doctor and my wife had kidnapped someone else's daughter. The child was safe enough and I decided that keeping her for a while would give Evelyn time to realise she was not Beth.

I know now that my wife is far more ill than I thought. It was wrong of me to act as I did. I can only pray for forgiveness.

Robert Berry

Sarah handed it back to Alec with a sigh. "Clearly, he feels supremely confident they won't be found before he's ready to part with Kate; what a strain on her parents! He is undoubtedly a sorely troubled man who needed to ease his conscience. Having written to them he can now put them out of mind for a while and deal with his own problems. I think we can ignore the postmark. It has been carried many miles – over water – since it left the writer."

"You're right. We located their travel agent who issued three return tickets for Valencia, Spain last week! They left on the tenth – last Monday, and their return flight is due on October 9th, when we are invited to his house. I suppose you noticed that he'd put his address, Southways, on the note?" He smiled grimly. "Dee and White found the place on Tuesday, exactly twenty-four hours too late." Sarah sympathised as he continued. "One of the numbers on Berry's 'phone pad with 'Gerald' against it turned out to be someone I know, Area Commander Mason! As soon as I found out I requested officially to see him. He said they played golf sometimes but was surprised when Berry rang him last weekend."

Berry had first discussed fixing a game, and then casually said an attempt had been made to kidnap his daughter and because of the circumstances he thought he should talk to whoever was in charge of the Mead case. "Me!" Alec snorted. "That explains how he got my name and location. Perhaps when he sent the photographs so badly addressed he didn't, deep down, care whether they arrived or not!"

"He doesn't refer to burying Beth," Sarah said, "He has probably drawn a mental veil over it, as his wife suppressed memories of the drowning but he could recall it at will – years of therapy might be needed before she can face what has happened."

"There isn't much he added to what we already knew, thanks to you!" Alec replied. "Taft left a message for Sgt. Dee, who had asked how many sets of boat keys there were. Cyril Taft didn't know whether it was important, but the spare set was left on the boat while he was away – by Berry! Taft was worried after he'd been questioned because he realised that all the keys hadn't actually been in his own possession since taking it over. After mulling it over until it was far too late to help us, he rang up!"

A flash of irritation crossed Alec's face as he resumed. "We're inquiring after the family in Spain but it seems unlikely we'll get any results. They might be with friends – and for all sorts of reasons it wouldn't be easy to find them. Unless, for instance, you first have the number of the escritura – the deeds – it's impossible to get property details from the registry: a real 'Catch 22'! And some house-owners don't bother to have the consumer's name changed for things like electricity bills in case their installation is inspected; re-wiring is expensive! The Spanish police are trying to help. Berry may have hired a car for instance, but Valencia is a very large Province."

He looked so glum that Sarah tried to cheer him. "We'll just hope then," she smiled, "that Kate has a lovely holiday – and don't ask me to spoil it by going there to join the hunt!"

***

That afternoon, in Granadella, a quiet little bay south of Jávea, Robert and Evelyn sat outside a small restaurant enjoying a drink under the shade of a colourful umbrella, watching a happy little girl play on the beach.

Their thoughts were very different.

Evelyn couldn't understand why Beth was no longer interested in the water and wouldn't even paddle.

Robert was glad that Kate, at first subdued when taken from all that was familiar, had settled down and was looking so healthy. She was already slightly tanned.

When she went back home he and Evelyn would soon be forgotten but he hoped she would remember the good things forever.

His letter must have reached the police by now. If he'd posted it in Spain it might not have arrived until after they returned themselves, but Jaime had a friend in the taxi business who gave it to a London-bound tourist to post in England.

He hadn't actually asked for it to be mailed anywhere other than Heathrow but it would be better if collected from a box away from the airport so that the police would concentrate the search on the mainland.

If only they could keep Kate and hide forever, he thought sadly. He might even have allowed the deception to continue had he not seen Kate's parents on television the night after he had taken Evelyn to her mother's with the strange child. Mrs Mead's frightened tear-stained face had haunted him day and night, but by now she must have his letter and he could forget her more easily.

These could be the last happy days of his entire life and he was determined not to mar them with self-recrimination.

51 – Polly

The week after Alec's visit was quiet for Sarah. Polly was out most of the time, on the trail of a second-hand gem to occupy the new carport. She had enlisted the help of her nephew, a mechanic who was between jobs; he provided her with transport as well as advice. It was a great opportunity, he said, to check out job opportunities and as Auntie was keeping his petrol tank full he had nothing to lose!

Apart from Polly and Frank the only person Sarah saw was Mr Green who came one morning to assess the building job and promised, subject to his estimate being acceptable, that work could start at the end of the month. A young woman telephoned on Friday morning and announced that she was Detective Constable Jean Stedman. The information Sarah had requested from the Chief Super was now collated but such files couldn't be copied or lent; she had his permission to bring them personally for Sarah to examine, was that acceptable? And if so, when? Of course it was! They agreed that DC Stedman should come on Monday morning. If Clarinda hadn't been due home within hours Sarah would have fixed the visit sooner, eager to get to grips with the facts.

When Frank brought Polly home for lunch they were in high spirits having been spectacularly successful. He was starting work on Monday at the garage where they'd found the perfect car! The garage owner hadn't planned to take on another mechanic but was so impressed by Frank's knowledge and enthusiasm, that he said he'd rather employ him than sell to him!

He also said that giving the car another going over could be Frank's first task when he reported for his new job, which, in turn, impressed Polly and Frank, so the deal was settled. Sarah produced a bottle of wine to toast both job and car and in consequence lunch dragged on well into the afternoon. She remarked after Frank left that it was not often, these days, one came across a young man willing to devote so much time to a pair of old ladies.

"Old ladies indeed!" Polly exploded. "Don't you call me old – I've not been drawing my pension all that long – and you are still under-age!"

"Well you don't look ancient I admit, but between him and us there are several generation gaps!" Sarah laughed.

"Which reminds me," Polly said. "You know the little girl you helped about five years ago ...her parents couldn't believe she was psychic. Jenny – Jenny something..."

"Of course I do: Jenny Muir. She was only ten."

"Well, I met her mother this morning; she was filling up at the pumps as we left the garage. She needs to talk to you and asked if we were still in touch; I gave her this number to ring." Polly frowned. "I'm sure you will hear from her soon – she looked ever so worried, I thought."

Mrs Muir's call came as Clarinda arrived. There wasn't time to say much other than give the address and invite her to come on Monday afternoon. Monday was going to be a busy day!

Although admiring all the paintings as Clarrie unloaded the car, Polly could not help comparing them with the painting of the cottage, which was already in the studio having been brought from Wales at the beginning of the week. "These are really lovely but there is something almost magical about the first one. I used to dream of retiring to a cottage like that." Polly touched Clarrie's arm lightly, looking slightly embarrassed. "If I had imagined it remotely possible, I would have dreamed of coming to live here. I am so grateful to you for inviting me, but when you feel it's time I moved back to my daughter, please don't be frightened to tell me."

"You can rest assured," said Clarrie, giving her a hug, "that you'll be welcome as long as you care to stay. It will be good for mother to have company; you have always got along well and know each other's worst faults already!"

During dinner Polly did almost all the talking. She was excited about the car, moving in permanently, her visits to the Latham's' and how amazing Sarah had been in helping find the kidnapped child. As soon as the meal was over she insisted on clearing up alone, then excused herself and went to her room.

Sarah and Clarrie had so much to tell each other that they still hadn't finished when the mantelpiece clock struck two and they reluctantly went to bed. Sarah was astonished that her daughter's psychic ability had made such a fantastic leap forward, so suddenly. She wasn't sure that it pleased her, even though she'd expected it to happen. It was hard not to be affected deeply by other people's problems. Clarinda would have to learn how to say no – not just to those whose motives were suspect, who would take advantage, but to sad, eager spirits on the other side that pressed for attention. Still, Sarah had learned to cope without a mother to lean on and if the Lord wanted them both in His army, who was she to argue?

By Monday morning the household had been re-arranged. Polly's son-in-law and a friend moved the wardrobes when they delivered her huge armchair, books and television set. He was impressed by the size of her new room and joked that they would have a hard time getting her away from it to baby-sit. He seemed fond of Polly but Sarah detected an air of relief that she was moving out. It was only natural; not many men invited their wife's mother to live with them in the first place! He did say, on the way out, that if ever she wanted to move back she would be welcome.

Frank's sister Patricia arrived several minutes before nine-thirty, eager to start work. She'd been a student nurse before she married at eighteen and retained an air of crisp efficiency. Six years later, with two infants at school, she had time on her hands but not enough to resume her career. When previously considering house-cleaning for others, even though the flexible hours appealed to her, she reluctantly abandoned the idea; Pat kept her own home well enough but hadn't a clue what an employer would expect. How did one go about cleaning a strange place? Would the standard expected be impossibly high? She was afraid of being found wanting. When her aunt Polly asked if she was interested in some pocket-money she didn't hesitate. With such a tutor, she might soon acquire the confidence to fill every morning, at other houses.

Polly gave her a conducted tour of the house, explaining how it was run. "I'll give you a back door key to the utility room, which you must not only keep unmarked in a safe place – you must never tell anyone else that you have it. On arrival, enter the kitchen quietly. In this establishment you'll probably find it clean and tidy, but in some houses – well, be prepared for a mess."

Looking around the gleaming modern kitchen, Pat was impressed. "I don't know why you need a daily," she said, "I hope you don't expect me to improve on this!"

"I don't, but if it's not as it is now when you arrive, I'll expect it to look like this when you leave!" Polly affirmed. "But before you tackle the kitchen, go through to the reception rooms. Your first task is to tidy them in case we have an early visitor. With this in mind, continue working downstairs. Unless otherwise instructed, never go upstairs until all in residence have vacated their bed and bathrooms." Polly continued in this vein until they again reached the kitchen. The front door bell rang and Pat jumped up.

"No," Polly checked her. "If you are working you are unlikely to be in a fit state to answer the door and would lower the tone. If you look presentable and the mistress of the house is within call you may offer to do so, but strictly speaking you should keep a low profile. If the house has other staff, no doubt one of them will..."

"Auntie! The doorbell is still ringing and no-one is answering at all," interrupted Pat.

Polly was rather breathless when she opened the door. At that moment Sarah came downstairs apologising. She had heard the bell, but was still dressing. The young woman in the porch announced herself as Jean Stedman and said she was expected. Re-joining Pat, Polly declared it time for a coffee break and put the kettle on. "When you make one for your employer you can also enjoy a drink, but don't abuse the privilege by sitting with it for more than five minutes. Always bear in mind that you are being paid by the hour and those who pay for service are entitled to be treated fairly."

Sarah took her visitor into the sitting room and was soon opening up the files she had brought with her.

"I'm sorry I can't leave them with you," said the young Detective Constable. "My name is Jean by the way... but you are at liberty to make notes of anything interesting." It wasn't a formidable pile but Sarah thought it would take her at least half an hour so she indicated a magazine rack, where Jean might find something to read while she studied the papers.

52 – Clarrie

Clarrie, in her studio, was sorting the paintings she had brought back from Wales. Only one apart from the cottage was ready for framing, so she would need to finish the others before the vibrant autumn colours faded from memory. As she looked around her she was satisfied. The room wasn't much more crowded than before. Standing together, along the far wall, the two wardrobes made little difference and the studio couch, her bed now, was only two feet nearer to the door. Before Tom died this had been their bedroom. Making it a workroom had not only forced her to continue using it but had given her an excuse to sleep somewhere else. It bore no resemblance now to the room they'd shared; the memories were painless.

In her mind she could conjure up the echo of his voice, singing as he showered in the adjacent bathroom, and felt the nearness of him, still caring. In quiet moments, as she painted, she imagined what he would think about her efforts. Knowing him so well she could put voice to his criticism and always persevered until the results would please him. Her recent vision of him was still intensely vivid, but with her new sense of her own psychic potential, she wondered if she'd ever have any real contact with him.

For the first time, she understood how her mother felt, when insensitively asked if she ever spoke to her dead husband. If ever Tom appeared to her she thought she could deal with it, but would never seek it. Love endured; Clarrie didn't need to see him to know that and she no longer dreaded the lonely small hours.

With this arrangement she could work, sleep or play at any time of the day or night, as the mood took her. It was good. Polly's presence would allow her much more freedom.

Clarrie was only dimly aware of movement in the rest of the house and was startled by the knock on her door. Polly hadn't wanted to interrupt earlier but was anxious to introduce her niece before she left, and to make sure Pat understood exactly what to do when cleaning the studio.

"It's mostly a case of what you should not do," laughed Clarrie. "Don't throw anything away that isn't in the waste basket. Anything you pick up off the floor prior to vacuum cleaning, please leave on the desk where I can vet it before making more mess! Don't dust or move anything on the work surfaces, I'd rather do it myself, but I'll be grateful if you make the bed and clean the bathroom."

As they left the studio Clarrie heard the front door close and guessed that her mother's visitor had gone. It was a convenient moment to stop work so she gave in to her curiosity and went downstairs. She could hardly wait to hear what else Sarah had discovered. Polly, with the same thing in mind, asked if she could join them; lunch was on but would be half-an-hour.

Sarah was poised, a writing pad on her lap. "Yes, come in, both of you," she agreed. "I'd like to marshal my thoughts. It would be a good idea if you each made your own notes as I talk." Deciding where to start was difficult but they knew the bare facts already, so Sarah advised, "Write down anything that occurs to you – ideas or questions, so you needn't interrupt my flow – I need to concentrate to sort out all this scribble!"...

Mrs Bane stated that her sister went out every Wednesday night to a literary-club meeting. Usually, Barbara – Babs – drove herself but her car needed servicing. By arrangement, she left it at the garage so they could start work on it first thing the following day and her friend picked her up from there to drive to the meeting. Bane worked late at least one night every week so it was no hardship for him to stay in town that evening to drive Babs home.

Bettina expected them around 9.30 and was perturbed when

ten-o-clock passed. She tried to ring her husband but finding his phone engaged she really began to worry about her sister's whereabouts and telephoned Ann Dodd, Bab's friend, who said she'd seen her onto the bus. The bus journey should have taken less than a quarter of an hour so when Babs had still not arrived at eleven, Mrs Bane (Bet) rang the police to ask if it had been delayed or had an accident. Ten minutes later, two uniformed constables – a man and a woman – came to tell her that Babs had been killed by a hit and run driver after leaving the bus. Mrs Bane said it was terrible that her sister should have had to walk alone down a badly lit road so late at night; she would never forgive David for not meeting her. He arrived home at 11.30pm. The policewoman was still there.

Bane stated that he had become so absorbed in paperwork he failed to notice his watch had stopped. He checked, found it said 20.15, and thought he had time to make a few 'phone calls before leaving ...he is an insurance broker and many of his clients prefer to discuss business at home after office hours. He gave the names and numbers of two people he'd called – the second was annoyed and asked why he couldn't have rung at a decent hour. It was only then that he discovered his watch had stopped.

It was actually 10.30pm. He looked up the number of Barbara's friend who assured him that when he was obviously not coming. She had driven Babs to the bus stop and waited with her until the bus came at ten-o-clock.

Deciding there was then no point in rushing, Bane finished what he had started and left the office at around 10.55. When he reached home the police were there and he learned of his sister-in-law's death.

Ann Dodd said that Babs sat in the car with her and they waited so long before deciding that her brother-in-law wasn't coming, that Ann couldn't afford the time to drive all the way to the other side of Caversham Heights. Her mother is a diabetic and Ann had to be home by 10.15 to tend her. It was impossible to ring David from the hall because the meeting was in a school and as soon as the hall emptied, the caretaker locked up and went home. If they had waited longer the last bus would have gone, so she drove Babs to the terminus where it was about to leave.

After arriving home (near the hospital), she had a call from David Bane and a second one later from Bettina. She told them both the same; Babs had caught the bus.

Sarah cleared her throat. "Well that's what happened according to statements from the three people closest to the tragedy. Any comments so far?"

"Why didn't they drive to Bane's office? It can't have been far out of town," asked Clarinda.

"And how on earth," interjected Polly, "Can anyone not notice the passing of over two hours!"

Sarah thumbed through her notes. "I think someone asked Ann that – about the office. She said Babs had only a vague idea where it was, never having been there. In any case, by the time they reached it he would most likely have left. As for noticing the time – when he first checked, it might already have been much later than indicated. What was the duration of the first call, I wonder." She looked up from her notes and made a cautionary comment. "Forgetfulness was probably his only crime. We must not assume he lied – or suspect him of worse, because of his present eccentric behaviour. The possibility was checked by the police of course. I have another batch of notes connected to their findings, but we'd better leave those until this evening. If we don't eat soon, Mrs Muir will arrive before we're ready for her!"

Polly hastily removed herself to the kitchen hoping to goodness the meal was still edible, while Clarrie set the table and Sarah sat lost in thought. It was well within the bounds of possibility that Bane really had committed murder but why? How? ...His alibi was perfect.

53 – Clarrie

Mrs Muir arrived at half-past-three. Polly absented herself again and Clarrie went back to her studio after being introduced. Four or five years ago when the Muirs first sought her mother's advice, her father and Tom were still alive. In 1971 when Grandma Grey died, Clarrie and her parents moved into the old family home. It was sad to give up their own house but Grandpa needed them and he refused to leave the place where he was born and brought up. Clarrie, unlike her parents, Sarah and Stephen, was thrilled to live there. It was rambling and solidly built of sand-coloured stone with a lovely garden.

Polly, the housekeeper, continued to live-in and had a daily woman to help her. There were also two gardeners who were indispensable, making the establishment expensive to maintain. Nevertheless, even after Grandpa also died a year later, they remained there; there was no question then of selling up. Ten years ago, Clarrie married and her parents would have loved them all to share the house but Tom preferred them to buy this, their own home. She sat reminiscing, gazing from the window across the garden to the unobstructed view ...the rolling hills of Berkshire. How Tom had loved to watch the sun sinking to the far horizon.

When Stephen, her father, died seven years later, Tom offered Sarah a home with them but she planned to buy an apartment of her own until Tom's accident led to his dying also, within a year. Sarah had a buyer for the old house but she postponed her own plans and, instead, moved in to help Clarrie.

Polly went to live with her daughter Jane.

Clarrie shook herself out of her reverie – she was getting depressed. The sooner she started work the better. What could Mrs Muir possibly want she wondered? It must have been frightening for Jenny, then only ten, to be clairvoyant and not be believed. Years before, when Jenny was three-years-old and talked to invisible playmates, Mr and Mrs Muir thought she was pretending, as most children do but the delusion, as they considered it, persisted as she grew up and they tried to talk her out of it.

When, at nine, Jenny persisted in speaking as if her friends were real and couldn't understand why others didn't see them, they panicked and took her to a psychiatrist. Jenny quickly learned not to discuss her visions. Even at that age she knew they considered her crazy and must have been half inclined to think they were right. She knew that insane people were taken away and locked up, so she stopped speaking of the strange things she saw. For over a year all seemed well … until the day her mother heard her holding a one-sided conversation and laughing.

Fortunately, the next doctor they took her to see was a friend of Sarah's and introduced them to her. She convinced them that Jenny was not only sane, but also very gifted and would probably have a bright successful future. Jenny kept in touch with Sarah for a couple of years – last time they had heard from her she was happy and doing exceptionally well at school but Clarrie was thankful that she hadn't seen ghosts when she was little!

It was almost five-o-clock when the slam of the front door indicated the departure of Mrs Muir. Clarrie heard her mother go into the kitchen and the temptation to put work aside for the day was too much to resist. There was so much of interest happening these days it was difficult to concentrate on anything else, even painting! Sarah had just started telling Polly what had transpired when Clarrie arrived. "Just a minute, let me pull up a chair too," she interrupted. "I know I wasn't in at the beginning of the saga, five years ago, but I remember feeling sorry for that poor child and being glad I wasn't psychic myself!"

"I was just wondering," mused Sarah, "what Jenny will

think of my advice? If she had come asking me for it herself, it would be a different matter." They waited expectantly as Sarah seemed lost in thought ... "Oh, sorry! I'd better explain her mother's problem."

Sarah sipped the tea Polly had just poured and told them about Jenny's recent years. While accepting that she really was psychic, her parents didn't want outsiders to discover her ability to communicate with the dead. They made her promise not to reveal the fact, even to her closest friends. It was partly embarrassment that made them do so, but they were genuinely worried that some people would shun her, causing her pain. Others might take advantage of her. They wanted her to grow up normally.

It had been difficult sometimes but Jenny was a good student and they were confident that when she became adult she would be capable of acting sensibly in her own best interest. "Now, at fifteen, when she should be planning her further education she wants to drop out to devote her life to becoming a healer." Sarah informed them. "To achieve this without running the risk of becoming a side-show in the entertainment business she feels she must join a religious Order. Her parents, naturally, are terribly upset. Being more aware than Jenny of all she would be giving up, they hate the idea of her being cut off from life."

"Is she very religious then? Has she been in touch with a convent?" Polly asked earnestly.

"Apparently not – in answer to both questions." Sarah said. "In a way, she's handling her problem quite sensibly. She wants to help people and, according to her mother, really does have the gift of Healing. They take for granted that she can cure their minor aches and pains but until a month ago she planned to go into scientific research ...in their words, a real career!"

Clarrie remarked that a scientific community wouldn't suit a sensitive; scientists were too down to earth. Polly said that even to consider a career like that Jenny must have a really good brain and she agreed with the parents, it would be a crime to waste it. "Why!" she cried, "Why doesn't she become a doctor if she wants to heal the sick?"

"And that," said Sarah, "is exactly what I suggested, Polly. We'll soon have you setting up on your own!" Polly almost purred with pleasure as Sarah voiced her own thought. "It would give her a good practical way of trying to cure by earthly means while enabling her to call her spiritual gifts into play. If she chooses not to tell her patients, they need never know that they are, so to speak, getting the best of both worlds!"

"Brilliant," Clarrie applauded, congratulating them both. "She is obviously good at science. I wonder what her other subjects are like."

Sarah reported that Jenny's best results were in Latin, Physics and Math. She attained 'A' grades in everything other than music and art. "And after all," Sarah laughed, "As her mother said, they are both of little use or importance!"

"I've rapidly gone off Mrs Muir," Clarrie declared. "Is she going to let you know how Jenny accepts the idea?"

"I think it likely that Jenny will eventually ring me herself, but I expect she'll need time to consider it fully." Sarah said.

"Well, completing her formal education is really the most important thing for now," declared Polly firmly. "She can decide later what she does with it." She stood, set her chair straight and went to the cooker. "Now let's have an early dinner then we can get back to our 'Who dun it'. It's much more fun than television!"

54 – David Bane

After dinner they spent two hours discussing the case but were no nearer to a firm conclusion. As Sarah pointed out, the police never found the car that had mown down poor Barbara even when the case was fresh. It wasn't within their scope to tackle the problem that way. If they found her murderer after all this time, and it was anyone other than Bane, it would be a miracle: they'd need divine intervention!

When the police interviewed David Bane originally he must have appeared to be a completely normal, sane individual, caught up in a terrible situation not of his making. "Two years on," Sarah pointed out, "we have the advantage of knowing that he has been anything but normal since the tragic death of his sister-in-law. We merely have to figure out why!"

"Before we leave the hit and run," Clarrie asked, "were there any witnesses? After all, there are quite a few houses near the junction where she was killed."

"And was his watch checked to see if it had really stopped," Polly queried. "I'd also like to know if anyone else in the building saw him entering or leaving his office."

Sarah checked her notes and confirmed that a repairer had replaced the battery. The watch showed the wrong time and he had no reason to doubt that the old one was flat. There were two witnesses who heard the engine roar after it started, followed by a scream. They ran to the window in time to see a small vehicle race away with no rear lights. Neither had noted the make or type. It could have been a van.

"Look," Clarrie said, "Why don't we do what the police are not supposed to do? Let's assume that Bane actually did it and try to prove it! If we can't, it will be easier to forget the possibility that his condition now has anything to do with a guilty conscience!"

The others were very happy to agree.

Sarah took a clean sheet of paper and divided it into two columns – FOR and AGAINST. "You are quite right dear. Whoever ran down Barbara is no concern of ours unless it actually was Bane, but before we ask why – because no motive is obvious, we'll see if we can figure out how." Sarah, pen poised, continued. "Let us first examine his alibi! Clarinda – take another sheet of paper and keep track of what was proved or unproved. Leave space under anything which was proved, we can decide later whether the proof provided satisfies us or not."

"May I have a sheet too please, Sarah," asked Polly. "I'd rather jot down anything that occurs to me as you go along, to avoid interrupting."

With renewed determination now that their thoughts were focusing on a definite approach, Sarah again went through what they knew of David Bane's actions that night. His office, in a converted old house, was one of a suite of three. His partner, who was abroad on holiday for several weeks on each side of the night in question, occupied one; the third was really a reception area. Their shared secretary was a middle-aged married woman who never worked late as she had a family to look after. Other offices in the building always closed at 5.30pm.

Sarah wrote under FOR, Not seen between 5.30 and about 10.45pm. She noted that on the day in question he parked his car outside some student flats where it was within sight of the porter's window. Bane actually went to the lobby and asked the man if he'd seen anyone hanging around it suspiciously – a coat was missing from the back seat. "It is almost," mused Sarah, "as if he went out of his way to make sure his time of departure was noticed!" She made a second heading on the left of her sheet, 'Unusual behaviour'.

"If he knew he would need an alibi," said Clarrie, "he must

have been very sure that Barbara would take the bus and walk home alone. Her friend might simply have driven her all the way."

Polly, disregarding her avowed intention not to interrupt pointed out that if he hadn't been able to carry out his plan that night he had nothing to lose anyway. "Mind you," she added, "he might not have expected her friend to wait with her. I know that school – it's a pretty isolated place with fields on each side of it. Perhaps he planned to run her down as she waited for him."

"We know he didn't move his own car, so whose car did he use to kill her. Where could he be sure of finding one and using it without the owner knowing?" Clarrie asked. "He'd hardly risk roaming up and down trying door-handles or wiring an ignition to start a strange vehicle!" Then she had another thought. "Could he have borrowed his partner's?"

This suggestion was greeted enthusiastically. Sarah rapidly searched her earlier notes again and at last concluded, "There's nothing here about the partner other than that he was away. He might not even have been interviewed." How could they find out after such a long time? It seemed hopeless.

"I wonder if Mrs Bane would know if her husband had access to his partner's car and keys." Polly suggested, "Bane may have been keeping an eye on the house for them or something."

"If we have the partner's name and address it would be better to ask him directly," Clarrie said. "Perhaps we could enlist the Reverend Kilroy to visit him, armed with a list of questions. He's obviously worried about Bane and is much more likely to elicit answers without arousing suspicion about a murder hunt!"

"Brilliant!" Polly applauded. "Ambrose can't possibly refuse, as we are doing all this for him anyway!"

"And I think we're doing very well, but let's not get carried away," Sarah cautioned. "Even if we find a car he could have used, how do we explain the fact that, even if no-one saw him, he spoke to at least three people on the telephone? Remember, when his wife rang she found the number engaged."

"Easy," Polly said firmly, reluctant to believe they weren't on the right track. "He could have rung them from somewhere else. They would assume he was in his office."

"Yes, I agree," Clarrie cried, "and he could easily have left the phone off the hook in case someone rang him back."

"Ambrose is sure to agree, so we'll prepare a list of questions for him to ask," said Sarah. After another debate, considering every angle carefully, they were all firmly convinced that Bane could have planned and carried out Barbara's murder. There were several points to re-check but after two years, how could they expect people to recall details that, to them, were trivial?

They regretted that there was no way of finding out how unusual it was for him to park so far from his own building. The road he'd used wasn't far from the centre of town but not near enough for shoppers to leave their cars and walk. Perhaps he parked in the afternoon of course, when more vehicles were about, but the houses there were large, double fronted, with drives of their own. Not many residents needed to park at kerbside at all. There was probably plenty of space so why did he choose the more crowded area in front of the students' residence? Did he deliberately draw his presence to the attention of the porter?

Leaving aside the actual murder they considered his later moves. Where could he have left the, perhaps damaged, car? The police never found it; how often were such cars found? They must invite Jean Stedman for a meal and ask her to explain the procedure.

Sarah's FOR column was almost full – the other amazingly empty. As she gazed at it her mind went back to her impressions of the dreadful moment when the car roared towards its prey. Exactly what had come to her when she handled Barbara's gold chain; she remembered the word 'red' clearly. Had she really said 'red carpet' before? She would have to ask Ambrose, as she could make no sense of what she'd said at the time.

Sarah was anxious to speak to Bettina too. When the young woman became better acquainted with the unexplained facts surrounding Barbara's death, surely she would agree to a meeting. Bettina was the only one who could help them to make any progress in understanding David Bane's bizarre conduct. Tired but gratified, after what they considered a fruitful evening, they at last gave up and went to bed. It had been an exhausting day for Sarah.

She didn't wake up until after nine-thirty on Tuesday morning.

Before joining the others for coffee Sarah made several telephone calls and afterwards told Clarinda and Polly that the remainder of the week was going to be pretty full too. Ambrose would be coming the following morning and Jean had accepted a supper invitation for Thursday night.

It was all very stimulating, Polly thought. She could not remember ever being so excited and on top of everything else – tomorrow they would have their new car!

55 – Monday October 1st...

The house, usually so quiet, was a hive of activity. Clarrie who had been away again since Saturday was due back for lunch and Alec had promised to join them. Sarah prepared the meal while Polly divided her time between supervising Pat and the builders. True to his promise, Mr Green had delivered a load of building materials on Saturday morning and his men turned up to start work on the foundations at half-past-eight. Sarah was glad to be apart from it all; she rather enjoyed cooking for guests. Polly had gradually taken over the kitchen since moving in and Sarah was normally glad to let her get on with it, if it made her happy, but with all the noise outside – doors opening and shutting and Pat shouting to her aunt over the roar of the vacuum cleaner, Sarah welcomed the excuse to shut herself away from it all.

Clarinda had been asked to do a painting of a house north of Oxford, so she'd combined a day's work with a visit to an old school chum who had invited her to stay over. Her daughter had so few close friends now, Sarah reflected sadly. It was always the same when a husband or wife died; acquaintances they had shared, gradually drifted away. It was hardly ever deliberate neglect; the severing of such ties was almost inevitable. Clarinda appeared happy enough. It was a blessing that she was able to become so absorbed in her work but it would do her good to be with people her own age.

As if in answer to her thoughts Sarah heard the garage door slam shut and soon afterwards the connecting door burst open. Clarrie came in and gave her mother a hug.

"I really enjoyed seeing Donna again – she looks so well and has two of the most beautiful babies. When they're a bit older I shall paint a picture of them. Donna insists I stay longer next time so I'll go for a couple of weeks. There are some stunning views to paint from her garden. I haven't discussed the portraits ...it will be a way of thanking her." Clarrie dashed back to unload the car without waiting for a reply ..."Something smells good. I'm starving!"

Pat volunteered to stay until after lunch, to clear up and make drinks for the builders who had eaten their pre-packed snacks and were back at work again long before Alec arrived at one-o-clock. He was astounded to find so much happening in what he had come to regard as a peaceful haven. Before inviting him into the house Polly took him to see their latest acquisition – the reason for the disturbance. He duly admired the little blue Mini – 'Old but clean, in excellent condition for its age' – and pleased Polly by agreeing that it would be a shame to have it standing outside unprotected. As they returned to the front door Polly assured him that before she drove it out on her own, her nephew was going to accompany her for a few hours.

Not until after lunch did they speak of murder.

"When you asked me for the facts about that old hit and run," Alec said at last, "I had no idea you thought David Bane might be the driver responsible. What on earth made you suspect him? He was thoroughly investigated at the time and everyone insisted there was no bad feeling between Bane and his wife's twin. Even her young man and friends of several years standing said they resided together in perfect harmony!"

"Well Alec, when I asked we had no fixed opinions. The police conducting the inquiry had no way of knowing how his behaviour would change almost immediately after her death, so it's no reflection on them." Sarah was anxious that he shouldn't imagine there was any implied criticism of the police in their minds. "However, we realise there's no evidence that his feelings towards her were other than socially acceptable, so if it wasn't sorrow that caused him to change, what was it? Because we can't attribute his mental disintegration to sorrow, our next step must be to eliminate guilt also. Approaching the crime this way, in the light of later events, we find it quite impossible to accept his alibi at face value." Looking slightly apprehensive, Sarah handed him her notes.

Alec took the list and studied it while the three friends waited silently for his reaction. When he looked up eventually it was with a rueful smile. "I have to hand it to you ladies – you have certainly made me wonder whether we were fooled by him. I'll round up as many as possible of the officers who were on the case. You can join us for lunchtime drinks sometime and question them yourselves. There's no way I can re-open the inquiry officially without new evidence, but if your efforts succeed in rooting out a cold-blooded killer we'll be in your debt yet again. No case is closed until it's solved."

Alec sighed heavily, and then brightened. "The kidnapping case is just about over. It is pointless trying to find Berry's hiding place in Spain, as he has three seats booked on a scheduled flight, due into Heathrow in the early hours next Monday. We won't pounce immediately. They'll be followed. We would like to know where he left his car, and I shall be mortified – not to mention extremely angry, if it's on a public car park! Depending on his actions I'll decide where and when to take the child from him. The poor little mite has had enough shocks already so I hope to hand her straight over to her parents."

Sarah appreciated the dilemma he faced. "If I can be of use," she offered, "perhaps with Mrs Berry, Beth's poor mother, please say." She hesitated, and added quickly, "Of course, I wouldn't want to be in the way."

"I'll take advantage of that offer because, to be honest, I'm not sure how to deal with her. She'll think we're abducting her own child by the sound of it. We are in Robert Berry's hands to some extent. If I can, I'd rather take Kate at a time which suits me, not go along blindly with his plans." He added hopefully, "Are you prepared to be on call after midnight on the ninth?"

Sarah waved aside the immediate protests of both Clarrie and Polly. If she could bring a little comfort to a woman already broken by the loss of two loved children she would willingly give up a night's sleep. She also felt she owed it to Beth to help her parents. Alec had a meeting arranged for two-thirty so he couldn't linger over coffee. He hurried away, promising to let them know when he'd spoken to the men concerned with investigating Barbara's death. He said it was unlikely they would still be serving together, so it might not be easy to get hold of them all without making too much of a stir but he'd do his best.

Clarrie spent the rest of the afternoon sorting herself out after her trip and Frank came to take Polly out for a test drive at five-o-clock. The building crew left around the same time and Sarah sat enjoying the sudden peace, until the telephone rang. When Ambrose came last week he had agreed to call on David Bane's partner; she thought the call would be from him. It was, however, Jenny Muir. The advice had not fallen on deaf ears and the idea really had appealed to her immediately. She had not rung Sarah straight away because her mother told her to discuss it with her teachers first. Everyone she consulted was enthusiastic and optimistic about her chances of success, so when she was qualified Jenny hoped Sarah would be proud of her – and willing still to advise her. Sarah wished her well and settled down again with one less thing to worry about.

When she had asked Ambrose about the strange exclamation she had made, he couldn't be sure what emphasis she had put on each word, but it didn't matter, Sarah suspected that the 'red' was more significant and she tried to recall the moment again and the words uttered in a tone of incredulity. There was something odd about the phrasing. Not 'red carpet': more apart too: 'RED' and 'CARPET'. Unlikely last words ...she gave up.

The call from Ambrose didn't come until the following day. He had eventually persuaded Bettina Bane to meet Sarah at the vicarage (neutral ground!) on Thursday if it suited her. Sarah agreed and said that Polly could drive them over if Elsie wouldn't mind entertaining her while they talked to Mrs Bane. Ambrose asserted that his wife would be delighted ...Sarah heard Elsie's voice in the background, saying they could swap cake recipes! He then informed her that, as promised, he had spoken with Mr Brown, Bane's partner. The meeting had been pleasant but unfruitful.

Mr Brown was not, nor had he ever been, closely associated with Bane. Although they shared premises their lines seldom crossed; they dealt with different types of insurance and had separate office suites but their relationship was good. When Bane's sister-in-law was killed he and his wife were on a six-week tour of the Far East. After their return he attributed Bane's air of distraction to worry and shock. Sarah was disappointed when Ambrose finished by saying the car theory was shot down. It had been securely locked in their garage, ten miles south of town near Beech Hill. Even had Bane possessed a key – which apparently he didn't – it was too far in the opposite direction for him to have used it within the time frame. Sarah assured Ambrose that he'd done well, and rang off.

The most interesting suggestion, which emerged during the after-dinner discussion that evening, was the possibility that Bane might have hired a car for a few days. If only slightly damaged but otherwise clean when he returned it, they would have charged him for the repair but would have had no reason to inform the police ...or would they? In such cases the police surely contacted hire companies and ask about accidental damages. Bane would have had to give his name too. On further reflection it was not after all a very promising line to follow.

On Thursday afternoon Polly rather nervously drove Sarah to the vicarage. It was only a few miles away but the roads were much more crowded, she said, than they used to be. She assured Sarah that Frank's verdict on her driving was favourable. "Said I'm inclined to be too slow ... I call it being careful, but he insists that slow isn't the same as good," Polly reported. Frank wasn't recommending that she should become a rally driver, he warned her, but other road-users tend to freak out if they have to follow little old ladies doing fifteen miles an hour! "Cheeky young devil," Polly snorted, changing gear and accelerating to thirty. "All the same, he's a good lad. It was kind of him to give up time to help me."

"You drive quite fast enough for me," Sarah declared. Then added quickly, "Oh, not that I feel at all nervous with you but it's pleasant having time to look at the scenery." Sarah wasn't saying so just to appease, out of politeness. With Polly to drive her she need not impose on Clarinda every time she needed a lift; she too felt exhilarated by a new sense of freedom.

When they arrived at the vicarage Mrs Bane was already there. She was dark-haired, attractive but rather severely dressed in a tailored suit. Sarah had expected her to be like the picture she had already formed of her twin, when handling the necklace – bright and fluffy. Perhaps she had looked, and been, less serious before Barbara died. Leaving Polly with Elsie in the rather austere sitting room, Ambrose took them to his study, which was much cosier. A stone fireplace stood centrally in a book-lined wall and a real log fire burned warmly, with complete disregard for the sunshine outside. Sarah looked about her approvingly. If unable to relax and talk freely in here, she thought, Bettina Bane would not be at ease anywhere.

56 – Ambrose

Ambrose seated his guests on each side of the fire and went to sit behind his desk. He was literally taking a back seat and made his intention quite clear by saying he hoped they would excuse his not joining them for a while – he had almost completed drafting his Sunday sermon and didn't want to lose the thread.

Sarah tried to put the young woman at ease by asking first about her early life; how difficult, or agreeable it was, being a twin. From her answers it was clear that the sisters had been identical except in temperament. "Babs always laughed more easily than I did," Bettina said sadly. To her a cup would appear half full – to me, half empty. We needed each other for balance. I kept her feet on the ground. She persuaded me to relax and enjoy life. Without her encouragement I'd never have married David."

From that point on it was fairly easy to put the whole story together. David had been a lot older and perhaps this made Bettina feel comfortable with him. He was 'every inch a gentleman' and very shy. They first met when he handled some insurance matters after their father's death but they didn't go out alone together until almost a year later. David's father had died years before, in 1960. Having always lived at home David naturally stayed on with his mother and appeared quite happy with the arrangement but rarely invited friends home. When their relationship became more serious David said his mother was very much looking forward to meeting her, but the encounter never took place because of Mrs Bane's terrible accident; she fell downstairs and died instantly.

Sarah probed cautiously to discover details of the accident. She learned that Mrs Bane, resting upstairs as she always did in the afternoon until David came, heard him arrive and started to come down. She slipped on the stairs and tumbled almost from top to bottom. The housekeeper, who heard her scream and fall, ran from the kitchen to find her unconscious in the hall. David also rushed out of the ground-floor cloakroom and immediately rang for a doctor. There was nothing obvious which could have caused her to trip – no loose mats or broken rods.

"It's such a shame you never met her. How long after her death did you marry?" Sarah asked. "It must have been a very lonely existence for your husband, but I suppose the housekeeper lived in." She privately hoped that the woman was still available: an impartial witness! Bettina confirmed that the housekeeper had her own apartment in the house and continued to work for them after they married in 1980. David, she said, was then forty-five, twenty years older than the twins. He was more worried than they, about coming between the sisters, and said from the beginning that if Babs wanted to live with them she would be welcome.

Actually, the twins had no qualms about being parted; they had different interests. "Still, I was pleased when Babs eventually decided to move in. She didn't eat properly; I worried about her."

"From what I've heard, Mrs Bane..."

"Oh, please don't be formal. Call me Bet."

"Yes, of course, and I'm Sarah. I'm impressed by your husband's generosity towards his sister-in-law." Bet looked puzzled so Sarah hastily continued. "Very few men would have done as he did: re-arranging his entire household to make her comfortable. I believe it all worked out well and there was no disharmony to upset him."

"We were all quite happy for years," agreed Bet, "right up to the day Babs was killed, there was never any friction – none at all, not even a cross word."

"Was there an immediate difference in David's behaviour

either before or after she died?" Sarah asked. "When in fact did you suspect that there was something wrong with him?"

Bet considered for a moment, and then described the events that led eventually to her leaving him. David was as devastated as Bet by what had happened and, Bettina confessed, she hadn't helped by blaming him for forgetting his promise to collect her sister from the hall. It was weeks before they settled down but life gradually returned to normal until about four months after Barbara's death when he became extremely jumpy, rounding on her, shouting hysterically, and accusing her of playing tricks – pretending to be Barbara.

He'd never before had a problem distinguishing one sister from the other; they wore their hair in distinctly different styles. Babs' hair was short, curled and streaked with blonde highlights; Bet's, long and dark, was coiled at the nape of her neck. Gradually his personality underwent a grave change. Whenever possible he avoided being with her and even though he stopped talking about it, he often jumped in alarm when he glanced at his wife, and ran from the room.

Bet guessed why and was at her wits' end to know how to deal with him. Half out of her own mind with worry she consulted Ambrose and David was persuaded to seek help. They thought the treatment was working for a while, he seemed less crazed but he wasn't the man Bet had loved and married – he was a morose stranger. They went to church but otherwise spent very little time together.

Bet became so unhappy that she was considering leaving him anyway, but things came to a head when he suddenly lapsed into his former madness. Over the previous months Bet had been sorting out Barbara's rooms, restoring them to their previous state. One evening, David saw her leaving the apartment. For a moment he stood, trembling. Then, in an uncontrollable fury, he grabbed her by the hair, shook her like a doll and yelled at her to take the wig off.

That was it. Bet went immediately to stay with a friend and collected some clothes the following day, while he was out. "I can't really say much about what happened to him after that, although the housekeeper did try to explain." Bet concluded. "Mrs Monk was very frightened. She said he was impossible. He even accused her of pretending to be Babs and trying to drive him insane. One Sunday morning he returned from church early, shouting that Barbara was hounding him. She wouldn't give him any peace – not even there! He quickly bolted all the doors and instructed Mrs Monk not to open them, so that Babs couldn't get in. At that point, she moved out too!"

As they stopped talking, Ambrose saw that Sarah looked slightly bemused so he shuffled his papers together and put them into a drawer. He re-joined them by swinging his chair out from behind the desk. "You can't be blamed for leaving him," he assured Bet kindly. "In his state of mind he could have harmed you physically. I dare say Sarah would like to speak with Mrs Monk, if you can tell us where to reach her. We both want to help and it appears that to do so we must discover the root cause of your husband's problem."

"An excellent suggestion, Ambrose, you read my mind." Sarah was grateful that he'd taken the initiative. "There are two other things I would like to talk about, Bet. Thanks by the way, for sending me the chain. It was most useful as she was wearing it that night..."

Bet looked astonished – she hadn't disclosed that fact to Ambrose! Sarah went on hastily, "The two words I heard – do they hold any significance for you?"

"None at all, I'm afraid. I can't think why Babs should have been thinking of a red carpet! There are many patterned carpets in the house with maroon in the pattern, but I wouldn't describe any of them as red. Why would Babs be concerned with such matters anyway?" She frowned and hesitated. "Oh! Well, come to think, she did ask – not exactly for a carpet, but for a piece of carpet – but that definitely wasn't red." Sarah and Ambrose looked at each other and both held their breath ...there was a slim chance they were on the verge of putting part of the jigsaw in place.

57 – Babs

With patience they extracted the whole story of the carpet piece from Bet. It was such a trivial thing to her that she had difficulty in recalling the issue. David, of course, knew that when they were children Babs often enjoyed teasing Bet and frightening her with ghost stories. Even after growing up Babs used to claim that she was psychic because she liked to intrigue people but – as Bet told David, it simply wasn't true.

The subject rarely came up until after David said she could use his mother's sitting room. It amused Babs to say things like, 'I can almost feel her presence in there'! One day Babs said, "I thought about taking the table from the bay window but I could just hear her telling me not to move her things without permission".

"It was stupid of her but didn't really matter," said Bet. "Only once was David really upset, after we found an old photograph of him, taken with his mother a few years after the war – black and white of course. David must have been about twelve."

With a puzzled frown, Bet explained that in the picture David's mother was wearing a housecoat with a large shawl collar and a full-length zip down the front. On the back she had written a note. 'Showing off my new housecoat, made from the old blue brocade curtains. Lucky they were my favourite colour!' They had replaced it in the album… If it hadn't come unstuck they wouldn't have seen what was written on the back and it wasn't significant enough to mention to David.

Bet was consequently as shocked as David when Babs later remarked that his mother had a very strong personality – her ghost still lingered – very regal in her lovely blue gown! He became so alarmed at the idea of his mother haunting the house that Bet had to remind him of the photograph to prove that the silly girl was just teasing.

"I told Babs she was behaving thoughtlessly and should have more regard for his feelings towards his mother, and she promised never to mention her again." Bet continued by saying that David readily accepted her apology and life went back to normal.

"You were going to tell us about the carpet," reminded Sarah, "and how long before her death did all this happen?"

"Oh, the photograph incident was about four weeks previously, but it was only a week before the accident, when David was out, that we found the carpet. We had never been in the attic and were inquisitive." Bet sensed their sharpened interest and looked puzzled. "I'll tell you about it, but I can't think it is of any importance." She saw from their expressions that they didn't agree and seemed about to ask why, but taking up the thread again she proceeded to explain.

"Babs was intrigued by the locked attic. It had never bothered me. I accepted that it was just a storeroom but when she nagged me I looked for the key on the kitchen rack. There wasn't one and I guessed it was on David's personal key ring... but why? I admit that the absurdity began to intrigue me too! I'm sure he would have let me go up there, I should have asked him, but our nosiness embarrassed me..." Bet hesitated, abashed, but they made no comment.

She went on to describe Babs' apartment. It was off a short corridor leading away from the main landing. Her door was on one side and the extra room David gave her for entertaining – his mother's sitting room – was opposite. The polished wood floor of the corridor was bare and allowed cold draughts to whistle under the doors. "So when we found an off-cut of stair runner in the attic, she seized on the idea of laying it sideways between the doors, to make both rooms warmer. The main landing is covered with a matching square and the stair carpet ends in a continuous strip along one side, so the addition wouldn't have offended the eye."

Bet looked shamefaced. She agreed it would have been an improvement, but there was one big problem. To satisfy Babs' curiosity she'd taken David's keys to unlock the attic door while he showered. It had been unlocked all day and re-locked secretly after his return. Bet was ashamed of her own deceit.

David would naturally have been upset and perhaps angry to discover how they had poked through his family and personal belongings without asking, so she told Babs not to mention it until she paved the way herself. Bet intended to tell him first about the draught and then she could ask if any suitable floor covering was available, but Babs grew impatient. When her sister had still not broached the subject after several days she tackled David herself. Bet wasn't there to hear exactly what was said, but apparently he promised to see if he could find a small piece the following weekend. To Bet's relief Babs didn't blurt out that they'd already been in the attic, knew one existed – and where it was!

"Well, that's it." Bet looked from one to the other, feeling that she had let them down. "No great drama. It was such a little thing and yet, you know, she was really looking forward to making her quarters more comfortable. Babs was like that. She took pleasure in things which to others would seem mundane."

Bet stared at Sarah intently, obviously wanting to say something but perhaps not sure how. Realising that she needed encouragement Sarah said, "You've been very kind giving up your time and speaking so frankly about a painful period in your life. Is there anything you want to ask me?"

"Well yes, actually there is," Bet answered timidly. "I've been told that you are a Spiritualist Medium and have been wondering... isn't it possible for you to contact my sister and find out from her if she saw her killer? It would solve the mystery immediately – and how can David's state have any bearing on Barbara, unless he believes he was responsible... not meeting her as arranged?"

"I'm not quite sure myself yet, but I can answer the first question. You see dear, it puzzled me too – that your sister had not come through to me at all." Sarah tried to explain in simple terms. "Usually when those on the other side are constantly in our mind it's easy for them to reach us." She stopped as an expression far removed from delight crossed Bet's face... "Oh, don't be alarmed. Your sister loved you in life although she teased you; death can't have changed that. I'm sure she'll never frighten you by appearing to you suddenly in the dark! But you can be sure she will be near and trying to help you for the rest of your life."

Bet looked a little less apprehensive and Sarah continued. "Not wishing to alarm you, I didn't speak of it when we first met, but now I understand her absence. You didn't arrive alone. An elderly lady has been with us all afternoon – your mother, I think. You are so like her in features but her hair is silver. She's wearing a mauve silk dress; it has a loose bow at the throat. She is showing me a brooch – a gold flower with a pearl centre."

Bet started to cry and Ambrose jumped up in alarm to comfort her. After accepting his handkerchief to dry her eyes Bet said, "It's incredible, but I do believe you have seen my mother. We gave her the brooch for her birthday, a few months before she died."

"Don't be upset Bet," said Sarah. "Be happy to accept the existence of an afterlife where we will all meet again one day. When you declared that Barbara haunts David, your mother shook her head in disagreement. She is telling me, Brabba still sleeps." This last disclosure caused a fresh flow of tears.

"I'd quite forgotten! When we were little my sister called herself Brabba – our parents got used to calling her that, as did I, until we went to school. You couldn't possibly have known that!" Bet declared.

Sarah smiled knowingly. "Which is why your mother said it, I'm sure. Have faith! Accept that you are not alone. Often when death is violent, a spirit needs time to accept the loss of earthly life. When Barbara wakes from that healing sleep she'll have your mother to care for her and I think you'll know when that time comes."

A faint ray of hope lit Bet's tear-stained face but she shook her head, not seeing how that could be... until Sarah continued. "Since your twin's death you often feel empty and pessimistic about the future. One day soon you'll awake hopeful and happy and know you are whole again."

To give the shaken young woman time to become composed again, Sarah carried on discussing the supposed haunting of her husband. "In light of what we've just heard, we know he couldn't possibly have been seeing Barbara's ghost – but did he ever actually say he was? When he spoke of being haunted did he actually mention her name? Or did everyone just assume he meant Babs? I will have to ask Mrs Monk the same question."

Ambrose considered carefully before speaking. "I am fairly sure now you've pointed it out – whenever he spoke to me he always said 'she', or 'her', and I assumed he meant Barbara."

"How strange," Bet agreed, "I think it was the same with me. Because Babs was uppermost in my own mind it didn't occur to me that he might not be speaking of my sister. I just jumped to the conclusion that our likeness triggered his guilt."

A tap at the door announced the arrival of Elsie with a tea trolley but they elected to join her and Polly in the other room. Having just about talked themselves out, they were glad to end the discussion for the time being. Polly, surrounded by cookery and home-knitting books, gathered them up hastily when they went in. She and Elsie seemed to have enjoyed the exchange and were planning to get together again soon. The conversation was impersonal and genial from then on.

When they parted eventually, Sarah invited Bet to visit her at home after she'd spoken with the housekeeper, Mrs Monk. She wanted Clarinda to meet Bet – they were only a few years apart in age. Polly drove even more carefully on the way back; it was dark and she had difficulty operating the headlights. Oncoming drivers who were dazzled and irritated because she was slow finding the dipswitch flashed them continually!

Agog to be brought up to date, but too occupied to concentrate, Polly agreed to wait until later, so that Sarah would not have to relate everything twice. Clarrie greeted them with some good news. The pub lunch date was fixed – Friday the twelfth, so Sarah immediately rang Mrs Monk to invite her for coffee on Thursday. Sounding surprised but pleased when she heard why, Mrs Monk accepted.

Sarah felt that things were moving forward satisfactorily, but now there was another awful possibility ...could they be investigating the wrong murder? Was there something about the stair carpet, which linked the two unfortunate victims? Could Bane actually have killed his own mother?

58 – Polly

The last week had culminated in an air of awed excitement. The added drama surrounding the death of David Bane's mother and his possible involvement in bringing it about, gave the three amateur detectives even more cause for stimulating speculation during their after-dinner sessions.

As the weekend turned into Monday morning however, the mood of the household changed. The return of the Berry 'family' from Spain was imminent and the likelihood of Sarah being carried off to London in the middle of the night influenced the day's activity. Clarrie and Polly insisted on her resting as much as possible and fussed until Sarah was driven to protest.

Alec telephoned to say he would be happier to have Sarah on hand anyway, so if she could be ready at five-o-clock he'd take her in his car, feed her and arrange accommodation overnight. It made more sense, as she was less likely to miss a whole night's sleep.

The afternoon dragged. It was almost a relief when Alec and Sarah at last drove off leaving them to settle down for the evening. After an early dinner Polly watched TV and Clarrie retired to her room upstairs, needing to plan her schedule for the next two months. Several people had commissioned pictures of houses; she would have to spare a few days to do preliminary sketches before the weather turned too cold to sit outside. They would certainly not want them depicted in grey December. A joint portrait had to be completed for Christmas: sisters: a surprise gift for daddy, so the children would come to sit in the studio.

The north facing room was much easier to work in than most places she had to use when visiting clients. Lights were available for effects and a daylight fluorescent tube over the window helped to boost the available light on dull days. Furthermore, she would be working at home, on hand if Sarah needed her support. She now knew from personal experience how draining it was to be 'used' by the Spirit world and felt much more protective towards her mother. In spite of herself she kept thinking of poor Mrs Berry, about to suffer the loss of a child for the third time.

Polly wasn't worrying about the kidnapping at all. From the beginning she'd had absolute faith in Sarah's conviction that Kate would be restored home safely.

She wasn't worrying about Sarah either now; she was sure to get a few hours sleep if not a completely undisturbed night. The TV news was on, but world events flashed before her eyes unheeded.

The possibility of Bane being a double murderer kept her brain churning. Now, alone in that big house, he was probably well on the way to complete insanity.

Polly could hardly wait to meet the woman who had kept house there for thirty-five years. From her own experience she knew there must be little about the Bane family not known to Mrs Monk! Babs' final thoughts might link the two deaths but why had 'red' been in her final thoughts? Could she have been thinking, not of a carpet but perhaps the car! That was it! A red car!

It was hard to resist the urge to ask Clarinda how the idea struck her but they had already said goodnight; she might be asleep.

59 – Kate

Alec had dinner with Sarah before leaving her at the hotel to rest. If the police decided to arrest Berry when he collected his car, which couldn't be far from Heathrow, Alec would telephone and Sarah would have about fifteen minutes to meet him in the lobby. Apparently Eddie and Ethel Mead were also in the hotel but there was nothing to be gained by disturbing them yet.

It was three in the morning when the call woke Sarah. She splashed her face with cold water to banish sleep and dressed quickly. The Meads were already down when she walked from the lift although she had taken only ten minutes to get ready. The poor things looked weary and dishevelled; they had probably not been to bed at all. Alec informed them that Kate was carried from the aircraft, asleep. The couple had taken her in a taxi to a private house about four miles away. The child was seen walking into the house; she was obviously okay. Kate's parents gripped hands thankfully.

An upstairs light had flashed inside the house, and was switched off almost immediately, but the lights downstairs were still on, so they had probably put Kate to bed and planned to stay the night. Alec intended taking them all there immediately to reclaim Kate. The exhausted child might not wake up if they were careful.

It was a quiet drive; no one wished to speculate on what would happen during the next hour. The house lights were still on when they drew up behind two parked police cars. Alec left them then, to take charge. They watched him approach the front door with another officer in plain clothes and a policewoman. A man answered their knock: after a moment they all went inside.

It seemed a lifetime before the door opened again.

The policewoman came out with a man who turned out to be Berry. He was carrying Kate and they came to the car where Eddie climbed out and took Kate without a word – she was fast asleep. He handed her gently to Ethel in the back seat, before climbing in himself to sit with them.

They both cried with relief.

The young woman asked Sarah if she would please follow her but didn't wait ...she conducted Berry back to the house. The scene that faced Sarah as she walked into the brightly lit room was like a theatrical tableau. Alec and his fellow officer stood with heads lowered, in conference. The policewoman stood alone behind a settee, on which were seated two women. One stared straight ahead looking stunned and seemingly unaware of the protective arm of the other, whose eyes were on Alec. In front of an artificial coal fire the plain-clothed officer she'd seen outside stood silently with another man, who looked agitated.

Alec abandoned his conversation as Sarah entered, took her to the two men and introduced Robert Berry. Alec informed him that, in his opinion, Mrs Berry would be greatly helped by talking with his friend Mrs Grey, a private citizen who had been of inestimable value in helping them to understand what had actually happened; without her, Alec said, there would have been no sympathy for Berry at all.

Berry, his wife and Sarah were conducted to the privacy of their host's study. The policewoman sat out of earshot, near the door, while Sarah surprised them both by speaking not of Kate, but of Tabitha. Berry took his wife's hand immediately and told Sarah that during the past two weeks she had gradually come to realise that Kate was not her own child but would Sarah please be very careful. Evelyn still didn't really appreciate what she had done or what had happened to Beth. He looked lost and beaten. It was a delicate situation – one of the most difficult Sarah had ever experienced. When they first sat down to talk she was at a loss to know how to begin and was glad when Berry had taken the initiative. As he spoke, Beth appeared to her – the first time for weeks – and with her help Sarah found the right approach. While they talked Alec drove the Meads back to the hotel and by the time he returned Sarah was ready to leave.

It would take a while for Beth's unfortunate parents to assimilate all Sarah had been able to prove to them and she promised to visit Evelyn in the future if needed again. A glance at her watch as they returned to the hotel indicated that it was hardly worth going to bed, but Alec said she must try to sleep. He had no intention of collecting her before eleven a.m. and they would lunch somewhere en-route. In looking after Sarah properly, he said, he was only following Polly's orders!

60 – Sarah

Mrs Monk telephoned Sarah on Thursday morning to be sure she could find the house. She was ringing from a public booth near the bus stop on the main road so Polly immediately went to fetch her and they were soon settled with coffee and cream cakes. Within minutes she was completely at ease. With Sarah alone she might have been more wary but Polly had already explained in the car that she used to be the family housekeeper and had known Sarah for over thirty years.

Without explaining the paranormal aspect of their inquiry – merely saying that in co-operation with his wife and vicar they were trying to learn more about Mr Bane's illness – they began to piece the story together again from yet another angle.

After she joined the household as a daily maid in 1955 David's father became ill and was bedridden two years later. The woman who was then the housekeeper, had been about to retire but under the circumstances, stayed on. Mrs Monk moved into the house to be of greater help; there were trays to carry up and down at all hours. Apart from that, she came from a large family and, at almost thirty years old, had never before had a room of her own so she was very happy to oblige. Mr Bane senior died in 1960 and the old housekeeper was still a fixture, so no one objected to her moving out again when she married Adam Monk. She continued to work part-time but her marriage didn't work out and she gladly returned there to take over when the housekeeper retired.

Not much happens in any house without the servants'

knowing but it is especially so when they live on the premises. Mrs Monk was always sorry for David because both parents were extremely religious and were highly suspicious of any activity outside the church. As a youngster he was allowed to help with fund-raising or bible classes for those even younger but he was never allowed to attend social evenings. They were frightened he would be 'led astray'! She suspected that neither spared the rod when David was little but in his final few months Mr Bane softened and worried a lot about his son.

David often sat with him for hours and their new closeness, instead of pleasing his mother, irritated her. His father thought it was time David socialised more – married, settled down and had a family. His mother said he was better off without a gold-digging floozy and told him not to put ideas into the boy's head. When she put her mind to it she was formidable and she allowed them fewer opportunities to be alone together.

The poor man died in his sleep one night. Mrs Monk had heard him ask for David several times during the previous two days but also heard the devious old woman tell David that his father was too ill to be disturbed. David was so full of self-reproach, not having been with him during his final hours that Mrs Monk had to say something to comfort him! Perhaps it was wrong of her, she admitted, but she told him he should blame his mother, not himself! After that, he stood up to her more and eventually set himself up in business, which enabled him to get out and make some real friends.

"Even so," Sarah said at last, "I understand Mrs Bane was eager to meet Bettina and a visit arranged." Pulling a wry face, Mrs Monk doubted that very much, in fact as far as she knew the subject never came up. It was at least a month after his mother's death before she, personally, even knew of Bettina's existence. She then made dinner for them several times – the twins came together as part of a foursome. Mrs Monk liked them both very much.

"It was nice to see him coming out of his shell and I was pleased to carry on working there after they married, but I think his mother must have turned in her grave!"

Sarah decided it was time to broach the subject that intrigued her most, the accident. She asked, "Did his mother always spend the day upstairs during David's absence? I believe she had a private sitting room"

"Yes. It's a lovely room ...overlooking the rear garden: comfortable and less formal then than the downstairs parlour. She used to come down when she heard him arrive, and then they'd have sherry together before he changed for dinner."

"On the night she died, was he still downstairs, or could he have gone straight up?" Sarah asked.

Mrs Monk shook her head. "I know what you're thinking. I went through all this with the police." She settled back in her chair apparently quite ready, even eager, to go over it again. "He always hung his topcoat and changed into slippers as soon as he arrived. I heard him go to the cloakroom, as usual, straight after the front door closed."

"What was the exact sequence of everything you heard and the time lapse between each sound, from that moment on," asked Sarah, thinking she was probably asking the impossible.

"Well, within a couple of minutes after I heard him go in, Mrs Bane's door closed upstairs. Then I heard the flush of the cloakroom toilet. The crash came almost straight after the flush and it couldn't have taken me more than ten seconds to cross the kitchen to the hall. He ran from the cloakroom at the same time. The door is in the wall under the stairs alongside that from the kitchen to the hall and we almost cannoned into each other."

Mrs Monk paused to take breath. The ensuing silence was not interrupted so she went on. "There is no way he could have been behind her and still had time to reach the cloakroom before I left the kitchen, absolutely impossible!" She shook her head to emphasise the point then made another. "And what possible reason could he have for killing his mother anyway? The old housekeeper told me he is a very wealthy man." She explained that each was financially independent and he could well afford a place of his own, having inherited from his grandparents. They left his mother an annuity but the bulk of the estate, three quarters, went to David, their only grandchild. "The house was

Mrs Bane's after his father died," she added, "and she could well afford the upkeep."

This statement was delivered with no trace of envy. Mrs Monk, like most of her breed, was proud to have cared for a family of substance. She suddenly looked sorrowful. "The quarter residue is in trust for David's children. What a shame," she sighed heavily, "I don't suppose there will be any now!"

Sarah smiled. She suspected there was already one on the way, even though Bettina hadn't mentioned it. "Do you know anything about the carpet which Barbara wanted to lay in her passage-way, Mrs Monk?"

"Now how on earth did you know about that? I heard them in the hallway – Mr David and his sister-in-law, a few days before she was killed. She was telling him what a problem she was having with draughts and said she could do with a mat or, ideally, a runner to match the one on the stairs, if he had any of the roll left over."

"Can you remember his reaction," Sarah asked, "better still, his exact words in reply?"

"Well, there was a long silence – I thought they must have gone out – then he said that he would find some for her." Mrs Monk broke off and re-iterated, "Well actually, he first said there was a small piece of it somewhere and asked how she knew about it. She laughed and answered – but in a low voice, I didn't hear what she said. Then he promised to look for it at the weekend. He was very good and generous to her. He said if there was anything else she needed she had only to ask."

"Did you know of any spare carpet?" Sarah asked. "Did you, in fact, have access to the attic?"

"Oh, I'd been in there several times helping to move things in or out, but only when he was with me. He kept the door locked – it was a real Aladdin's cave! It's no good asking how Barbara knew what was in there. Perhaps she really was psychic!" So, Sarah thought, the reason for his panic was obvious – he perceived Barbara as a threat he had to remove! He must have been suddenly convinced that she really was in contact with his mother's ghost! How else, he must have postulated, could she know of the carpet's existence?

Sarah pieced together his probable thought process.

He felt threatened by her knowledge, or more conceivably, her 'proven' access to it. And the most likely reason for his fear? What else? His potential exposure as a murderer! They might not discover how he committed the appalling crime or even why, as the reason was not financial, but he must have harboured a deep hatred for his mother. It was all so long ago; perhaps it would be better after all to forget the matricide and concentrate on the 'hit and run'.

There was little else she could expect to discover from Mrs Monk but Sarah verified that, although in her late seventies, there hadn't been much wrong with his mother's eyesight; she wore glasses only for reading. Mrs Monk also maintained that the servicing arrangement for Babs' car was not unusual. It was better to have a lift home, leaving it overnight in town, than drive it there in the early morning, making it difficult for her to get to work on time. Sarah then remembered to ask if, in his wild accusations of pretending to be 'her', David ever referred to Barbara by name and wasn't at all surprised to hear that he hadn't. Mrs Monk finally admitted how frightened she had become of David. She endured as long as she could – she'd always been fond him – but enough was enough! Glancing at the clock, she exclaimed how late it was and gratefully accepted Polly's offer to drive her home.

After they left Sarah went over her notes again and wrote out the case against David Bane as she saw it. Her private conviction, based on intuition must be set aside. Tomorrow they would meet the trained investigators. She needed to martial her thoughts and put them concisely without wasting time. Hard-headed professionals were concerned only with facts and would probably scorn their amateur theories. The idea that Bane was involved must surely have occurred to them and been rejected so they would be unwilling to believe he was, after all, the killer. They would be on the defensive.

Still, what they could not tell her might be just as revealing as the things they could! Sarah no longer doubted Bane's guilt but policemen need proof. If only she knew how, when he needed one, he had first found and then abandoned a car without arousing suspicion ...if only!

61 – Friday October 12th...

When Clarrie drove her mother and Polly to the Bull Inn there was only one space left to park on the small forecourt although they were not late. "Perhaps the whole force is here," remarked Polly. Inside, two tables were occupied and there were actually six men with Alec at the bar. Only two had come together – four came from widely different directions and Alec had also driven alone. Regular customers would have farther to walk than usual!

Introductions over, Alec ordered a Ploughman's Lunch for everyone but himself and left when the food arrived. Polly, eyeing the variety of cheeses and breathing in the sweet heady aroma of newly baked rolls wondered how he could tear himself away! He had given the men only the briefest explanation for calling the meeting but made it clear that he expected their full co-operation. They were consequently very curious to know why the old case should be under discussion in the complete absence of new evidence.

At first, a couple of officers were openly hostile, assuming that they were under scrutiny themselves. Soon realising that, although the ladies were friends of the dead woman's family, they were in no way being criticised for not finding her killer, they relaxed.

Hearing their hypothesis that the driver had been none other than the girl's own brother-in-law they were all intrigued but dismissive. His car was the first they inspected. Ray Jenkins, now a sergeant, said that any vehicle involved in such a collision might be more bloody than damaged but it was likely to be dented somewhere across the front. Garages were routinely asked to report any repairs booked in or undertaken after accidents, where the driver had fled the scene. The same applied to hire firms; each reported incident was investigated. All such inquiries cover adjoining counties and then extend to the rest of the country. A high percentage of perpetrators were caught.

They enjoyed a sociable hour or two but Sarah had to admit their progress was nil. Three of the men had already gone and those who remained were taking their leave outside. Sgt. Jenkins lingered, trying to arrange a future meeting with Clarrie who was doing her best to discourage him without being rude. "I might think of something later which would be useful," he was insisting. "If you give me your telephone number, I can keep in touch."

Clarrie unlocked her own car door and ducked inside quickly, saying he could always find her through Alec. With a hint of desperation, before she slammed her door, the sergeant said, "Funny thing, my beat covered the garage where she left her own car earlier that night and some idiot had run into that too!"

Sarah, about to climb into the car herself, stopped and stared at him incredulously. "Do you mean to say that her car was damaged? And if it was, does that mean it was not inside the building?"

"Why... No." Ray answered hesitantly, not quite knowing whether to be pleased to have captured their attention or apologetic because he hadn't thought it sufficiently important to mention before. "She left it on the forecourt. It's quiet as the grave around there after seven, but apart from the fact that it was locked, she always dropped the key through the garage letter slot – the smashed headlight glass was lying on the concrete where it stood. By the time I got there they'd begun the repair, but I saw the debris being swept up."

"Did you examine the front of the car or the glass bits for blood?" asked Clarrie.

"Well, I didn't look through a magnifier but I saw nothing to suggest that it was anything other than a routine thump." He saw the looks they exchanged and added defensively, "Anyway there were two tenners wrapped in a strip of newspaper and tucked under the wiper. The bloke responsible had scribbled 'SORRY' down the margin and you don't get many hit and run drivers doing that!"

They eventually managed to get away from him, taking a number where he could be reached and promising to let him know if they made any progress. Sarah was jubilant; they all were. It was diabolical: a masterstroke on Bane's part: diabolical and clever. "It was the one car which he could be absolutely certain to find quickly," declared Sarah, "being party to the usual servicing arrangement."

"Of course," cried Clarrie, "she parked her car outside on the forecourt after it closed. He could have used it without anyone knowing it had been moved. It would have been simple for him to obtain a key – she probably had a spare."

Polly was still gasping with horror. "Killing her was terrible, but to run her down with her own car! What a monster." She shuddered and the others fell silent, each absorbed in thought. Suddenly remembering her own theory, that the hit-car might have been red, she asked, "Does anyone know what colour Barbara's car was?"

"When we get back I'll ring Bettina and Ambrose to invite them for lunch to discuss everything we have theorised about." Sarah decided. "We'll have to break it gently that we seriously suspect her husband of murder."

While Polly bustled straight to the kitchen insisting that she had the evening meal planned and needed no help, Sarah telephoned Bettina and the vicarage, and immediately afterwards went to tell Polly that the car was green, so if it was the hit car, the significance of 'red' was still a mystery. Both lunch invitations had been accepted for next Friday ... Ambrose would come early to discuss their findings and plan the next step, but what of the outcome? Sarah suspected there could only be one end for Bane: imprisonment for life, either in gaol or committed to an insane asylum.

The air of anticipation increased as the week wore on. They

discussed their theory from every angle but couldn't fault it. Instead of going to her studio every evening after dinner Clarrie couldn't tear herself away from nightly deliberations. They went over every aspect of David Bane's life and, if they were right, his facility for getting away with murder! Polly said it was no wonder his guilty conscience convinced him that their angry ghosts were in hot pursuit! Clarrie doubted that he owned a conscience at all and Sarah was inclined to agree.

In spite of the gruesome topic it was good to relax after the last few gruelling weeks. Their talk became more desultory and the companionable silences grew. As always, halfway through October, the nights were growing colder, summer a memory and Christmas still far enough ahead to postpone panic, so they were all content to rest.

A fragrant log fire blazed in the hearth and the heavy drapes smothered the low monody of a biting wind.

***

A few miles away, David Bane was also listening to the eerie moaning of the elements. He shrank into the depths of an easy chair staring at an empty grate, which still held the grey ashes of a long-dead fire. He glanced fearfully into impenetrable shadows thrown by table lamps ...she was here. He knew it! He wondered, quivering in the grip of wild panic, would he ever be rid of her on this side of the grave – or the other!

62 – Friday October 19th...

After a restless night, unable to stop her mind turning over – she was not looking forward to facing Bettina – Sarah found it difficult to leave her comfortable bed when the alarm clock sounded. She forced herself to rise; from experience she knew there was no way Polly would wake her until absolutely unavoidable. Even with guests coming Polly would cope alone rather than disturb what she referred to as Sarah's much-needed rest. Being reminded that she was a few years older than Sarah cut no ice; she said she had only her body to worry about, whereas Sarah must get 'brain tired'! When Sarah went down Polly was already busy at the kitchen sink, humming happily as she prepared vegetables. "I wish you didn't get up so early Polly," Sarah chided, "you must have been here for hours, seeing all you've done!"

"It's not that much and I'd rather get it out of the way before Pat comes. I've told her we'll need her later, to clear up again after we've eaten, so she won't be here until ten-thirty." Polly was happy and obviously had things well under control. She added reassuringly, "Pat will have ample time to do the sitting-room before Ambrose arrives at eleven-thirty and can do the dining room while he's here." Finally placing lids on all the saucepans Polly dried her hands. "That reminds me ...Pat has asked me to teach her how to serve. Do you think it would be in order for her to practice today?"

"It might look a little ostentatious," Sarah observed, "but it would certainly curtail hard-to-digest topics at the table!" They decided to explain Pat's presence and allow her to serve, on the grounds that it might amuse their guests and even help to relax them more. Fortunately, it did exactly that. Aware that they were being accepted into a family scheme to help Polly's niece, Ambrose and Bet thoroughly enjoyed their lunch.

By the time they both settled quietly in front of the sitting-room fire for coffee alone with Sarah, she felt more ready to tackle the delicate matter of David's present, and most probably past, insanity. Before Bettina had arrived Ambrose and Sarah had already decided that, subject to her approval, they would go to the house and attempt to speak with her husband. Neither felt confident of achieving much but each was reluctant to bring the police into the matter again when all they could offer was speculation. If he incriminated himself they would be together to bear witness and could call Alec for advice afterwards. But now they had to apprise his poor wife of their suspicions.

When Sarah spoke, Bet grew paler and almost froze to complete stillness. As if mesmerised, she heard how her sister might have been murdered to cover up an earlier crime. Even in the absence of positive proof it made sense. Bet recalled odd actions of David's: strange looks, isolated phrases, which lent credence to what she was hearing. But she still defended him, unable to accept that he was a monster. When Sarah finished and asked if she would take them to see him, Bet at first refused. Ambrose and Sarah looked at each other helplessly; without her co-operation they could take matters no further. They conversed in undertones allowing the distraught woman to re-consider without interruption.

Eventually Bet spoke haltingly. "I know you would never have said all those terrible things if you hadn't been sure in your own minds that you were right, but it is so horrible and incredible. Mrs Monk knows much more about his early life than I do, he never spoke about his childhood or his mother unless asked. I can believe she beat him as a child and repressed him later, but it would have been so much easier for him to leave home than to kill her. If you are right, he must have been planning her murder even as he was inviting me to meet her!"

"If you remember dear," Sarah said, "Mrs Monk hadn't heard your name mentioned until after Mrs Bane died. David never took friends to meet her, male or female. It was as though he had no life outside home or office." Sarah paused to allow the point to be assimilated then continued gently. "He was forty-five years old when you married, an enormous step anyway at that age, but leaving the only home he'd ever known would have made it even more so. If he could have been sure of having his mother's approval for marrying, moving to his own house would perhaps have been possible, but by acting against her wishes he would have risked being banned from going there again, ever! I suspect he saw no alternative to killing her."

"I've just thought of something else." Bettina suddenly blurted out, crumpling visibly. She started to shake and groped in her handbag for her handkerchief... Ambrose started to rise, offering his, but she waved him away nervously. "You asked me why Babs should have been thinking of anything red. I know the answer!" She was unable to control her sobs and it was some time before she recovered sufficiently to tell them.

"When you wanted to know the colour of Babs' car I couldn't understand the significance so it didn't occur to me then. It was second-hand about six years ago. The engine was good but the bodywork terrible. There was so much rust on it that she affectionately named it 'Red'. Continuing to call it that, even after it was re-sprayed green, amused her. As she saw it coming straight at her she must instantly have recognised it!" In a flood of fresh tears Bet's voice trailed away. While Ambrose tried to comfort her, Sarah watched sadly, wishing it had been possible to help without first hurting her.

Any lingering doubts that Bane murdered his sister-in-law were gone. Shuddering as she thought of the girl walking alone, she imagined the sudden roar of the car speeding towards her. Babs would not have been blinded by dazzle because the headlights were off. It had been easy to recognise her own car intent on running her down. As she shouted 'RED' in horror, she probably realised that David was driving it. The speed of a brain in moments of stress is incredible and recognition was followed by instant awareness that his rage was connected to the carpet in the attic. She probably sensed his hostility when they spoke of it, and even though he had apparently promised to find it for her, she must have known he was extremely upset.

Bet recovered some of her poise and to their great relief changed her mind about introducing Sarah to David. "It would have been easier to refuse," she said, "but I'm pregnant. For my baby's sake as well as my own I must do everything possible to help him, whether he's innocent or guilty."

"You are being very wise," Ambrose consoled her. "Even if our accusations are proved false his behaviour isn't sane. He needs professional help and it is our Christian duty to see that he gets it, even against his will. His child – and I'm so pleased you will be blessed – his child should have a father restored to health if it is within our power."

According to neighbours' gossip, David was seldom seen leaving the house; Bet telephoned every week and he usually answered. More often than not he'd been vague – uncertain who she was, a client or his secretary, but sometimes he was pleased to hear her and asked her to come home. Bet said she might have to try several times before he was lucid enough to agree to the visit. Although Bane answered at the first ring, it was obvious from Bet's side of the exchange that it was one of his bad days. She gave up, frustrated, and promised to continue ringing until she made him understand.

Ambrose gave Sarah a nod of encouragement – they had been talking earnestly while Bet was trying to call David. In answer to a query from Sarah, Bet acknowledged she still had a key to the house and after some persuasion from Ambrose she reluctantly agreed to a change of plan... they would visit him anyway: unannounced!

63 – David

David Bane stared vaguely at the telephone, his hand still on the receiver. Had it rung? Had he just answered it? He relaxed slowly and went back to work. For a fleeting moment he thought his secretary must have taken the call... then perceived with a bewildered frown – he was not in the office. Since the departure of both his wife and housekeeper he had gradually transferred his files home to his study. Sometimes, functioning almost normally, he wondered why his list of clients was dwindling, but most of the time he wandered around the large house fearfully.

After days of existing hazily, he would emerge feeling weak and hungry, find something to eat and rally his senses enough to telephone an order to the local grocery store.

In his clearer moments he could not understand why Bettina had gone, forgetting he had frightened her away. Mrs Monk too had deserted him – whatever could have upset her? Well, they weren't indispensable. Any fool could push a vacuum cleaner and boil an egg! He wondered fleetingly if their going had anything to do with Barbara but rejected the idea; neither of them suspected he had been forced to kill her. He knew she had scared her twin when they were little, claiming to see ghosts, but when he asked Bet if Babs really was psychic, she scoffed at the idea instead of telling him the truth!

If only she hadn't lied!

He should never have opened up that room again. After his mother's death he had often felt oppressed by her presence in there and fancied he saw her sometimes from the corner of his eye. Only by locking it up had he succeeded in banishing his mother and her ghost from his mind.

He had grave misgivings when asked, but could think of no reasonable excuse for refusing Babs the use of his mother's parlour. After she took it over he had ample cause to regret his generosity. She became more and more sly and stupidly playful. She would glance over her shoulder making pointed comments in stage whispers: his mother's eye was on her; she hoped the old lady would not mind the antimacassars and lace tablecloths being removed and so on. She handed them over to him, together with an antique clock and – how could she know, unless in contact with her? – How could she have selected all his mother's favourite ornaments, saying they were so terribly valuable she couldn't be responsible for their safety?

One day she tripped on a loose rug as she went into the room and he distinctly heard her say, "It's the Duchess's way of saying I should watch my step. Can't you just see her standing there – so regal in her blue brocade – wagging a long bony finger?" Then, realising he'd heard her, she said that being extremely sensitive to atmosphere, she knew his mother didn't really object to her presence. Babs said the dear lady understood that no disrespect was meant and still smiled benignly on her.

To reassure him, seeing how upset he still was by the accuracy of the image, Bettina had given him some cock and bull story about a snapshot in an old album and at the time he had believed her. Bet must have chastised Babs because she apologised to him very sweetly and promised to stop being silly. Later, it dawned on him ...Babs couldn't possibly have known it was blue brocade from a black and white photograph! Of course, he pretended to accept what she said but watched her even more closely from then on. He tried to ignore her insidious glances when they met or passed each other, particularly when near the stairs. Bet never noticed. To all appearances they were a happy family again but almost daily he perceived new indications that Babs was in contact with his mother.

Sometimes she even sounded like her – beginning sentences with the dreaded words, 'I thought you were going to' ...a reproach that echoed from his earliest memory, through all the years of his life. He could tell by the way she tilted her head that she was taunting him, but he was too shrewd to let anyone see that it bothered him. He was in the hall one afternoon. Seeing him there, Babs started coming downstairs then swayed and almost fell. She saved herself dramatically by grabbing the rail and from the way she looked down at him he knew exactly what was in her mind. He wished she had broken her neck too! Wishing her dead was merely a short step away from planning how it could be expedited, but he knew it would hurt Bet and shrank from actually doing anything about it, until she stupidly gave herself away and left him no choice.

Leaving the house one morning she asked if he had anything to stop the cold draught in her corridor. He had not suspected a deeper motive until she pointed to the stair carpet and lowered her voice slyly, "A little strip of that – if you have any of the roll left over, hidden away somewhere – would be absolutely perfect!" He had been shaken: confused, but asked what made her think there would be any. She sealed her own fate by whispering, "A little bird told me!"

Within a week she was dead.

He laughed aloud recalling how clever he'd been – remembering even to take with him a sponge and a flagon of water to clean up her car. The headlight housing was dented so he smashed the glass completely when he parked it afterwards: real genius! Nobody suspected him, any more than they had suspected him of killing his mother. Memories held at bay for years, came flooding back. It had been difficult to avoid laughing aloud when the police examined the stairs where she had fallen.

The doctor was first on the scene. He arrived just before the ambulance and assured the attendants that he'd looked straight away for anything that might have tripped her but no loose object had been on, or near, the stairway. Of course there wasn't – he was no dummy!

It was so very lonely in the house now. Sometimes he was sorry about his mother and even regretted that she was no longer with him. The feeling surprised him. From his infancy she was extremely possessive, wanting to control his every waking moment. His resentment had always been there but he harboured it silently, without protest because, at the first hint of insubordination, she would reach purposefully for one of his father's leather belts. When his father found out, the beatings stopped, but she had other ways of making his life miserable.

In spite of everything he didn't doubt her love for him. He'd loved her too but she would never have accepted Bet and allowed her to live happily under the same roof. Barbara too became a threat to his happiness with Bet. One day she might have revealed how he used the carpet and spoiled everything for them. David longed for Bet to come back home. He fell asleep at his desk and when he woke still could not remember why she had left him. Babs hadn't been around either, for ages ...it must have something to do with that; twins didn't like to be apart. They had gone to live together; that was it – but where?

Like thin wisps of smoke, his memories drifted into focus only to swirl away as he tried to grasp them more firmly. Eventually, feeling a little better, he walked downstairs and searched, unsuccessfully, for Mrs Monk. He made himself a sandwich in the vast empty kitchen. He ate, staring at the white tiled walls, which gleamed dully as darkness fell. He sat without lights until he felt a stab of fear. It was easier for ghosts to come in the dark. After switching on all the lights he experienced a moment of clarity ...he remembered that Barbara wasn't living anywhere. She was dead!

Knowing her car would be left on the garage forecourt in an industrial area where it was quiet at night, he had taken her spare keys. Leaving the telephone off the hook he slipped from his office and, on the main road, took a taxi to a bar where he was unknown. He'd thought of everything. He went in, exited by the rear door and walked through the back streets to the car. He drove it to the school and was parked in a side road out of sight when Barbara emerged with her friends. He had expected her to wait alone and would have killed her as soon as all was quiet but Ann had stayed with her. Knowing he must account for his time, he drove away, found a pay phone and rang a client as though phoning from his office. It was then about 9.30pm. The girls were still together when he returned and he followed when they eventually drove off. He was enraged when, after all his pains, he thought Babs was getting a lift home...

The house was cold. There had been no housekeeper to attend to the central heating controls for weeks – but he began to sweat. The wild panic which gripped him when he saw his quarry moving beyond reach, returned. To control his shaking he gripped the arms of his chair as tightly as he had gripped the steering wheel that night, but he had gradually regained his composure when he saw her climb onto the bus. He remembered with a satisfied smile how calmly he had acted.

He knew where the bus would drop her and the quiet side streets on the Heights along which Babs would have to walk home, but time was his problem. He'd planned to return to his office after running her down at the school, to replace the phone and telephone Bet immediately to say he'd forgotten to collect her sister. He would have asked if Babs had rung home. When she said no, he would have promised to go directly to the school anyway. Her body would have been removed by then ...so, of course, he couldn't be expected to know that she'd been killed, could he?

His next step would have been to meet the bus, then drive home and be amazed not to find her already there! It could have been perfect, but he hadn't lost his head. He had followed the bus, eventually overtook it and turned into a side road near the stop where it would soon arrive. He drove over several intersections to a stretch where the houses were spaced farther apart. It was a quiet residential area where few people tended to move about on foot, even by day, and waited in a tree-lined avenue that crossed her route. There was enough of a glow from the street lamps to identify her, so his vehicle lights were off – if anyone did see him he couldn't risk their reading the number plates.

As soon as he saw Babs coming he had started the engine, raised the revs slightly and eased his foot off the clutch. He released it fully and the car was rolling when she reached the middle of the cross section ...then he jammed his foot hard down on the accelerator and drove straight at her. There was no point in stopping to make sure she was dead. If she survived she certainly couldn't have recognised him. He'd been far too quick; ingeniously resourceful!

He then drove as fast as he dared to return the car to the garage forecourt, stopping on the way to telephone a second client who asked what the hell he was thinking of, ringing at half past ten! David chuckled, recalling how angry the man had been. There was no way he would forget that his conscientious broker had been working late! It had been another master touch, ringing Ann Dodd too... Ringing!

Something was ringing now... the telephone.

Picking up the receiver he heard Bet's voice and burst into tears. "Where are you Bet? Please come home," he gasped between sobs. At the other end, Bet too was nearly crying, thinking that perhaps it had all been a ghastly nightmare and he was recovering from whatever had been troubling him – until he spoke again. "You know mother wants to meet you. She doesn't mind at all that we got married. Bring Babs tomorrow, for one of Mrs Monk's special dinners." He stared at the instrument in his hand and thought for a moment. "Where is Mrs Monk? Is she with you?" He heard a click at the other end and knew Bet wouldn't answer.

How could she treat him like this when she knew how much he loved her? The more he wondered, the more convinced he became that it was his mother's fault. He would have to get rid of her. He'd worked out how to do it. That was why he couldn't let Babs have the carpet: not yet. She could have it afterwards, but first, he had a use for it himself. Before he forgot it again he decided to fetch it from the attic. When he carried it into the cloakroom and was about to hide it in the shoe cupboard, he remembered that he didn't need to hide it from Mrs Monk because she'd gone with Bet and Babs. He left it leaning against the wall.

A spasm of hunger drove David back to the kitchen but the store cupboard was almost empty. How could Mrs Monk have let stocks run so low ...sheer incompetence! All that remained in the freezer were some packets of vegetable, two chickens and a huge leg of lamb ...no fast food. As he searched, he repeatedly lost his grip on reality and his irritation increased with his hunger. He rang the call-bell to the housekeeper's room and when no one came, stormed up to look for her. He banged on her door and, when she didn't come out, rushed in and was astonished to find the apartment empty. David sagged dejectedly as he remembered again that Mrs Monk had deserted him too!

He slumped on her bed staring at the furniture, carpets and curtains: all unfamiliar. Surely they could not be part of his house? He had rarely, if ever, been in there before, not in his whole life! Disorientated by the sudden strangeness of his surroundings he held his head, sick with fear. With no recollection of wandering down, he found himself in the kitchen again, making coffee. He cooked the last scrap of bacon and then stared at it for so long, lost in thought, that it was greasy and cold when he ate it.

At three-o-clock in the morning he wrote out a long grocery list, rang the shop and went into a violent rage when nobody answered!

64 – Tuesday October 23rd...

After lunch, Bet picked up Sarah for their visit to her old home. Ambrose was already in the car. They had decided it would be wiser to use Bet's car in case David saw it arrive; he might not otherwise open the door, even for his vicar. The house, hidden by trees, stood farther from the road than the neighbouring properties.

Both gates to the semi-circular drive were open, so Bet was able to drive straight in to park at the front porch. All was quiet; they saw no movement at any of the windows. She rang several times, before returning to the car, crestfallen, to say he must have felt fit enough to go to his office. As he wasn't in to talk to them, it was another day wasted; their mission seemed to have failed. However, Bet was reluctant to give up. She was anxious to go in and see for herself how her husband was living and looking after himself. "I've often wanted to come, but was apprehensive about facing him alone. There is no other friend I would care to ask," she admitted, "so if you don't mind, will you come in with me? He might come back soon. Perhaps we could wait a while."

Sarah agreed willingly, unable to resist the chance to see for herself if restless ghosts haunted the place where two hapless women had lived and where one had met a violent death. Bet would not have used her key had he been at home; she felt awkward about intruding unannounced. At least, her car outside would warn him of her presence when he returned, she said, as she invited them into the spacious hall, which was rather gloomy even in mid-afternoon.

The curved rail of the banister led the eye up to an even darker landing. Bet said the upstairs curtains must be drawn. They looked through all the ground floor rooms including the cloakroom where Sarah pointed to the roll of carpet propped inside. Bet confirmed that it was the one she and Babs saw in the attic but couldn't understand why David had suddenly brought it downstairs – two years after Babs reminded him of it. Sarah asked if Bet would mind showing her the sitting room that had been Mrs Bane's exclusively, so Bet took her up to see the rest of the house, leaving Ambrose in the library keenly examining the shelves of books, unwilling to tear himself away from such treasures.

Centred on the left side of the square landing were two doors. One opened into David's dressing room, which used to be the nursery; the other revealed a half-landing on the service stairs from which one flight went down to the kitchen and a narrower staircase went up to the floor above.

Seeing Sarah's interest as she peered into the darkness, Bet clicked on the light switch and invited her to walk up. Leading the way she explained – the whole upper floor was actually roof space. The original rooms, for two servants, now constituted the housekeeper's self-contained apartment and occupied the greater part. Opposite the recess that gave entry to the living space was another door. Bet tried the knob and was not surprised to find it locked. It was the door to the attic.

Sarah felt nothing oppressive about the atmosphere and was unconcerned about the attic's being inaccessible. Now she could concentrate on David's mother. Returning to the first floor landing, Bet offered to show her the main suite which ran across the front of the house, but Sarah declined... she felt more drawn to the small hallway which led to the rooms once occupied by Barbara, particularly to the door opposite her bedroom. As soon as they went into Mrs Bane's parlour Bet sensed Sarah's change of mood. For a few moments she watched in silence but when Sarah started to shake, as though gripped with fever, Bet was terrified. In the short time she'd known Sarah, Bet had forgotten her pre-conceived notions about mediums being weird and going into trances. Sick with fear, she backed out of the room and ran down to Ambrose.

"What can we do?" she gasped, "I'm scared. I can't go back to her!"

Ambrose couldn't avoid being infected by the note of hysteria in Bet's voice but, pretending to greater nonchalance than he felt, he patted her arm gently. "I'm quite sure that Sarah knew what she was doing when she came here. Rather than risk anything going wrong, I'm sure she would have brought her daughter along, for spiritual support. We will wait here quietly and pray for her, as I'm sure she would want us to do." Bet looked unconvinced so he promised that if Sarah didn't come out of her trance soon, he would telephone Clarinda.

Upstairs, Sarah was fighting for self-control. Immediately on entering this, her private domain, David's mother had tried to take her over, mind and body. Others had tried before and Sarah had always won the battle by prayer and sheer will-power. The idea of abandoning herself, wholly, to domination by a departed spirit was terrifying. She knew that some mediums always worked that way, but seldom when alone. They liked support: another experienced medium observing, ready to banish an invasive presence and bring them out of their trance.

Sarah adamantly refused to accept the strong, forceful personality, which was forcing itself upon her. With her inner ear she perceived, as from a vast distance, a voice, "Allow me to help my son. Please! I must save his soul. I beg you not to stand in my way..." Torn between self-preservation and her desire to help the restless shade of Bane's mother, Sarah relented. With a fervent prayer of her own Sarah mentally took a pace back and found herself walking to the window. She pulled the curtain aside and saw Bane wandering in the garden. She unlatched the window and threw it wide open. In a voice unlike her own she called to him... "David, come inside at once. We must talk."

Startled, Bane looked up and stared: wild-eyed. He began to run away then stopped, bewildered. With his head lowered, he turned slowly and walked back, totally confused again. He was only enjoying the fresh air ...what did she want now? It was typical of his mother to ruin even his simplest pleasures. He felt harassed. Something vital was slipping away …it was important that he remember. Was it something he'd done or had not done, or something he planned to do? He went into the kitchen and turned the key in the heavy door. She told him always to make sure it was kept locked. Already, he couldn't remember why he had come inside. He had been happy looking at the flowers.

He went into the hall and was shocked to see it ablaze with light. The ceiling and wall lights were all on. He heard his mother's door open and shut and looked up expectantly. The landing lights were on too! With a rush of excitement David remembered. He had just come in from the office. This was the night he had planned for! Tonight his mother would die.

Ambrose and Bet also heard the door upstairs. They realised too that David had entered the house but were stunned to silence when they saw his gaunt, haggard appearance and witnessed his furtive behaviour. He darted towards the cloakroom and picked up the narrow carpet roll. He held it above his head and pushed it sideways between the uprights of the banister until it was in line with the stair runner, tucked into the angle of the highest step he could reach. He backed away and looked up to where Sarah stood, about to descend.

Ambrose followed his gaze and was shocked to immobility when he didn't recognise Sarah – seeing instead, a complete stranger! She started to descend, smiling down at David, a hand raised in greeting. Bet saw only Sarah, solemnly staring straight ahead... about to take a fatal step down. She was not looking where she was going...

"Sarah!" Bet screamed. She ran from the library followed closely by a thoroughly shaken Ambrose, who in a split second saw the tall unfamiliar figure transformed into his friend. He was mortified. Just when Sarah needed him he had failed her! "Sarah!" screamed Bet again. "Stay there! Don't move!"

Bane whirled round and gaped when he saw his wife. His face was bloodless... his eyes wide and full of pain. "Why did you warn her?" he bellowed. "How could you?"

Bet fell back, sobbing with terror, "Why David? What have

I done?"

Still he strode towards her, shouting. "Now we'll never be together. It was the only way and you've ruined everything! I only wanted to make you happy." He ran to the front door, wrenched it open and, before they could stop him, was running down the drive, tearing at his clothes and hair wildly, completely out of control.

Sarah held on to the banister rail and gradually emerged from the trance. Bet, halfway up the stairs, helped her to step over David's lethal trap. Viewed from above, the continuity of the pattern rendered it almost invisible.

Ambrose slumped in the doorway. As Sarah walked to him he straightened up and took her hands. "I am so ashamed. I simply could not function. I was completely stunned. Someone other than you was standing there, at the top of the stairs." He mopped his face and brow and went to sit down. "The shock of realising it was Mrs Bane's ghost, drained the use from my legs and took my voice. Thank the Good Lord for Bet and her presence of mind, otherwise you would have fallen as that poor lady did twelve years ago." He was pale and shaken.

"She wouldn't have let me fall," Sarah said to console him. "I was prepared to carry on descending, but she made me freeze." Sarah didn't seem at all perturbed. "I was gripping the rail tightly a fraction of a second before Bet shouted. David's mother had materialised through me; I knew that, but had not entirely lost consciousness."

Now that it was over, Sarah seemed unusually excited as she explained. "She wanted him to see her. The fact that he did proves what I already suspected." The others, recovering a little, looked astonished …what else was to be revealed? "He is clairvoyant," Sarah continued. "That's why he was so ready to accept that Barbara was too, but I doubt whether, since his mother's death, he ever saw her as solidly in the flesh as he did today!"

Bet declared that she'd seen only Sarah, whose glazed look alone was enough to scare her out of her wits without also seeing the dead walk! While they were speaking, Sarah dialled Alec's number. He advised them to leave the carpet roll in place and wait. Dee and White, with a photographer, were on their way, and not to worry, Bane would soon be picked up.

Because they already knew Sarah, the two detectives were quick to take in the import of what Ambrose and Bettina had witnessed. Sarah explained the connection with the earlier death of Bane's mother and they lost no time in reporting back to Alec. He told them to stay at the house until relief arrived, but to send the Reverend Kilroy, Mrs Bane and Sarah home. If Bane returned to the house it would be better for him not to see a horde of people.

The drive back wasn't long. They were all wrapped in thought and hardly spoke until Bet turned the car into the driveway. Sarah suggested they stay together for a while. Clarinda and Polly would be anxious to hear what had happened and she felt that both Ambrose and Bet needed a sympathetic audience to talk it out of their systems. Both agreed without persuasion. The trauma was wearing off and they were eager to go over everything; only by doing so could they convince themselves it had ever really happened.

Ambrose rang Elsie and she arranged to call for him on her way back from town. He had about an hour to unwind before she came for him at six-o-clock but Bet accepted an invitation to stay for dinner.

Although it was a relief to have the situation brought to a head, Bet's troubles weren't over and she was not yet ready to be alone. Just after eight-thirty they heard from Alec that David had been found and was safe in hospital, under guard. Alec was pleased that Bet was present and told her that the house had been secured; she could collect the keys at her own convenience. She would not have to lie awake worrying about her husband's whereabouts, he was in good hands and would be able to do no more harm either to himself or others.

65 – Sarah

Sarah was soon caught up again with her own affairs but it was difficult to put either the Berry family or the Bane's completely out of mind. Just before Christmas she received a letter from Bettina Bane. 'It would have been quick and easy,' she wrote, 'to pick up the telephone,' but went on to explain that in talking she might not have been able to convey her very deep gratitude for all that Sarah had done for her. She was pleased to say that David, although he would need treatment for the foreseeable future and might one day have to stand trial, did have lucid moments and understood why the old house should be closed up. He was thrilled about the baby, which was expected early in the New Year.

Bet said she would soon be leaving her friend's flat as she was buying a small place of her own and had persuaded Mrs Monk to move in and continue keeping house for her; she would need her help and support with the baby. She expressed the hope that she and Clarrie could get together soon, promising to ring when she could give them her new address and telephone number. Polly read the letter approvingly and commented that it was a nice gesture and showed good breeding. Clarrie said, in the words of her old school motto, 'Manners Maketh Man'!

Apart from being taken out to dinner by Alec and Algy as a foursome on Christmas day, which Polly spent with her family, and Boxing Day, when they entertained a gathering of friends at home, the season came and went uneventfully. Bettina had a baby boy on the third day of January and a week or two afterwards rang to thank them all for the flowers. Sarah was pleased to hear that she was coping with her changed circumstances and even sounding happy but a warning bell reverberated at the back of her mind! It was disturbing but nothing she could pin down. She was therefore not really surprised when less than two weeks later Bet rang again, to tell her that David had suffered a stroke from which he hadn't recovered. She asked if Sarah would come to his funeral. By the end of February Bet's life was returning to normal, in her new home with baby Adam.

Alec, bringing them up to date, rang to say that Mrs Berry had been referred to psychiatric care and was unlikely ever to stand trial for either the kidnapping or Ozzie's death. Both the Meads and the Crown Prosecution Service were unwilling to press charges against Robert Berry in view of the unusual extenuating circumstances. Ozzie's family, the Lathams were bitter that their son's murderer seemed to be going unpunished, but appreciated that, thanks to Sarah, they knew how bravely he had died.

The household went back to the normal routine …Clarrie in her studio eight or nine hours a day, Sarah going out twice a week to play bridge and Polly mothering them both, happily organising Pat and the meals. She commented, when April arrived, that the year so far, had been much less traumatic than the last, for most of which they had all been worried stiff about little Kate, Beth's parents and David Bane: one thing after another!

Within moments of her speaking there was a call from Bettina Bane. Returning to the kitchen Sarah informed Polly, "Bet wants to call in today if we're not busy. Of course I said we would be delighted to see her. She should be here in about half an hour …we have just enough time to defrost some scones!"

To their surprise when Bet arrived, a small van pulled in alongside her car. Two men alighted and unloaded a piece of furniture. While they did so, Bet explained that it was a writing desk that had belonged to David's mother. Without quite realising what was happening, or why – it all happened so fast,

Sarah and Polly watched the desk being deposited in the (fortunately) wide entrance hall before the men departed with cheerful waves.

Bet explained breathlessly that apart from the library, which she had catalogued during the years she'd lived there, she was selling the house and most of its contents.

She was going into business and the extensive collection of old volumes would be the nucleus of her Antique Book Shop.

She intended making a substantial donation to the church on behalf of David's parents – sure they would have approved, as they were both very religious and staunch supporters of local charities.

"I've always had a generous monthly allowance," she said, "and David gave me sizeable cheques for my birthdays and Christmas so I have enough saved to buy my new premises without eating far into his estate. Even if my business fails I won't starve!"

She appeared unaware of the fact that the other two were still staring, totally bewildered, at both her and the desk.

Bettina hardly paused for breath. "I knew he used to run a successful company but had no idea he was independently wealthy, and a trust fund from his grandfather will cover all Adam's needs."

She stopped talking at last, looking rather embarrassed. "I'm sorry! It came out like a boast, but I didn't mean it like that. I only told you so that you won't hesitate to accept the desk: beautiful isn't it?"

Bet enjoyed their looks of utter astonishment as they stared at the fine piece of furniture. "It was in my mind to give you something old from the house – to thank you, but I couldn't decide what, until after Mrs Monk and I finished clearing out. I can't imagine how we missed it, but when the dealer opened a drawer in this desk we found part of a letter in Mrs Bane's own hand. The rest has been thrown out, but no matter. Whoever was the intended recipient is unimportant, it struck me as a sign. This desk has to be yours, as a gift from her!"

Sarah was stunned. It was a valuable antique and she

immediately said that Bet mustn't be offended, but she had to refuse it, no matter whether Bet needed to sell it or not – it was just too much! Bet held up a hand to halt Sarah's protestations. She had expected that Sarah would be reluctant to accept the gift and had her own argument ready...

Proving that it wasn't a spur of the moment decision, Bet said, "I've had all the furniture assessed, so I know exactly what I'm doing. This is a Carlton House desk – a lady's writing table called a 'Bonheur du jour', probably pre- 1795! The antique dealer left his card in it, in case you ever wish to sell it."

Sarah attempted to stem Bet's flow of enthusiasm, not being able to conceive of anything that would persuade her to accept such a valuable gift. Bet, however, would not be interrupted and carried on talking excitedly.

"Before you say anything else, please look at this. When I read it myself I was stupefied ...it could have been written especially with you in mind!"

Sarah glanced quickly at the letter and understood, but even so, looked earnestly at Bet and tried again to refuse. "It is extremely beautiful and I'm really touched that you want me to have it, but the letter alone, owing to the circumstances in which it was found, is quite sufficient, if I may keep it." Refusing to listen to Sarah's protests, Bet lifted one side of the bureau and asked for Polly's help to ease it nearer the wall ...until they decided where it should stand permanently she said.

Polly glanced apologetically at Sarah, but complied. She agreed with Bet. Sarah did deserve recognition for all she had done. Bet terminated the discussion by opening the front door and walking back to her car. "If it makes you any happier Sarah dear," she called over her shoulder, "consider it a permanent loan. Just enjoy using it! Sorry I can't stay for tea. I have to get back to feed Adam, Please tell Clarrie I'll ring her next week."

After she had gone, they carried the desk into the sitting room and re-arranged the furniture. Polly was bursting with curiosity wondering what on earth the letter could have to do with Sarah. She didn't have to wait long before Sarah unfolded the sheet of linen paper again and handed it to her.

It was apparently the end of a letter, in faded, elegant script:

'... having given of yourself so generously, I can never hope to repay you. Few would have acted as selflessly in such demanding and difficult circumstances. You have the undying gratitude of my family and myself. Please accept this token, with our thanks.

Mary M. Bane.

Sarah re-folded the letter and touched the polished satinwood surface of the desk. She could picture the old lady sitting at it to write. She was still slightly bemused but conceded with good grace that she had lost the argument and, for once, Sarah was happy to accept defeat.

Mai Griffin

During her successful career as an artist, travelling the world and painting portraits of Royalty, Heads of State and other prominent figures, Mai has never stopped writing. The Echoes series may be built around purely fictional characters, but Sarah Grey and her late husband Stephen were inspired by Mai's parents. Mai now lives in Spain. Dividing her time between painting and writing is a challenge, but helps to still her own ghosts...

Renaming an already published book series was a heart-wrenching decision – the contents of the books and the stories has not changed, however, so for your convenience and that of booksellers the new and the old titles are below

by Mai Griffin

~~Deadly Shades of Grey~~ 'Ghostly Echoes'
~~A Poisonous Shade of Grey~~ 'A Poisonous Echo'
~~Grey Masque of Death~~ 'Dangerous Echoes'
~~Haunting Shades of Grey~~ 'Haunting Echoes'
And Coming Next 'Chasing Echoes'

Watch www.uppublications.ltd.uk for more information or follow Mai on www.maiwriting.com